THE COLLISION OF THE PAST AND THE FUTURE . . .

Frank King and Joyce Fisher walked around the stone altar, to look up at the enigmatic faces, in the moonlight.

"Think of all they've seen," Joyce whispered.

"Open canoes," the NASA pilot mused, "sailing ships, steamboats, jet planes, and now spacecraft."

"Gods, chiefs, explorers, sea captains, warriors . . . and astronauts."

"All far from home."

"Where's 'home,' Frank?"

King looked into the darkness, in the direction of the crippled Space Shuttle. "I'm not sure . . . maybe somewhere in space, ultimately. God knows I've spent most of my life trying to get there. Maybe I'm just trying to go home again."

SHUTTLE DOWN

Lee Correy

A Del Rey Book

BALLANTINE BOOKS • NEW YORK

TO:
Margaret and John

'O Hotu Matu'a i-unga-mai-ai
Ia Hau Maka, i toona tuura
Ka-kimi te maara mo te ariki
Mo te ariki, mo toma

Hotu Matu's sent here
His servant Hau Maka
To search out a landing place
For the king to land.

—Rapa Nui folk saga

CHAPTER ONE

"T-minus thirty seconds and counting!"

"Launch Control, *Atlantis*. We're showing a low-pressure light on the SSME manifold." Frank King seemed calm and cool as always just before a launch. But external appearances were deceiving. Inside, he was just as uptight as before the flight of any hot airplane or Shuttle mission.

"We don't see it on telemetry, *Atlantis*," the voice of Launch Control came back over Frank's headphones.

"Another damned glitch," copilot Lew Clay muttered. "This bird has always been squirrelly, Frank."

"T-minus twenty and counting!"

"Yeah, if it's real, the main engines'll shut down before they reach full thrust, and we won't get booster ignition," Frank observed. "Let's ride her." He triggered his mike switch. "*Atlantis* is go."

"Ten . . . nine . . . eight . . . seven . . ."

The hellfire of a Space Shuttle launch was now so routine at Vandenberg Air Force Base that hardly anybody bothered to look up from his work. The Los Angelenos to the southeast might bother to look up through their smog to see the *Atlantis* climb into the blue morning sky on the tail of flame from her main engines and two solid propellant boosters. It was just another Shuttle mission into sun-synchronous polar orbit carrying either a Department of Defense satellite or a NASA Landsat. This time, it was the latter that was tucked into the cargo bay of the *Atlantis*, Space Shuttle OV-104. The ship was running light to get into polar orbit without the assist of the Earth's eastward rotation, an additional Orbital Maneuvering System (OMS) kit, or the external boost of a pair of Titan engines under the External Tank.

Frank King rode out the liftoff impassively, his eyes

making their standard scan of the panel in front of him. He noted the movement of the points of light along the nominal trajectory plots projected on the display in the center of the panel. Things seemed to be going normally.

But he couldn't shake the nagging feeling that something was *wrong*.

Nothing showed on the instrument panel. There were no alarms from the highly automated systems. The three digital computers that controlled the *Atlantis* during her boost into space signaled nothing amiss.

Yet he knew something was wrong.

He began to think about abort mode options . . . just in case.

He had too many years of flight in him—too many years of F-15s and F-16s screaming across the southwestern desert, too many years of handling SR-71 Blackbirds through the thin air of near-space, and too many years of boring supersonic holes through the sky in NASA T-38s. More than 5000 hours of hot-airplane jet time crowded his memory.

Frank King had that elusive psychic connection with every aerospace vehicle he flew—and with his car as well. He seemed able to reach out and make any machine an extension of his own senses. He had spent his life doing this, being the master of machines that would and often did kill very quickly.

In fact, it had been practically his whole life.

And he was still alive, which was testimony not only to his skill as a pilot but also to the extension of his ego into the machines he flew. Deep within him, however, he knew that it was because he was deathly afraid of every one of those machines and therefore *had* to master each of them to assert his human superiority.

Something was wrong with the *Atlantis*, and he tensed inwardly, waiting for it to happen, ready to take any one of a number of actions, no matter what.

Lew Clay didn't sense anything amiss as the increasing g-load pinned him deeper into the cushions of his copilot's seat. He, too, was an experienced pilot of hot airplanes that screamed through the skies of Earth, and he had more than a dozen Shuttle missions under his belt as well. As he scanned the panel both out of habit and from training, an inner part of his mind was elsewhere . . . because, in spite of the glitch, this seemed to be a normal flight. That little inner part of his mind was living last night over again with vicarious pleasure. Lew enjoyed being a Shuttle pilot for the same reason that motivated a lot of other hot pilots: women.

The most sensual, the most desirable, and the most eager young women had always been attracted to the men of danger: the sailors of the high seas, the railway engineers, and—since the beginning of the twentieth century—the intrepid aeroplane, airplane, and aerospace pilots. Just outside the gates of Vandenberg in Lompoc, a Shuttle pilot could live like a sheik of far Araby. The same held true for the Cape as it always had for Edwards Air Force Base.

It was a great life, Lew was telling himself. Someday he might end up as the command pilot in the left seat, but he didn't need to sit there in order to take advantage of the fringe benefits that accrued to a Shuttle pilot. He was content. He had struggled hard to make it this far. Now he intended to enjoy the most advanced flying job in the world and everything that went with it. If ever there was a happy man, it was Lew Clay. At least, right at that moment.

The same could not be said for George Hazard, whose nickname was obviously "Hap." As the payload specialist, Hap was primarily responsible for the NASA Landsat—it would be known as Landsat-XIII once Hap had powered it up and used the payload arm to place it in orbit—riding in its cradles in the payload bay. Hap Hazard was doing a job he wanted to do, but he wanted to do more. He knew what the Shuttle was ultimately capable of: regular and inexpensive access to space for anyone who wanted it. And he was an angry man because the program wasn't working out that way. Instead of riding herd on a Landsat, he wanted to be shepherding a load of structural components for a space station, a solar-power satellite, or even a space colony.

His mind wasn't yet with the Landsat riding behind him in the bay. His part of the mission wouldn't start until King and Clay had stabilized the orbit so he could get to work.

If it weren't for the pinch-penny Administration, coupled

with a Congress that doted on social programs at the expense of such high-technology efforts as space, he told himself, the United States could be well on its way to becoming the major space power as well as operating on the leading edge of the technology of the high frontier.

There was so much to do! Hap always fretted about this.

But right then he could only do this job, and he was good at it. He was known for being one of the best payload specialists in NASA. He didn't do much flying; this was only his third Shuttle mission. He spent most of his time with his payloads, from the day they were first turned on in the contractor's plant until he placed them in orbit.

But for now, as the *Atlantis* climbed to orbit, Hap had to be content to dream that he was taking part of a space station into orbit rather than merely a prosaic Earth-oriented Landsat.

In the seat beside him on the flight deck, mission specialist Jacqueline Hart had been over the flight plan until it was committed to memory. She wanted to be known as the best mission specialist in the program, and her reputation was already growing. She was good. The best, some said.

She was a pilot, too—and a good one, as might be expected. As the *Atlantis* climbed on its back to space, her eyes focused on Frank King. She was not looking at him as a man, but as a pilot. Having never flown with him before, she was watching Frank's every move because he was known to be one of the best. Another couple hundred hours in the T-38s, she was thinking, and I'll have the high-performance jet hours to qualify as a Shuttle pilot. That she wanted more than anything else in her life, and she realized that an outstanding reputation as a mission specialist certainly would not hurt her chances of upgrading to pilot status.

The gang of hot pilots at Houston who ran the Shuttle manpower scheduling knew that she wanted to be a Shuttle pilot at any expense. But if Jackie Hart ever made the upgrade to pilot status, it would be because she was an outstanding pilot, period. She never would or never could make the grade through proper utilization of feminine wiles. Though an attractive woman, she was almost a female caricature of a man, of the hot pilots she was counted among. She was, as one former fighter jock put it, hard as nails and capable of whipping her weight in wildcats.

"*Atlantis,* Houston. Coming up on SRB burnout. Everything looks copacetic."

"Uh, roger, Houston," Frank grunted as the g-load was now rising to three-gees, making it difficult for him to talk. "Joe, anything showing on that . . . low-level indication . . . we got before liftoff?"

"Negative, *Atlantis.* All telemetry looks good. As old Shorty used to say, all systems A-Okay! Does something appear wrong?"

"Ah . . . negative . . . okay, SRB burnout! We've got SRB separation indication. Both SRBs away." The acceleration had dropped back to one-gee as the two big solid-fuel units burned the last of their propellants and were separated from the External Tank. The acceleration would build slowly back up to three-gees again as the liquid hydrogen and liquid oxygen were burned out of the big tank, making the Shuttle lighter and requiring that the three main rocket engines in the tail of *Atlantis* be throttled back by the computer to keep the acceleration low.

"Okay, *Atlantis,* flight path's nominal . . . going right down the pike," the voice from Houston told him unnecessarily.

"Roger that, Joe. Panel looks normal," Frank said, his eyes continuing to scan because he *knew* that something was wrong somewhere. Still time for a "return to launch site" abort, he told himself.

But the *Atlantis* continued to drive for orbit on her back. Her trajectory was, according to the display on the panel before him, somewhat east of due south, an ascent path that would put her in a slightly retrograde circular orbit 200 nautical miles above the surface. The orbit had been designed so the Landsat would be in "sunsynchronous" orbit, meaning the cameras in the satellite would be looking down at the Earth at the same local or sun time on every orbit.

Four minutes and ten seconds. Frank scratched the "return to launch site" abort possibility from his mind. They couldn't make it back now; they would have to go into the "abort once around" mode—if they could. But it would be another five minutes before the *Atlantis* would achieve sufficient velocity to make that possible.

Frank began to relax inwardly. His experience told him that if something were going to happen, it probably would have happened before now. The solid boosters had separated cleanly and on schedule. The displays told him the *Atlantis* was thrusting along according to plan. There were no caution lights, no warning lights, no malfunctions, and no indications of any impending malfunction. The entire flight thus far had been that way.

Maybe I'm getting jumpy, he told himself. Maybe it was time to take that vacation with Ellie that he had been promising her for so long. The last four years of their married life hadn't been that smooth, but the life of a Shuttle pilot's wife wasn't supposed to be smooth. Not with NASA's policy of running its pilots on a minimum of six missions per year—preferably twelve—to permit them to maintain a high level of proficiency that ground-based simulators could not provide.

In the Houston simulators, the technicians could throw all sorts of emergencies and malfunctions at him without endangering an expensive Shuttle Orbiter. In some ways, the simulator runs with their emergencies were fun for Frank, a big game in which he tried to outwit the technicians. Flying a simulator helps, he thought, but it isn't the same as having your pink bod strapped into the real thing. You can't throw up your hands in defeat and walk off the flight deck on a real mission . . .

A strange sensation brought him back to the reality of the flight of the *Atlantis*. The acceleration was no longer holding him into the back cushions of his pilot's seat.

"MECO!" Lew snapped.

"Main Engine Cutoff? Why?" Frank snapped back, scanning the panel.

There were red lights everywhere.

"Don't know."

They were back in the simulator again. They had to be! This couldn't be real. In all the years of Shuttle operations, there had never been a premature cutoff of main engine operation.

Frank reacted as he would in a simulator, except now he felt that dry-mouth and hard-stomach fear that never occurred in a simulator. Lew worked in unison with him. They both knew what to do, and they responded almost instinctively.

"Jettison the ET." There was no sense in carrying the extra weight of the big External Tank. There was no way to restart those three main engines, and Frank knew that the ET was now penalty weight for whatever they had to do to get down safely.

He felt a slight jolt, then the feeble acceleration of the *Atlantis*'s thrusters pushing the ship away from the tank. "External Tank away," Lew replied in a calm voice.

"Houston, *Atlantis*, ah . . . trouble here." In spite of the fact that adrenalin was pounding through his system and fear was a lump in his throat, Frank managed to maintain the cool, calm, drawling voice of the professional pilot.

"We see it, Frank," Joe Marvin replied from Mission Control in Houston, his calm, cool drawl being transmitted through the Tracking and Data Relay Satellite 23,400 miles above the Earth and back to the *Atlantis*. "Don't know what caused it. Worry about that later. Computer coming up with a landing point for you. Stand by for a possible OMS burn."

"Roger, Joe."

"There isn't a hell of a lot out there ahead of us except water," Lew observed. He began punching data into the shipboard computer. A pictorial of the South Pacific Ocean appeared on the display with the track of the *Atlantis* superimposed on it. The track of the *Atlantis* ended in the South Pacific Ocean. Another manipulation on the computer keypad produced the landing footprint of the *Atlantis* on the screen.

Frank looked at it. "Can't quite make the coast of Peru or Chile. Too far cross-range. Any islands out there, Lew?"

"*Atlantis,* Houston. You have *a* landing point, Frank. You can't make the west coast of South America or any of the Polynesian islands. You've got just one piece of dry ground between you and Antarctica—"

Lew came up with the answer simultaneously with the computer from Houston.

"Isla de Pascua," the copilot announced.

"Easter Island," Mission Control said.

"Has it got an airstrip we can use?" Frank asked.

"Stand by, Frank. We're on the horn to National Ocean Survey right now. We'll get the latest data on whatever airport's there."

"Coordinates: twenty-seven degrees ten minutes south, one-oh-nine degrees twenty-six minutes west." Lew read the computer display unnecessarily. "Forty-eight hundred nautical miles from Vandenberg and a little more than two thousand nautical from the coast of Chile. It's four hundred sixty miles left of our ground track."

Frank was also keying his computer pad. "Sixty-three-second OMS burn," he remarked, referring to the additional velocity that would be needed to reach Easter Island from their present position, said velocity to be provided by the pair of 6000-pound-thrust engines of the Orbital Maneuvering System housed in the two bumps on either side of the *Atlantis's* tail fin.

"*Atlantis*, Houston. Frank, you're lucky. Then again, you're not. You've got an airstrip waiting for you. Stand by to copy the data." Joe Marvin's voice crackled.

"Ready to copy, Joe."

"Mataveri Aerodrome, Isla de Pascua." Joe Marvin at Houston was obviously repeating what he was hearing over a telephone from the National Ocean Survey offices, where the charts were located. "Hard-surfaced runway. Eight thousand eight hundred fifty-eight feet long by a hundred feet wide. Runway One-Zero or Two-Eight. Suggest using Runway One-Zero because of runway slope. Approach end elevation one-thirty, departure end two-twenty-three. No TACAN. VOR frequency one-one-seven-point-one. Nondirectional radio beacon, frequency three-oh-five kilohertz. Both the VOR and the NDB are at the approach end of Runway One-Zero. Control tower frequency one-one-eight-point-one. Stand by one, NOS says the VOR, NDB, and tower are on request."

"Get 'em on the air for us," Frank snapped. "I can land this brick manually, but not without some sort of radio aid to tell me where to aim it. And we can't work the NDB because nobody put a good old low-frequency Automatic Direction Finder aboard this flying anvil." As a matter of fact, Frank thought, they wouldn't have put a standard VHF omnirange receiver and indicator aboard if the Shuttle pilots hadn't pointed out that a lot of potential contingency landing fields around the world did not possess the TACAN radio navigational system of the U.S. Department of Defense.

"Stand by, Frank."

"Roger. Okay, Lew, let's set this thing up for Easter Island." He turned and handed the scrap of paper with Mataveri's numbers to Jackie Hart. "Here. Hang on to these. Read them off to us if we call for them."

Jackie gazed at the numbers and shook her head. "I was afraid that's what I heard. Frank, you'll have to hit that runway dead-nuts. Start your final flare long before you cross the threshold or you'll never have room to stop."

"You just let me worry about that, Jackie. We've got a runway. That's better than finding out whether or not this brick'll float long enough for us to get out of it."

The two pilots calmly set things up for the necessary OMS burn that would provide the added velocity to stretch the glide of the *Atlantis* to Easter Island. It was a puny boost when it came, a mere 12,000 pounds of thrust pushing against the 150,000-pound mass of the *Atlantis*. But a little over a minute's worth of that puny shove was enough. Frank made the cross-range correction with the vernier engines and waited until the *Atlantis* had dropped low enough into the atmosphere for the aerodynamic controls to have an effect.

"*Atlantis,* Houston. Frank, I told you you're lucky." Joe Marvin's voice came through to them. "We reached Santiago by phone, direct dial, believe it or not. The operations office of the Chilean national airline, LAN-Chile, tells us that one of their Seven-Oh-Sevens just took off from Isla de Pascua . . . So the VOR's operating and the tower's manned. You're doubly lucky because there's only one flight a week out of there—and that was it."

"Roger, Joe. We're on our way," Frank replied.

"Any problem with making it, Frank?" Joe asked.

"Yes and no. But we've got to make it, so we will." He didn't tell Houston he was saving some OMS burn time for contingency. He intended to shoot the approach short and use some OMS rocket thrust to stretch the glide if necessary. After hours in the Houston simulators, it was a trick he had worked out for himself. It didn't have NASA's blessing, but he was the spacecraft commander who was between the rock and the hard place at the moment. He would do what he had to do in order to get the *Atlantis* down in one piece. After that, it was Houston's worry.

Lew had dialed-in the VOR frequency for Easter Island. "Too far out," he muttered. "Still have a flag, and I can't get the Morse code identifier yet. Pick it up in about . . . two minutes."

"Can you land this thing manually without the microwave landing system, Frank?" Hap inquired.

"Nobody's ever done it before," Jackie pointed out.

Frank nodded. "Did it in the simulator. Had to fight like hell to get them to set it up for me, but I've practiced it. It won't be easy, but I've got lots of runway with an uphill slope," the pilot replied, concentrating. "Okay, Lew, I've got control response on the sidearm controller."

There was never any question in his mind at the time—only later, when he thought about it and got the shakes—that he could land the *Atlantis* on an 8858-foot runway with no automatic landing system to help him. Shuttle Orbiters usually landed under automatic control, guided by the superaccurate Microwave Scanning Beam Landing System on the ground. To attempt to land with only a VHF Omnirange station to provide horizontal direction, and without any distance information or vertical-glide slope data, would take everything he knew about flying the Shuttle Orbiter.

The fear was still there, but it was a different kind of fear this time. He understood the situation and knew what he could do and would do. This was much different from riding along and wondering what was going to happen. The emergency *had* happened. The malfunction *had* occurred. The mission *was* aborted. Now he knew exactly what he and Lew would have to do.

The same sort of quiet fear welled up in copilot Lew Clay, who now realized why Shuttle pilots were the jocks of their day, why the fringe benefits were so good, and why he was sitting in the right seat. He was going to earn his salary for a change. But the judgment calls would be Frank's; Lew was just a backup man. He didn't know right then whether he could handle the sort of responsibility that was resting on Frank at the moment. Maybe it was just as well, he told himself, that he was riding the right seat.

Maybe he never wanted to move into the left seat. Maybe that was why he was happy where he was.

The *Atlantis* dropped through the upper atmosphere, her stubby wings reaching for lift to glide and her black bottom hardly getting warm in comparison with the searing heat of an ordinary entry into the atmosphere from orbit. True, her tiles became hot, but not the white-hot ablative heat of entry.

"Two hundred thousand feet," Lew called out. "Okay, I've got the VOR signal."

"Set me up for the two-eight-zero radial inbound on the reciprocal, Lew," Frank ordered. "Houston, *Atlantis*. You wouldn't by chance happen to have the current Mataveri weather, would you?"

"Negative, *Atlantis*. Best we've got is the satellite photo, shows generally clear in the area, maybe some high, thin clouds. Suggest you try the tower."

Frank wanted to say something, but he didn't. The comm panel was over on Lew's side of the flight deck. "Lew, dial-up the Pascua tower."

Lew's right hand went quickly to the overhead panel. "You've got it."

Frank's course plot on the display showed they were about fifty miles out—if he could rely on the inertial data from the guidance system. But he had to. He had no TACAN, with its distance-measuring equipment, to guide him in. In fact, he didn't have even the simplest commercial distance-measuring equipment, because Isla de Pascua had nothing more than an ordinary, everyday, commercial VHF Omnirange station and an even more primitive non-directional radio beacon which the *Atlantis* lacked the receivers for anyway.

The island was set up to handle an occasional commercial flight, not an emergency landing of the supersophisticated NASA Space Shuttle with its advanced electronics and communications equipment—UHF, TACAN, Microwave Scanning Beam Landing System, and S-band, pulse-modulated voice transmissions to orbiting relay satellites.

Somewhere along the line, Frank thought fleetingly, maybe the supersophisticated technology should have left a little room for a lot of the old technology that was already in place and working just fine.

"Pascua Tower, Shuttle Orbiter *Atlantis*. Mayday! Mayday! How do you read? Over."

A voice tinged with a heavy Latin accent came back. Frank had heard it before: Spanish-speaking air traffic control operators over the Caribbean or Spain. English might be the international language of air traffic control, but that didn't mean that pronunciation and accent were universal. "*Atlantis,* theese ees Pascua Tower. I read you loud and clear. What ees the nature of your emergency, please?"

"Pascua Tower, *Atlantis*. We're a United States Space Shuttle Orbiter. We've had a propulsion malfunction that prevented us from going into orbit. We *must* land at Easter Island because we have no power. We're forty miles northwest at one-five-zero thousand feet, landing Mataveri in less than five minutes. I've got only one chance to make it. What's your weather, please?" Frank snapped back curtly. Time to worry about the consequences of such undiplomatic language later. He was getting pushed for time.

"*Atlantis,* Mataveri weather is thirty thousand, high thin broken, visibility ten kilometers, wind one-three-zero at ten, altimeter one-zero-six-five millibars. Landing Runway One-Zero. I do not have a visual on you yet. Please report the field in sight. Over."

"One hundred thousand feet," Lew reminded Frank.

"Roger. Watch that display and call out the distances according to the inertial navigator. I want to keep heads-up for the island."

"Three-five miles."

"Okay, we've got the VOR needle in the center. Setting up a twenty-four-degree glide slope. Lew, the OMS system hot?"

"Roger."

The conversation became terse but not panicky. White knuckles gripped the armrests where Hap Hazard and Jackie Hart sat, but not in the pilots' seats. The cockpit recording tapes would later reveal an unreal professional calmness in the voices of the two men.

The *Atlantis* broke through the thin cloud layer at 30,000 feet, and the South Pacific Ocean sparkled below. Frank peered intently through the forward windows, straining to see the one single spot of land in 2000 miles of ocean.

"Twenty thousand feet. You're drifting left of the radial."

"Tally ho!" Frank called out at the same instant that both Hap and Jackie, watching over the shoulders of the two pilots, saw it, too. Easter Island lay dead ahead. The black strip of Mataveri Aerodrome cut across the narrow southwest neck of the island.

"Pascua Tower, *Atlantis*. We have the field in sight."

"*Atlantis*, thees ees Pascua Tower. You are cleared to land, but we have no fire trucks available."

"I hope we won't need them, Pascua Tower. But we may have to evacuate the ship quickly once we've landed."

"Roger, *Atlantis*. We will do what we can to help you."

"Hang on, gang, we may make it without an OMS burn," Frank muttered. He began to talk to himself aloud as he manually flew the *Atlantis* down to the ground, a habit he had picked up years ago as a green student pilot shooting his first instrument approaches into Cincinnati's Lunken Field. This time, however, he had no instruments other than his experienced eyes to rely on, no data other than his own memories of shooting landings like this in the Houston simulators, and absolutely no expertise at all doing it in a full Space Shuttle Orbiter operating with a payload aboard. He was glad that the avionics and computers hadn't failed; he was getting the right amount of computer-generated feedback through the stubby sidearm controller that was the *Atlantis*'s version of the old control stick of airplanes past. "Hold her in there. Drifting right now. Down on the nose. Keep that airspeed up. Lew, give me altitude and airspeed call-outs."

"Ten thousand five hundred. Three hundred knots."

"Sounds good. We'll make it. Like landing a brick. Who told NASA this thing was a glider? Keep the nose down . . ."

"Five thousand. Three hundred knots."

"Turbulence. Steady her in there. Little high. Energy management, that's what we need. Got plenty of energy, plenty of altitude and airspeed to make the strip."

"Two thousand. Three hundred knots. Inertial system says one mile."

"Not that accurate this close. Okay, pull up. Here we go.

Three degrees. Looks good. Hold it. Hold it. *Gear down!* Bleed off the airspeed. Runway threshold coming up."

The end of the Easter Island runway was rushing at him. He fought a pilot's natural instinct to haul back on the stick and get the nose up more to lose airspeed. It was the first instinct of any green pilot when trying to land in the Shuttle simulator.

"Altitude too low to read. Three hundred maybe. Two-twenty knots . . . bleeding off . . . two-oh-five . . ."

"Over the fence." It was almost a shout from Frank. Not willing to use up a single foot more of the runway than he had to, he popped the speed brakes on the vertical fin and dropped the *Atlantis* to the runway. It hit with a cloud of smoke as the four tires of the main gear contacted the asphalt at more than 200 miles per hour. The impact almost drove the wheels through a runway designed and built to handle the gentler landings of commercial jets.

Frank pulled the sidearm control stick back as far as possible, keeping the nose high. "Brakes," he snapped. "Override the antiskid if you have to, Lew. We're running out of runway."

Two parking aprons on either side of the runway flashed past. The nose wheels dropped to the pavement as the brakes came on. Frank really wasn't worried. The *Atlantis* could be stopped in 5000 feet if necessary—and he had touched down within 1000 feet of the end of an almost 9000-foot-long runway with an uphill gradient. He would get it stopped in time.

But slowing 150,000 pounds of Orbiter from 200 miles per hour to a dead stop can't be done quickly—or without a lot of braking effort. The designers said that it could be done in 5000 feet, but the designers weren't flying the craft. This wasn't the drawing board or the computer terminal.

But the designers were right. The computers were right. And Shuttle Command Pilot Frank King had done everything just right. The Space Shuttle Orbiter *Atlantis*, with four people and a Landsat aboard, came to a shuddering halt 800 feet from the end of the runway on Easter Island in the South Pacific Ocean.

Lew was covered with cold sweat. "Jesus H. P. Christ, Frank! That was one hell of a job."

Hap said nothing. His face was white, but color was beginning to return to his cheeks.

"Damned fine landing, Frank," Jackie snapped. If she looked cool, Frank knew she wasn't. The slip of paper with the Mataveri data on it was crumpled and wilted in her damp hands.

Frank sighed. He wasn't sweating. He hadn't had time to sweat. He had been very busy. Now he looked around out the side windows of the flight deck. "We're down. The worst is over."

CHAPTER TWO

The telephone rang.

Casey Laskewitz swung his desk chair around from where he was typing the latest news release into the word processor:

> *The NASA Space Shuttle* Atlantis *lifted from Vandenberg Air Force Base, California, this morning carrying Landsat-XIII into orbit around the Earth. The Landsat-XIII is the latest in the modern generation of satellites designed to monitor Earth resources and detect pollution . . .*

He hated to be interrupted when he was cranking out a news release on the Shuttle. It was important that each of them was done correctly to project the proper image of the Shuttle to both the media and the general public. At least, it was important to K. C. Laskewitz.

He grabbed the phone. "NASA Public Affairs, Space Shuttle Media Relations, Laskewitz speaking."

"Casey, Reed Richardson."

A grin broke over Laskewitz's long face. "Hey, Red, how'd the launch go?"

"It didn't," came the flat reply from the NASA mission manager in Houston. "Casey, move on Project Shuttle Down."

"Ohmigawd." Casey Laskewitz made it sound like a single word. He grabbed a pencil and a sheet of scratch paper. "Where? Anybody hurt? Details?"

"Easter Island."

"Easter Island? That's ten million miles from *anywhere!*"

"How right you are. King reports the *Atlantis* is on the ground at the Mataveri airstrip there. All personnel are okay. The Orbiter is apparently undamaged. We don't know what happened, but there was a premature MECO. Your shots current?"

"Uh, yeah. Were the last time I checked."

"Okay, get moving. The team's meeting here in Houston at sixteen hundred hours, local, this afternoon. We'll try to be on our way by nineteen hundred from Ellington, the Air Force willing."

"That's fast, Red, but I'll get the media clued in right away," the Public Affairs man replied. "Use your name on the Shuttle Down Release Number Three?"

"Yeah, okay, but nobody'll be able to reach me. Joe Marvin'll handle things here in Houston until you get your shop set up on Easter Island. Uh, Casey, maybe you oughta let old Uncivil Service himself handle the release. He'll have to coordinate it with the State Department. We've got no agreement with Chile for contingency landing rights on Easter Island. Gotta go now. See ya at sixteen hundred." The phone went dead.

"Sonofabitch," Laskewitz growled under his breath. He slammed the phone into its cradle, his mind racing. This wasn't the ordinary Shuttle Down contingency landing that NASA had tried to prepare for in advance. Several years of delicate negotiations conducted by State had resulted in contingency landing rights in Spain and Okinawa. But nothing with Chile!

Somebody had forgotten to cover the bases for polar orbits.

Wait a minute, Laskewitz thought. Somewhere there was a United Nations treaty on rescue and return of astronauts and space objects. He grabbed the phone and dialed a number.

"June, Casey Laskewitz. Get me the full text of the UN treaty on astronaut rescue, and get it up here *fast!*" Without waiting for an answer from the girl in the NASA library archives, he turned back to his console, punched the code for Shuttle Contingency Releases, and peered at the directory that flashed on the screen.

Why, Casey asked himself, had the Front Office tried to weasel-word an emergency by calling it a "contingency"?

In anticipation of the Shuttle Down possibility, he had prewritten several press releases using bogus Orbiter and crew member names. He had only to call up the releases from the computer memory, run global search and replace to insert the right names and other data, and run out a hard copy. Quickly, he checked the text of four releases, selected one, typed the data into his keypad, and told the word processor to print it. Then he swung around and grabbed the telephone again.

Reed Richardson was playing it as cool as he could in spite of the incredible situation. Mission Control had calmed down following King's landing at Mataveri. Now the monkey was on Richardson's back as the mission manager in overall charge of the flight of the *Atlantis* from checkout to final unloading and refurbishment.

First things first, as far as he was concerned. Although the procedures manual said one thing, he had done what he considered to be the Number One Job: notify Casey Laskewitz and get the proper story out to the media before somebody leaked a rumor. It was easier to get the story out first and worry about the possibility of dealing with the bureaucrats on top of him than to wait and then attempt to explain away the nonfacts of unfounded rumors. The possibility remained that some eager science reporter had been monitoring the Shuttle frequencies on a scanner or that some eager science buff might have picked up some of the satellite transmissions from the TDRS and figured out that the *Atlantis* was down. But the chances were slim. Hardly any reporter covered a Shuttle launch any more, and it didn't even rate mention as a sidebar on page 86 these days.

But Reed Richardson knew that Project Shuttle Down would be the top news story of the day—and he thought he knew how the media would handle it. After all, hadn't they been on NASA's ass for spending all that money in space ever since Armstrong and Aldrin landed on the moon? Now, the news media couldn't care less, except occasionally to blast the space program as an unnecessary government boondoggle, a waste of tax money that could be better put into social programs so that, in effect, the Department of Social Welfare could spend the NASA annual budget in less than four days.

Reed Richardson was very bitter.

So the Shuttle mission manager in charge of the Landsat-XIII flight of the *Atlantis* knew exactly whom he should call first: Casey Laskewitz at Public Affairs.

Having done so, he then started to follow the NASA procedure for Shuttle Down and, with considerable trepidation, called Duke Kellogg.

The Shuttle missions and their technical problems weren't his biggest headaches. Because of the "System" his boss was his Number One Problem. In order to eliminate as far as possible the appointment of civil service personnel as part of a political spoils arrangement, the Civil Service Commission had, over the course of decades, built a monumental edifice of rules, regulations, and policies that, when put into action, usually accomplished what they were designed to prevent: the retention of incompetents in the top-level GS grades.

The System could be manipulated, and it was. A negative power system consisting of rules and regulations concerning "thou shalt not," it left room aplenty for those who would bend the rules. And it was set up so that any advance in grade was determined by the number of people a person supervised—*not* on the quality of his work.

To say that Reed Richardson was bitter was an understatement. He hung on because he felt the only way to get Man into space was to play the game in the main tent. But Kellogg was a perfect product of the System.

"Duke, Red," Richardson said over the phone after Kellogg's secretary connected them. "The *Atlantis* just went down on Easter Island in the Pacific. Frank King and Lew Clay made a beautiful manual landing on the Mataveri airstrip there. Premature MECO. I need your authority to initiate Shuttle Down."

Duke Kellogg was an old Air Force jet jock who hadn't made the grade to flight-astronaut status in Apollo or Sky-Lab, and he was now considered too old to fly the Shuttle. "Well, now, let's not get our water hot, Red. Crew okay?"

"Yes."

"How about the Orbiter?"

"King reports he got it on the ground without any landing aids except his calibrated eyeballs," Red replied curtly.

"The man's good," Kellogg observed unnecessarily. "Can you patch me into the net with him? I want to talk to him."

"Duke, their communications are down," Red reminded him. "King and Clay have their hands full right now powering-down the *Atlantis* without any ground-support equipment to help cool things off. They shut down the fuel cells right after they reported a successful landing. We know they're down, and we know they're okay. I've got to get Shuttle Down moving right away."

"Okay, wait one. Let me get the procedures manual here."

"I've got it in front of me, Duke. What do you want to know?"

"Just want to make sure we proceed in an orderly fashion, Red. We spent a lot of time and effort working out the plans for contingency landing on foreign soil. When the crunch comes and the panic button gets pushed, we've got the procedures manual with everything worked out ahead of time. Keeps us from making mistakes."

"For God's sake, Duke, I know what has to be done! All I need is your authorization to proceed. We've got twenty-five percent of the United States' manned space flight capability sitting helpless on a runway two thousand miles from anywhere. I need to get the teams moving, the equipment lined up, the Air Force off the dime—in short, Shuttle Down activated. Your office and Headquarters can worry about the implications and rescheduling the next three months' flights . . ." He didn't tell Kellogg that some of his people were already on the horn to Marshall Space Flight Center to get the stiffleg derrick ready and a mobile crane rented, and to Dryden Center at Edwards for the 747 carrier aircraft, NASA 905. "And, Duke, you'll have to coordinate with somebody at Headquarters. We don't have a contingency landing agreement with the government of Chile."

"What's that got to do with it?"

"Easter Island's owned by Chile," Red reminded him.

"Oh. In that case, we've got to interface with State."

"Probably, but that's not my worry."

"Okay, I'll handle it. You notified Headquarters?"

"Negative," Red lied. Then he couldn't resist tweaking Duke's tail a little bit, so he added, "According to the procedures manual, that's your job, Duke. Give me clearance to get started, then you probably ought to call the Front Office. The bird's been on the deck for seven minutes now."

"Ah, you're right, Red. Okay, you obviously know what you're doing there, and you've read the book. Go on Shuttle Down! I'll call Headquarters, then scat right down to Mission Control there. That way, I can stay on top of things with you."

Great! Red thought. Thank God I'll be on a plane to Easter Island before the day is out! He knew the Mission Control crew would keep things in order here. They wouldn't start working the next mission of the *Columbia* out of the Cape for another five days. And they knew better than to let Duke Kellogg try to take over. Joe Marvin would see to that. Even Duke Kellogg found it hard to argue with a Shuttle pilot who had been retired off active flight status after twenty missions and burned hands from opening the hatch on an emergency basis after an otherwise normal Cape landing.

"Hi, hon. Casey. Look, I've gotta go to Easter Island, so I won't be home for about two months . . . Sorry, hon, but we've got a Shuttle down there. And it's my job . . . I know, I know . . . But we've talked about the possibility of this . . . I'm leaving for Houston with Jake Hardin in less than thirty minutes. He's up here from the Astronaut Office with a T-38, and he'll fly me back to Houston with him. I've gotta be there by five o'clock, our time, this afternoon . . . Yeah, Jessica will mail my check directly to you while I'm gone . . ."

"Colonel Hubbard."

"Matt, Reed Richardson in Houston."

"What's the good word, Red?"

"Shuttle Down."

"Oh, great! Where?"

"Easter Island in the South Pacific."

"Can't you pick a better place, Red?" the Air Force officer asked, looking up at a map of the world behind his desk. Just as he thought: the Military Airlift Command didn't have a base within thousands of miles.

"I didn't pick it, Matt. Frank King and Lew Clay had an emergency out of Vandenberg," Red told him flatly. "It was either Easter Island or the drink."

"Okay, listen, I'll get the staff working on the problems," the young bird-colonel replied, thinking that this might be one that would justify his getting out of his Military Airlift Command office at Andrews Air Force Base and maybe logging some time. He could see from the map that it was going to be a big, long-range operation, and he didn't think that the Air Force had developed any contingency plans for Easter Island. "There's going to be problems with operations into Easter Island, Red. I'll tell you more about them in a few hours. In the meantime, we'll get a C-5 Galaxy out of Dover to Huntsville to pick up the stiffleg. Anything else while I'm at it? Need fighter cover?"

"Got anything available to airlift our initial team of fifteen people into Easter Island?"

"I'll check. What's the airfield like? I'm running through my FLIP chart book here, but I don't find Easter Island listed at all."

"Try looking for Isla de Pascua, Chile, on your Jepp charts."

"Hoo boy! Yeah, I've got it in front of me now. I don't know if we've got landing rights . . ."

"We will. Just get things moving, Matt. Going to take this one yourself?"

"You read my mind, Red. Stay at Mission Control. I'll be back with you shortly."

"I'll be here. We're not going anywhere without the Air Force."

"Hell, Joe, NASA Nine-Oh-Five's in the shop with the engines undergoing maintenance. There's a new Airworthiness Directive out on the burner cans," Hank Hoffman said into the phone, looking out his window to where he could see the huge tail of the 747 Shuttle carrier sticking out of the hangar of NASA's Dryden Flight Research Center at Edwards Air Force Base in California's Mohave Desert. "It'll be at least a month before the shop gets those cans reworked, at the rate we have to move around here on the tight budget . . ."

"Hank, we've got Shuttle Down operations going here with full authority to proceed according to the manual," Joe Marvin explained. "Consider that you've got full authority to go to Pan Am or American or United or *anybody* who flies Seven-Forty-Sevens—even to Pratt and Whitney if you have to. Get your engines any way you can, but get them fast. Let me know what you need in the way of purchase orders or contract obligations or whatever. We're pulling in Danny Davis from JPL as contracting officer. He'll be here until the team leaves for Easter Island. You gotta have NASA Nine-Oh-Five on Easter Island according to schedule for the recovery."

Casey Laskewitz burst out of his office at Headquarters and started down the long corridor toward the corner office occupied by his boss, Roger Service. But he didn't get there. He met the NASA Public Affairs deputy coming down the hallway almost at a full run toward him.

"Laskewitz, we've got the *Atlantis* down!"

Casey nodded. "I know, Roger. Here's the release, ready for your approval."

"How did you find out?" Roger Service asked. "The Administrator himself just called me . . ."

"Richardson phoned me from Houston," Casey explained as he led his boss back into the Shuttle PA office.

"Why did he call you first? Why did I have to find out from the top?"

"Because that's the way it's laid out in the Shuttle Down procedures manual," Casey reminded him.

"Oh. Well, if that's what the book says, that's the way we do it. I want to call a meeting with you and your people for two o'clock."

"They already know what to do, and they're doing it—and, besides, I'll be on my way to Houston with Jake Hardin in a T-38," Casey said, indicating the bags sitting next to his desk. He always kept four bags there, each fully packed with a week's worth of clothing for tropics, arctic, desert, or temperate climates. "But, Roger, there's a big, fat problem here that you've got to handle, because it isn't in the book and I'll be out on Easter Island."

Roger Service hesitated for a moment. If it wasn't in the book, there were no plans laid out. And that meant new plans and procedures would have to be worked up in a hurry, probably in some all-night sessions. He had grown tired of that sort of thing in the old public relations rat race on Madison Avenue, where decisions often had to be made fast and furiously in reaction to any number of happenstances. Here at NASA, he had found a very comfortable job. Service did his work by the book. Procedures were everything these days. Even planning the procedures involved procedures that were scrupulously followed. "What's the problem?" he asked.

"Easter Island," Casey explained. "We have no contingency landing-rights agreement with Chile, which owns it."

"So? Isn't there a UN treaty or something?"

Laskewitz picked up a sheaf of papers from his desk and handed them to his boss. "Yup. Here's the text of the treaty itself. Haven't read it. Haven't had time. I didn't clear the news release myself according to the book because the Department of State is probably going to have to get involved in this."

"I haven't the authority to interface with State," Service complained. "The Administrator's going to have to do that."

"It'd make the Office look pretty good if you were the one to bring one matter to his attention, wouldn't it?"

"Uh . . . yeah, it would, Casey. Thanks. I'll get right up there to him."

"Okay, Roger, I'll call you from Houston. I'll feed you stuff out of Houston and Easter Island for official release here—according to the procedures manual." Casey Laskewitz glanced at his watch. "Jake's waiting for me down in the parking garage right now."

"Wait a minute." Roger Service tried to bring his subordinate up short. "I haven't signed your travel authorization yet."

Casey grinned and waved a manila envelope as he picked up Suitcase Number One. "Sure you did. Remember? Couple of months ago, after I got my shots. It was part of the procedure, Roger. See ya!"

"We can't get through to them?"

"We can't get through to them, Red," Joe Marvin explained. "There's no telephone link to Easter Island. No cable. No satellite ground station. Just an old low-frequency radio station at Hangaroa, the only village on the island."

"How about checking with the Chileans in Santiago?" Richardson suggested. The pressure of the past hour was getting to him now. His stomach was upset, and he was fighting off the tension hiccups he usually got when under extreme stress. Ordinarily, he was a cool customer, and he had been selected for his position because of that. He wasn't a former fighter pilot, but the old fighter jocks who ran so much of the manned space flight program had decided that Reed Richardson was, in essence, One Of Them and could therefore be trusted to keep a cool stool and a hot pot. The boys with the Right Stuff felt they could trust guys like Richardson, just as they trusted most of the experienced FAA air traffic controllers they worked with.

Joe Marvin sighed and placed his gnarled hands on the edge of the controller's console. "Red, who do I call? Who do I talk to there? What do I say? And am I authorized to make such a call? Dammit, you've trained us all in the detailed procedures that this outfit dearly loves, but there's *no* provision for calling the President of Chile. Not only is my Spanish lousy, but that recent problem down there is something even the CIA doesn't like to think about."

At that point Red almost lost his cool. He grabbed for a telephone handset. "Dammit, we've got four people and several billion dollars' worth of Orbiter sitting down there! I'll call *somebody* and get through to them!" He reached out to punch the dialing buttons.

Joe rested a hand on his boss's arm. "Red, sit down and take five. Our team is safe for now. They'll get that bird cooled down because it didn't go through much of an entry." As Richardson slowly replaced the handset in its cradle, the former astronaut continued. "So what are you going to say to them? 'Hey, man, we landed one of our spaceships on one of your islands by mistake, and we'd like to come and get it. And we're arriving with our military C-5 transports and other aircraft, plus at least a hundred people.' Red, their so-called students tried to storm our Embassy in Santiago six months ago."

"Sorry, you're right," Richardson sighed. "I've gotta assume that Headquarters has been in touch with the Department of State and something's in the mill. But it just galls the hell out of me to be sitting here surrounded by all this supertechnology that's totally *worthless* right now. We can communicate with the Voyagers out a couple of billion miles in the outer Solar System, but we can't even make a telephone call—much less a simple radio contact—to an island in the Pacific Ocean! Right now, Easter Island could be as far away as the stars for all we can do . . ."

Alfred M. Dewey sighed and looked at the pad of notes he had just made during the telephone call from his boss, the Assistant Secretary of State. He didn't like what he saw. And he didn't relish the nasty job that had just been dropped in his lap—with full authority to do whatever was necessary, but please coordinate with the Assistant Secretary to make certain that no diplomatic protocol got crossed up in the process.

In spite of the fact that Dewey was a State Department specialist in high-technology interfaces with South American nations, he still had an ancient, wood-cased, vacuum-tube intercom set on his desk. He flipped two switches down, pushed the talk handle, and said, "Miss Fisher? Mr. Sullivan? Please come into my office immediately. This is reasonably urgent, so drop whatever you're doing and bring something to take notes on."

In the hallowed corridors of what was called Old Foggy Bottom, that simple understated request amounted to something that would have been classed as a direct order across the river in the Pentagon. Joyce Fisher and Nash Sullivan walked into Dewey's office less than two minutes later.

Youngsters! Dewey thought with some disdain. What

was State coming to? These two had been the bane of his existence since coming aboard in June following their graduation from MIT and Cornell, respectively. The seasoned State Department administrator had immediately found himself on the defensive when they had been assigned to his office staff, not because they were young, but because they were both bright and aware of current technology.

Sullivan was a tall, gangling redhead who might have been more at home on a basketball court. The young man was, instead, an electronic engineer, Phi Beta Kappa, and summa cum laude. Unlike many young, technical people, he had picked up a minor in political science. To some extent, Dewey felt threatened by Nash Sullivan in spite of the fact that the young man had a very pleasing personality and no apparent willingness to play the little games of internal politics that went on around him. His puppylike eagerness showed in his greeting to Dewey. "Hi, Boss, glad you called. I just worked out a solution to that Honeywell computer deal in Argentina."

"It'll have to wait a bit. Sit down, please," Dewey told him.

On the other hand, Joyce Fisher disturbed Alfred M. Dewey as she followed Sullivan into the office. She had disturbed him ever since her initial interview. He had wanted to tell Personnel he couldn't use her, but he instead found himself confirming her for one of the two slots he had available. As a bachelor in his middle years, Alfred M. Dewey had found women either unattractive and therefore unstimulating—or so overpowerfully attractive that he was afraid of them. However, Joyce Fisher affected him as no other young woman had. Not that her dark-haired, sultry appearance was provocative or even exceptionally attractive. Nor was it her soft voice, whether speaking in Spanish or in English. To Dewey, it was the way she moved and acted and spoke that stirred strange feelings within him. If only she weren't young enough to be my daughter! he had once thought. But he had no daughter. Like Sullivan, Joyce Fisher exhibited the eagerness of youth and the enthusiasm for her job that would probably wear off after several years of battling the Department and its policies and protocols. She merely nodded and sat down, smoothing a wrinkle out of her pants suit as she settled back in the chair.

Dewey cleared his throat. "I'm going to have to pull both of you off your present assignments temporarily and put you on a rather urgent matter that's just come up." At his words, Sullivan raised his thin eyebrows. Joyce Fisher cocked her head sideways, an intent expression on her face.

"It seems the chaps over at the space agency have created a small international incident." He continued slowly, filling them in while trying to keep his eyes off Joyce and on the notes he had taken. His presentation finally wound down with, "The situation is confused, to say the least."

"I'd expect as much," Sullivan said. "From what I know of the area, Isla de Pascua is probably the most remote place on the face of the Earth."

"It's known to the natives as Rapa Nui," Joyce Fisher put in. "But they also call it *te Pito o te Henua*, which means 'the navel of the world' or 'the center of the world,' depending on translation."

"So the Shuttle went down," Sullivan mused. "It was bound to happen sooner or later. But, Chief, don't we have international agreements giving us emergency landing rights?"

"With Spain and Japan," Dewey pointed out, "but not with Chile. True, Chile signed the UN treaty on astronaut and space-vehicle rescue and return. That doesn't seem to be adequate for the space people. Seems they've got only four of these Space Shuttles, and they've booked flights and taken money down and a whole list of other things. So they want that Shuttle back as quickly as possible."

"Boss, if I remember that UN treaty, the Chileans have to return the craft to us . . ." Sullivan began, then stopped to think for a moment. "However, I don't know how they're going to manage it. They don't have the capability. That thing must weigh more than fifty tons, and it doesn't have any engines of its own that would permit it to be flown through the atmosphere."

"The Assistant Secretary made me well aware of the technical facts," Dewey said testily, trying not to let this youngster get the better of him when it came to such things. "The United States has to go in and retrieve the *Atlantis*. According to NASA, that will require C-5 Galaxy military transport planes, plus other military transports carrying about a hundred people, plus the NASA Nine-Oh-Five, the Seven-Forty-Seven airplane that can carry the *Atlantis* on its back."

"Can't NASA do it alone, without help from the Air Force?" Joyce inquired.

"They own only the Seven-Forty-Seven," Dewey explained. "Because they've been on such a tight budget for the last decade or so, they couldn't afford to buy and maintain the fleet of large transports required to carry out an emergency rescue mission such as this."

"Yes, they've always relied on DOD for spacecraft recovery and other emergency facilities," Nash Sullivan observed, taking notes. He looked up suddenly. "Chief, is the current Chilean government going to let us land military aircraft on their territory to pick up the *Atlantis*?"

"*That* is only *one* problem," Dewey said, tapping his pencil on his note pad. "Diplomatic relations are slightly strained at the moment following the recent difficulties." He sighed and continued. "We've been given the job of handling the diplomatic side of this rescue operation. According to the Assistant Secretary, the Secretary himself has given me carte blanche to handle this, and it's on a rush priority basis. NASA wants to get its recovery teams on their way *this afternoon*."

Nash Sullivan whistled.

Joyce Fisher shook her head in disbelief.

State didn't usually work that fast, and all three of them knew it.

"So this conference is going to be short," Alfred M. Dewey asserted. "We're not to let either NASA or DOD accuse State of dragging its feet on this one. We've been given priority orders. Full use of discretionary funds has been approved. Sullivan, I want you on the next plane to New York; you're going to be the Department's technical man at the UN—and we have to interface on that level because of the UN treaty. Miss Fisher, because of your familiarity with the region and your fluency in the language, I want you to be State's direct representative on the NASA recovery team. Get to Houston as quickly as you can and contact the NASA people—I have their names here. I'll coordinate from this end." Dewey got to his feet and looked at his watch. "I'm due at the Chilean Embassy in twenty minutes for a meeting with the chargé d'affaires. Sullivan, stay in touch with me through our UN mission. Miss Fisher, I'll stay in touch with you through NASA until you get to Santiago; then use our Embassy's diplomatic channels—but I want you in either Santiago or Isla de Pascua, wherever you feel the situation requires you. And you've got a very difficult job, given the current situation."

Joyce Fisher replied coolly, "It may not be as difficult as you've told me. I think I can handle it, Mr. Dewey." Her reaction was also one of quiet eagerness. She was finally going into the field to work on a delicate diplomatic mission concerning high technology. True, her degree in chemical engineering from MIT hadn't covered many of the aspects of astronautics, but she felt her familiarity with South America was far more important than a detailed technical background.

Sullivan was grinning from ear to ear. This was just the sort of assignment he had always dreamed of. What other young college graduate had ever had such an important job dropped in his lap within months of joining a large government operation? "Yessir, I'll be on the first flight to New York once I can get a bag packed."

In a large, concrete building near the Potomac River, in Langley, Virginia, another conversation was in progress: "Chief, NASA's dropped a Shuttle Orbiter onto Easter Island. State's certain to be involved in the recovery plans, which are going to be extensive. I felt you should know about this because it's probably going to severely impact our operations in Santiago. I want to activate three of our sleeper agents, including the one on Easter Island . . ."

Another report was being given at an embassy located at 1125 Sixteenth Street N.W.: "Comrade Ambassador, as the KGB representative here, I must inform you that the Americans have made an unauthorized emergency landing of their Space Shuttle *Atlantis* on Chile's Isla de Pascua. The recovery effort of the Americans will drastically affect our programs in Chile. But this accident of theirs will give us an opportunity to hamper their competitive space effort. The *Atlantis* was launched from the military Vandenberg Air Force Base complex and is carrying what NASA claims is an Earth-resources satellite. However, why would the Americans devote an entire expensive Shuttle payload to a single Earth-resources satellite? My information says that the payload is actually a nuclear-powered satellite carrying a high-energy laser-beam weapon for the military purposes of their Department of Defense."

CHAPTER THREE

"Emergency power-down. We have no ground-support cooling equipment," Frank said crisply.

Although they hadn't gone through a full entry with the maximum heat load that would be encountered in such a maneuver, the *Atlantis* had picked up some aerodynamic heating. And the operation of the three fuel cells providing electrical power, plus the two auxiliary units powering the hydraulic system, had created internal heat loads. Normally, ground-service trucks would quickly pull alongside after landing to blow cool air into the *Atlantis* to keep these heat-generating devices and the electronic equipment cool. It was different here on the runway at Mataveri, however. Very different.

Lew shut down the last fuel cell, thereby cutting off their communications with the TDRS satellite and with Mission Control at Houston. But Frank's last brief message from the *Atlantis* had told Joe Marvin they were safely on the runway at Mataveri, there was no damage to the ship, and the four of them were okay.

In Frank's opinion, there was no time for worry or concern about what Mission Control and NASA would do. He was familiar with the gross details of the contingency landing program—help would be on the way shortly.

Meanwhile, he was still in command of the *Atlantis* and fully responsible for her. Not only did he have to worry about doing the right things for the Orbiter, he also had the well-being of his crew to think about. "Hap! Jackie! Get the hatch open. Get the survival kits off-loaded. And get out of this bird. Lew and I will be out just as soon as we get everything shut down. We've still got a couple thousand pounds of toxic hypergolics aboard."

The mission specialist and the payload specialist did not need any further urging. They had been through the emergency drills before. They knew the hazards associated with a contingency landing without benefit of ground-support elements to cool off the critical systems, drain off the hypergolic propellants—chemicals which would ignite spontaneously on contact—that were also highly toxic, and disarm those pyrotechnics that were still functional. The two of them were unstrapping almost at once, and as the two pilots worked over the panels, the specialists dropped through the hatch to the mid-deck.

As they extracted the emergency egress equipment from the lockers on the mid-deck, Jackie couldn't help commenting to Hap, "Damn, that was one hell of a fine landing!"

Hap didn't look up from where he was removing equipment from a locker. "Could you do as well, Jackie?" he asked quietly.

"Probably."

"Well, when you can honestly say you know you can, maybe Duke'll give you a try." He let it drop at that.

Jackie straightened up and put her hands on her hips. "Listen, Hap . . ." she began.

Hap still didn't look up. "Jackie, if the hypergolics are leaking in the tail section, we'll get a free ride back to Vandenberg on the shock wave. So let's fight later, okay?" He tossed part of the emergency ground-survival kit at her. She caught it. He dug the rest of the components out of the storage areas while she stacked them by the still-closed side hatch.

"That it?" she asked, now cooled down.

"Yeah."

"I'm opening the side hatch. It's getting hot in here."

As the side hatch flopped horizontally outward, the thermal apron deployed around its edges and a breath of warm, moist, ocean-scented air rushed in. Jackie crawled out onto the hatch and looked around.

"It's like landing on the Moon!" she exclaimed.

"What do you mean?" Hap stuck his head through the opening and stared.

There wasn't a tree to be seen anywhere. To the north, several volcanic cones rose into the sky, their slopes covered with brownish-green grass. Rocks were everywhere. Except for the black asphalt runway of Mataveri Aerodrome, there was no sign of humanity.

And it was quiet.

Save for the soft whisper of the sea breeze blowing along the runway and the creaking of the *Atlantis* as her structure cooled, there was no sound, not even the squall of sea gulls.

Jackie tossed a glance toward the tail of the *Atlantis*. "Visually, we look okay back there, Hap. Drag out the rope ladder."

"What rope ladder?"

"That's right, you don't know about it." Jackie crawled back into the mid-deck and went to her personal-effects locker on the forward bulkhead. Months ago, she had argued with the experts at the Cape about some means of getting back aboard the Orbiter after a contingency landing. Standard "emergency egress" consisted of a chinning bar attached to the hatch from which a crew member could swing down and then drop the distance of ten feet to the ground. But there was no way to get back in. After fighting a losing battle against experts who maintained that (a) there was a slim chance of any contingency landing now that the Shuttle System was operational, and (b) if there *did* happen to be an emergency, she wouldn't want to get back aboard anyway, Jackie had bought an eight-foot hemp rope ladder normally sold as an emergency home fire escape and simply put it in her personal-effects package that accompanied her on every flight. Maybe the NASA engineers who didn't fly Orbiters didn't think such a device was necessary, but Jackie wasn't going to fly without it. She had learned the game of J.I.C.—Just In Case— early in her flying career.

By the time Frank and Lew climbed down from the flight deck, she and Hap had the ladder installed.

"What's that?" Frank asked.

"You want to be able to get back aboard?" Jackie said.

"I've been carrying that rope ladder in my kit for the last seven flights."

"Good thing they don't know everything we carry along, isn't it?" was Frank's only comment. "We're all powered down, but let's get out of here just in case we've got propellant vapors accumulating in the tail section." He waved at Jackie. "Ladies first."

"This is supposed to be an equal opportunity crew," Jackie reminded him.

"Okay, then, ancient law of the sea takes precedence: women and children first," Frank fired back. "And don't ask which I consider you to be right now. Just get out that hatch before I spank you."

He looked as if he meant it, so Jackie moved.

After dropping the survival kits to the ground, Frank was the last to crawl out the hatch and clamber down the rope ladder to the runway. "Okay, let's get away from this bird. Down the runway, back toward the tower over there."

"Wonder why nobody's come out," Hap mused as the four of them shouldered the survival kits and started along the strip.

"Yeah, no 'Follow Me' jeep. Hell of a reception," Lew grunted. "Man, what a desolate place! Not a tree anywhere. If it weren't for the grass and the bushes, I'd think we landed on another planet."

"For all practical purposes, we did," Hap said. "If we'd landed on the Moon or Mars, we'd be on TV right now with two-way communications. But when Frank makes a landing like that one, naturally nobody's around to see it."

"Don't be so sure," Frank remarked, shifting his part of the survival kit to his other shoulder. "Here comes your Follow Me jeep, Lew."

From down the runway, a jeep sped toward them. It drew up and came to a stop. Three men disembarked.

One wore a military uniform with strange pips on the shoulder boards. He was short, wiry, and clean-shaven, with carefully slipped and groomed black hair.

The second was obviously a Catholic priest, attired in the usual long, flowing white robe, a gold cross dangling from a neck chain. He was about the same age as the military man but wore a long, untrimmed black beard with streaks of white running through it. He peered at the world through a pair of round, rimless eyeglasses and bore an expression of interest and concern.

The third, a civilian with a bushy black mustache, carried a black bag. A fat belly hung over his belted white trousers.

Frank broke the ice. "Good afternoon, gentlemen. Thank you for letting us use your airfield. Otherwise, we'd be in the ocean."

"Good afternoon," the military man replied in excellent, unaccented English. There was no hint of caution, aggression, or suspicion in his voice. In fact, there was no hint of any emotion whatsoever. "I'm Captain Ernesto Obregon, Armada de Chile, and the military governor of Isla de Pascua." He extended his hand to Frank.

Frank took it and shook hands, replying, "Governor, I'm Frank King, command pilot, United States Space Shuttle Orbiter *Atlantis*."

Obregon looked past him at the *Atlantis*. "Yes, I recognize the aircraft and your space agency's markings. I didn't think I'd ever see one on Chilean soil, much less on Isla de Pascua."

"Neither did we, sir," Frank told him pleasantly. It was quite obvious that the governor was a well-educated Latin American who had been raised and trained in the upper class of the South American culture. *La dignidad de hombre* would be sacred to this man, even on this remote South Pacific island which he governed, and Frank was therefore going to treat him with all the deference and protocol possible. After all, the commander of the *Atlantis* knew he was in no position to do less. Besides, there would probably be enough problems generated anyway before they got the *Atlantis* off this island.

"Permit me to introduce the members of my crew," Frank went on. "My second in command and copilot, Lewis Clay . . . my payload specialist, George Hazard . . . and my mission specialist, Jacqueline Hart." He didn't give a damn what Jackie thought; he had deliberately introduced her last for the simple reason that women's lib hadn't yet made the slightest dent in the governor's culture, but chivalry, on the other hand, was an integral part of it.

Obregon shook hands with the other two men, then raised Jackie's hand and kissed it. "Gentlemen, señorita, welcome to Isla de Pascua."

Jackie blushed at the Chilean's suave greeting. What thoughts she might have had about insisting on being treated equally were never expressed. In all her life, she had never had her hand kissed before. Americans didn't do that sort of thing, and she found herself wishing more American men would.

"You're all civilians?" Obregon asked.

"The National Aeronautics and Space Administration of the United States is a civilian organization," Frank explained. He gestured toward the *Atlantis*. "As you can see, there are no military markings on the ship, and none of us wears military uniforms. Oh, our flight suits are alike because they're fireproof, and we bear the United States flag. But we're all civilians." Frank was, in fact, a full colonel in the Air Force on assignment to NASA as a Shuttle pilot, and Lew was a commander in the U.S. Navy on the same sort of assignment. But as far as *this* situation went, they were NASA civilians, and Frank intended to keep it that way.

"Excellent. There might be problems otherwise." Obregon seemed greatly relieved and moved to the next item on his obviously well-thought-out if hastily planned agenda. "Please permit me to introduce the members of my welcoming party."

The priest was Father Francisco. His only remark, uttered upon shaking Frank's hand, told the Shuttle pilot why the military governor had brought him along: "Welcome to my island."

The plump man was not Chilean at all, in spite of his obviously Latin appearance. Dr. Victor Esteban was introduced as the doctor on the island—the only doctor—and it was apparent from the black bag that he had come along in case there had been injuries. "*Ia orana oe!* Welcome to Rapa Nui," he exclaimed as he shook hands, even with Jackie. He spoke English well, with an accent that was not Spanish but rather a strange mixture of Spanish and something else. The matter was partly resolved as he added, "The world may know it as Isla de Pascua, but those of us who were born here still call it by its real name: Rapa Nui. Are you all well? Any injuries? Any others aboard your aircraft who might need my help?"

When the crew of the *Atlantis* looked at one another briefly in some confusion about this, Dr. Esteban said, "Have no fear. I'm no Polynesian witch doctor. I know the idea enters the minds of some of the few tourists we get here. University of Mexico, residency in Valparaiso, then back here to my people . . ."

"Governor," Frank put in, "it's urgent that I be permitted to use your radio to contact the United States. They're awaiting word from us, and we must start making the necessary arrangements to get the *Atlantis* off the island and back to the United States."

"I'll be happy to cooperate, Mr. King, but first things first," Obregon replied, holding up his hand. "Chilean law requires that I take care of a few items of protocol. Nothing serious, but I have to make regular reports to Santiago. May I see your passports, please?"

"Passports?" Lew repeated in disbelief.

"Captain, we have no passports with us," Frank broke in. "We never anticipated having to land the *Atlantis* on foreign soil."

Captain Obregon thought about this for a moment. Then he sighed. "No passports, and no visas? Do you have *any* documents with you that will serve as identification and proof of national origin?"

Frank looked baffled but managed to answer, "No, but we have our names on our flight coveralls here. That serves to identify us."

"Hardly an identification document, Mr. King."

It was the quiet Hap Hazard who stepped in at this point. "Your Excellency"—he addressed the military governor by his proper title—"I realize that we've landed here without the necessary personal documents required for international travel. But we beg your indulgence because this was an unanticipated landing. And the problems of weight in space travel prevent us from carrying along everything that might be necessary in the way of international documents." Hap had been around, especially in Europe, and knew the ins and outs of immigration and Customs. "If our commander can use your radio to contact the United

States, all the necessary documents will be provided to you when the rescue team comes here to retrieve the *Atlantis*."

The military governor shrugged. "Under the circumstances, no great problem for the moment. I'm sure we can work something out before I make my monthly report. However, I'll have to inspect your aircraft and its cargo. Customs regulations, you know. May I see your aircraft's license, its Certificate of Airworthiness, and its cargo and passenger manifest, please?"

Again, the request set Frank back on his heels. The *Atlantis*, in common with the other three Orbiters, didn't have a U.S. Certificate of Airworthiness, issued by the Federal Aeronautics Administration, because of an agreement more than a decade old between NASA and the FAA, when NASA had convinced that agency that the Space Shuttles were not aircraft and therefore did not have to conform to FAA specifications. As a matter of fact, Frank thought, the *Atlantis* didn't even carry radio transmitter licenses, which were required under international law. He had flown enough nonmilitary aircraft to know of these things, but it had never occurred to him that the *Atlantis* would need those items aboard in the event of a contingency landing.

"I'm afraid space vehicles don't carry such things, sir," he told the governor.

Obregon sighed again. "International law requires them, Mr. King. How do we know what you're carrying? How do we know the origin of the aircraft and its airworthiness?"

"Well, there's a builder's plate attached to the bulkhead that says the *Atlantis* was built by Rockwell International at Palmdale, California."

Again Hap intervened. "Your Excellency, if you'll let us know what documents you require, we'll talk to the United States and have them available for your inspection as soon as the first members of the rescue team arrive here. None of these standard requirements for ships and aircraft was considered valid for spacecraft because of the UN treaty relating to the rescue and return of astronauts and space vehicles—and I believe your government signed that treaty."

Captain Obregon was obviously becoming as confused about this as Frank. He really didn't know what to do with this huge black and white monster covered with bricklike tiles that was sitting on the runway of the island he governed. It was *obviously* a United States spacecraft, and these people were *obviously* Americans. But they had *nothing* in the way of documents to prove anything they said, and he would be out on a limb if he didn't demand to see such things.

On the other hand, he thought, what could he do? He couldn't deny them entry to Isla de Pascua. They had no means of getting off the island. And he couldn't impound the *Atlantis*; he had no machinery that could move it off the runway.

He took the easy way out because his report to Santiago wasn't due until the end of the month. Perhaps the Americans would come up with the necessary documents before that time. "Ah, well, we'll make allowances in this case, Mr. King. I'm sure your rescue teams will bring along the documents for me to see. In the meantime, however, it would put my mind at ease if Dr. Esteban and I could inspect your aircraft and its cargo. Dr. Esteban enters and inspects all incoming aircraft for public health purposes, and . . ."

"Be happy to have you do so, Governor," Frank told him with a slight smile, "except we're much too close to the *Atlantis* right now. There're still rocket-propellant chemicals aboard her that are highly toxic to human beings. Until we can get experts with the proper equipment here, it may be dangerous to go aboard, much less to be within a kilometer of her." Catching the quick look that flashed across Obregon's face, Frank added, "But you're welcome to look. You won't be able to see much in the payload bay; there's no light there."

As a military man, Obregon was familiar with the nature of rocket chemicals used in rocket-powered guided missiles. He didn't want to deal with such things right then because he wasn't equipped to do so. "Can you get it off the runway?" he asked.

"Do you have a tow tug?"

Obregon shook his head. "The LAN-Chile jets that fly into here don't stay. They leave for Tahiti or return to Santiago within an hour after arrival. We have no means of towing them or refueling them."

"Then the *Atlantis* will have to sit where it is," Frank concluded.

"Can't you taxi down to the south ramp?" Dr. Esteban inquired.

Frank shook his head. "The *Atlantis* is an unpowered glider. It can't move on its own once it's on the ground." He looked at his ship sitting in the middle of a runway only ninety-eight feet wide. "There isn't room to turn it around, even if you did have a tow tug." It was beginning to dawn on Frank that the situation was considerably more complex than he had originally thought. And he was growing more convinced every second that all aspects of a contingency landing had *not* been considered and prepared for.

"You mentioned that the rocket chemicals still in the *Atlantis* are toxic," Dr. Esteban said, looking toward the Orbiter with obvious unease. "What are the chemicals?"

"Nitrogen tetroxide," Jackie Hart told him.

Esteban thought about this for a moment, then stated, "Your Excellency, it will indeed be necessary to talk to Santiago by radio immediately. I am not equipped to handle any emergency involving human inhalation of nitrogen tetroxide fumes. It's known as a poison gas!"

"I believe this jeep will carry the seven of us," Captain Obregon observed.

"Red, Matt Hubbard," the voice of the Air Force colonel came over the telephone handset. "You've made my day, buddy. The problems we've got with Shuttle Down you wouldn't believe."

Richardson sighed. "Solving problems or finding people who can is what I get paid for, Matt. What's the matter?"

"Oh, nothing very serious . . . except that Easter Island is so gawddamned far out in the boonies that it hasn't got *anything* except a barely adequate runway. And no fuel; I've got to bring in every drop of jet fuel we use if I need to refuel any aircraft there. And the bloody place is two thousand nautical miles from Santiago *or* Tahiti."

"Look, you guys fly the Atlantic and Pacific nonstop every day," Red pointed out.

"Yeah, I know, we're the supermen of the airways—except we put our pants on one leg at a time, just like you guys at NASA," the colonel retorted. "Listen, Red, I wasn't kidding. We've got real problems supporting your operation on Easter Island. For example, no C-5s, to begin with."

"What?"

"We can't get a C-5 Galaxy into Mataveri."

"Hell, Matt, that runway's almost nine thousand feet long! Frank King got the *Atlantis* down there—and that's a very hot item."

"It may be a nine-thousand-foot runway, Red, but the Jepp charts—which are all we've got available on it—say it's only ninety-eight feet wide with no turnarounds at either end," the colonel from MAC explained. "C-5s have been restricted to runways a hundred and fifty feet wide. We can't turn them around on any runway narrower than that without turnarounds. *Plus* the fact that there isn't parking space *off* the runway to put more than two of them at a time to unload them."

"Well, stick some landing mats aboard the first one to land, and we'll help you put down a turnaround," Red suggested.

"No dice. When we tried that a couple years ago at Dyess Air Force Base, we damaged ten tires, the landing-gear pods, and the flaps. The C-5 is *heavy*, man. It just bends the hell out of steel landing mats."

"Have you got any answers, Matt?" Red queried. "We've got one-fourth of our manned space capability sitting in the middle of the Pacific Ocean. How do we modify the plans to get her out of there?"

"Got a cement mixer or an asphalt machine?"

"I don't get you."

"Okay, listen, I've got three C-130 Herks for you. One of them takes you and your contingency landing crew in, along with some of the equipment necessary to build an asphalt or concrete turnaround at both ends of the Mataveri runway. The second C-130 brings the rest of that equipment. The third is a flying fuel tank, carrying enough JP-4 to refuel the C-130s already there, and we run it as a shuttle back and forth to Santiago to bring in more fuel. Once we have turnarounds and larger ramps built, I can get the C-5s into Pascua according to plan."

"I knew you'd figure something out." A smile played over Red's face for the first time in hours.

"And, as luck would have it, I've got three Herks available that'll be into Ellington by nineteen hundred hours, your time, tonight, ready to take you and your crew to Easter Island by way of Panama, Lima, and Santiago." The Air Force colonel paused for a second, then asked, "You got the construction crews available to modify that runway?"

"I'll get 'em, Matt."

"Try Commander Block of the Navy Seabees at the Pentagon," Hubbard suggested. "He's always been helpful to us here when we found ourselves in a tight spot."

"Okay, I'll do that," Red replied, making a note to run it through Headquarters, since he didn't have the authority. He also made a note to check on Houston contractors as a second source in case he ran into too much DOD red tape.

"Uh, one thing, however, Red," Hubbard added. "I know Chile's part of the 1952 military assistance pact—if the Allende government didn't abrogate it back in the late sixties. And we've always got the Rio treaty to fall back on. But are you sure I've got military landing rights in Santiago and on Easter Island?"

"We've got somebody working on it at State. I'll check with them," Red promised. "Assume you have all the permissions required."

"Man, I hope you're right."

Red Richardson hung up, leaned back in his chair, put his hands behind his neck, and tried to stretch to relieve the tension. In another ninety minutes, the crew from Kennedy would be arriving, and the Shuttle Down task force would be pulling itself together in Houston. He had put a number of people to work digging out facts about Easter Island that might pose problems. He knew there were going to be a lot of problems.

The plot projected on the wall of Mission Control showed the delta-shaped symbol of the *Atlantis* sitting smack atop a speck named Easter Island. The longer he looked at that projection, the more pessimistic he became, the more he began to worry, and the more potential problems began to form in his mind.

"Damn!" he swore aloud. That island was literally at the end of the Earth.

Roger Service stared stupefied at the headline on the early-afternoon edition of the *Washington Post*.

SPACE SHUTTLE DOWN ON EASTER ISLAND! the banner head screamed at him in huge black letters.

The story that followed wasn't much better.

Service cringed because of two little letters, *AP*, that appeared at the beginning of the story following the Washington dateline. And because of the byline, "by Alice Arnold."

Damn Laskewitz! Service thought savagely. He shouldn't have given the story to AP, especially to that bitch Arnold! Of all the sensationalist, antitechnology, antispace, hyperthyroids running around trying to act like reporters and screaming about women's lib and the dangers of technology, Alice Arnold was considered by Service to be the worst. Why did Laskewitz have to deal with her at all?

In his other hand he held a scrap of paper torn off the teletype machine connected to UPI. Herb Haynes had written a short but accurate account of what was going on. Service didn't have a quibble when the media people chose Herb Haynes as their pool reporter to go to Easter Island with the first planes. He didn't like Haynes; he didn't really trust any newsperson. But Haynes was at least honest about what he wrote.

Roger Service knew he was going to catch pure, unadulterated hell from the Administrator once the Boss had seen the *Post*. He was just waiting for the telephone to ring.

It did.

"Public Affairs. Roger Service speaking."

But it wasn't the Administrator's office. A sharp female voice jumped out of the receiver. "Service? Alice Arnold, AP. I understand Herb Haynes is going with you people to Easter Island. Get me aboard, Roger!"

"Hi, Alice," Service managed weakly. "Look, sweetheart, we've got only limited space aboard the Air Force cargo plane that's going in there—and no seats or amenities for women."

"Dammit, Service, I'll buy my own commercial ticket,

then—but I'll tell my readers that your chauvinistic attitude—"

"Alice, we can't take the whole world down there—not when our budget's been cut to the bone, thanks to your harping about the waste of money on space." The instant he said it, he knew he shouldn't have.

"Get me on your flight, or you haven't seen anything yet! Or do I have to call the White House to make you behave yourself?"

The last thing Service wanted was to get the Presidential Science Adviser involved. He was going to have enough trouble with the Administrator anyway. "I'll get you aboard, Alice. Just be in Houston tonight. Maybe you can make the meeting of the recovery team at four P.M., Houston time, if you get moving. I'll tell Laskewitz you're coming."

"How the hell am I gonna get to Houston that fast? How is Casey getting there? Can I hitch a ride on the same NASA plane?"

"Only if you want to ride in his lap, Alice. But he left in a T-38 about ten minutes ago. I'd suggest you quit talking and start moving."

"I sincerely hope we'll be able to work out the many problems in this matter, señor," Alfred M. Dewey said smoothly to the chargé d'affaires. "Please be assured that the United States government is more than anxious to cooperate very closely with the government of Chile. It was most fortunate that Isla de Pascua has a new airfield large enough for the *Atlantis* to make a safe landing on. Your government's to be commended for constructing that aerodrome."

"The government of Chile is always happy to assist the United States, especially when it comes to the space program," the slim and dapper chargé replied smoothly. "Please sit down, and we can get most of the details arranged quickly." He indicated an ornate chair beside an ornate desk.

"I believe I explained the basic problem to you, señor," Dewey continued. "My government will need the permission and support of your government to recover the Space

Shuttle *Atlantis* from Mataveri Aerodrome on Isla de Pascua."

"And what will that entail, Señor Dewey?"

"The National Aeronautics and Space Administration has had contingency plans for such a thing for years," Dewey pointed out. "They've already set their operational elements in motion. We'll have to land at least two Lockheed C-5 Galaxy transports at Mataveri, along with several other aircraft carrying personnel and equipment. We'll have to bring in the Shuttle carrier aircraft, a Boeing Seven-Forty-Seven modified to carry the *Atlantis* on its back. The Galaxy transports will bring in the necessary cranes to lift the Shuttle aboard the carrier aircraft. Then we'll depart, leaving nothing behind to mar the beauty of your Pacific island."

The chargé was taking notes in Spanish. "How many people do you anticipate bringing to Isla de Pascua for this operation, Señor Dewey?"

"NASA tells me that seventy-five people will be required for the recovery operation itself, and we believe there will be another twenty-five to fifty people involved—news media, supervisors, and others to coordinate the effort."

"So you're planning for more than a hundred people, señor?"

Dewey nodded.

"For how long?"

"NASA estimates forty-five days."

The Chilean shook his head sadly. "Señor, Isla de Pascua has a total population of about twelve hundred people. There is a sharply limited water supply on the island, and only limited food available because the island does not lend itself well to extensive agriculture. Electrical power is extremely limited as well—certainly far less than that required to support your operation. I think it will be impossible for the facilities available on Isla de Pascua to accommodate more than a hundred people for almost two months."

"I . . . uh . . . I'll have to relay this information to NASA," Dewey replied.

"Also, no fuel is available for your aircraft. They will have to fly in with enough fuel to return to Santiago or Valparaiso."

Dewey swallowed.

The telephone rang. The chargé d'affaires picked it up, spoke in Spanish for a moment, then handed the handset to Dewey. "It is someone from your space agency."

"This is Alfred Dewey," the State Department man began.

"Mr. Dewey, Reed Richardson at NASA Houston. I'm glad I caught you at the Chilean Embassy. We've run into some problems planning the recovery of the *Atlantis* from Easter Island."

"So have I, Mr. Richardson. But what is your problem?"

"According to the Air Force, we'll need to make some additions to the airport there in order to get their transport planes turned around on the runway," Richardson explained. "We've also got to arrange to pour some concrete pads in order to set up the crane to lift the *Atlantis* aboard NASA Nine-Oh-Five."

"Richardson, give me your number and let me call you back after I discuss this with the Chilean chargé d'affaires here." Dewey took down Richardson's number and then added, "I'll be right back to you, because we've got some other problems, too."

Dewey hung up and relayed Richardson's information.

"Señor Dewey." The man was shaking his head. "This matter is becoming considerably more than just a simple recovery operation. The Chilean government has had to put severe restrictions on any construction or excavation activities on the island because of the extreme interest exhibited in Isla de Pascua by both scientists and entrepreneurs. It is our policy to maintain the island in its current natural environment as much as possible, and we do not wish to see it turned into another South Sea paradise. We can and do welcome a limited number of tourists, but even the new Mataveri Hotel cannot handle many people."

He steepled his fingers and looked thoughtfully at the ceiling. "It is the intention of the government of Chile to be as cooperative as possible since we are signatories to the United Nations treaty covering rescue and return of astronauts and space vehicles. But this operation will require many people and a great deal of equipment. You will have to bring in food, water, fuel, living arrangements—in short, you will have to transport a significant number of people and material to Isla de Pascua. The environmental and cultural impacts may be tremendous. In addition, you will be bringing in military aircraft and equipment which, given the delicate situation in the South Pacific, may cause diplomatic problems for my government. I am afraid that this matter goes far beyond the authority of the Ambassador here to grant the necessary permissions."

It would be even more than that, the chargé told himself, since the Soviets were pressuring Santiago either to permit them to establish a leased base on one of Chile's Pacific islands or, barring that, to deny the islands' use as military bases to any other nation, especially the United States. The Soviets were trying to build their naval power in the Pacific. And for all he knew, this might well be a ploy on the part of the United States to establish the basis for a future military base on Isla de Pascua. There *had* been rumors . . .

He stood up, signifying that the meeting was over. "I shall have the Ambassador communicate with Santiago on this matter."

As far as Alfred M. Dewey was concerned, the meeting was *not* over, and he didn't stand up. "Señor, my government has a very expensive device sitting on the Mataveri runway. It amounts to one-fourth of our national manned space capability. We have a number of international payloads, bought and paid for, that will require rescheduling and perhaps reassignment to other launch vehicles. I would respectfully request the most expeditious handling of the matter, especially of the permissions required. I have people waiting in Houston, and there are four Americans on Isla de Pascua awaiting rescue."

"Señor," the somewhat vexed chargé replied gently, "I will act as quickly as possible. However, it may take several days, communication being what it is. In the meantime, I am certain that your astronauts on Isla de Pascua are being treated with warm hospitality and that there is nothing to worry about that would justify such extreme haste."

CHAPTER FOUR

After the Mataveri control tower, the Isla de Pascua radio station building was probably the newest edifice on the island. But "new" to the crew of the *Atlantis* was something different than "new" to the natives of Rapa Nui. The radio shack had been built from the volcanic rock of the island, with very little wood or concrete in its construction. And even the concrete looked well weathered, leading Frank to assume that it hadn't been mixed or poured properly. The building itself, at the base of the control tower, housed the transmitters for the Isla de Pascua aeronautical radio beacons, the VHF tower transceiver, and the en-route aeronautical traffic-control equipment. It also housed low-frequency communications gear that served aeronautical and other purposes, and there were additional rooms, most of which hadn't been occupied yet and were bare to the walls.

The young enlisted man of the Chilean garrison was visibly nervous at the presence of the military governor as well as Father Francisco and the four strangely dressed American space farers. However, he behaved as professionally as possible, tuning up various pieces of equipment and then calling Santiago in a stream of rapid-fire Spanish.

When contact was established, Obregon got on the microphone and made a verbal report of what had happened.

Frank couldn't follow the conversation; he looked questioningly at his three crew members, and each of them replied with a silent shrug or shake of the head.

"Governor," Frank finally broke in during a pause in the exchange, "once you've given your report, please ask them to get in touch with Reed Richardson, Mission Control, Johnson Space Center, Houston, Texas. See if they can arrange a two-way communication for me. I must talk to him and explain the technical details he needs to know. And, Governor, if you're worried about the cost of the call, the United States government will take care of things."

Obregon considered this for a moment, then engaged in more rapid-fire Spanish over the radio. After long minutes, the military governor replied, "They're attempting to make the telephone connection now. It'll take several hours, Mr. King."

"Several hours?" Jackie burst out.

Frank motioned her to be quiet. "Governor, have them get in touch with the American Embassy in Santiago and make the connection through the Embassy's diplomatic radio channel."

Obregon nodded. "Mr. King, you're a man who knows how to get things done."

The auditorium was jammed with the seventy-five people from the Cape who made up the contingency landing team, plus the others who had joined the group—Casey Laskewitz and Joyce Fisher among them. Over the objections of Reed Richardson, Casey Laskewitz had admitted the news media. Television cameras lined the back of the auditorium, and Casey promised all the reporters a full press briefing following the general planning meeting.

Fortunately for NASA, Casey Laskewitz knew the reporters by name. "Herb, you made it; good! Walter, I'm glad you're here! Charley, just keep your shirt on, we'll get you some library footage after this meeting is over! Hi, Alice, your boss let you come after all, huh? Howdy, Frank, welcome back to Houston! How goes the special series, Hugh?"

Some meetings between reporters weren't as cordial, however. "Well, if it isn't Lois Lane herself," Herb Haynes remarked to Alice Arnold. "Still looking for Superman?"

Of all the men she had met, Alice Arnold reserved a special dislike for Herb Haynes, not only because he worked for the competition at UPI but also because he had her number and didn't hesitate to let the world know it. There was no friendliness in her voice when she replied, "Well, such a surprise to see you here, Herb. I thought you'd be sitting on your fat ass up in Washington and clipping from other people's stories."

Before their repartée could soar to even greater heights, the hubbub in the auditorium quieted. Red Richardson clambered onto the low stage and stepped to the podium. "Ladies and gentlemen, let's get settled down here. This is a planning meeting for Shuttle Down. Have we got the rest of the people on the net?"

A small loudspeaker set up on the table on the stage was connected by telephone lines and microwave links to other locations for people who couldn't get to Houston, hadn't had time to get there, or wouldn't be needed in Houston in order to bring off Shuttle Down.

Seeing a nod from the communications tech, Red spoke up. "Military Airlift Command? Matt, are you there?"

"Read you loud and clear," the speaker replied.

"Dryden? Hank, are you on?"

"We're here!" came the voice of Hank Hoffman from Dryden Flight Research Center.

"Marshall? George?"

"We're here," came the slightly Southern drawl from Marshall Space Flight Center in Huntsville, Alabama.

"Headquarters? Mike?"

"Headquarters here," came an echoing voice, indicating that a large contingent had gathered in the sixth-floor conference room at 400 Maryland Avenue.

A technician waved to Red from the side of the stage. "We've just got Frank King on the line via radio link from Easter Island through the Santiago Embassy," the tech reported.

A ripple of excited sound ran through the room.

"Hi, Frank. You okay? Read us all right?"

A slight pause, then some static, then Frank's voice came through, barely audible. "Connection isn't very good, Red, but we hear you. When you guys going to come and get us?"

"As soon as we can get this operation organized. Let's get started here. Everybody has the details. First off, transportation: Colonel Matt Hubbard, MAC. What's it look like in your shop, Matt?"

"We'll have three C-130s ready at Ellington in about two hours."

"I'll need more airlift than that."

"I know. I'm getting a Pan Am charter Seven-Oh-Seven

for the press and some of the contingency recovery team that doesn't get on those first C-130s," the Air Force colonel replied.

"Uh, we've got a problem," Frank said from Easter Island. "The *Atlantis* is still on the runway, so you've got about eight thousand feet of Runway One-Zero available. We can't tow her off the runway; they haven't got a tow tug here. You might get the C-130s in, but nothing bigger."

"Matt, see if we can borrow a tow tug from Ellington— or somewhere—and put it aboard one of the first C-130s to land," Red said.

"What kind of tow tug do you need to pull the *Atlantis*, Frank?"

"It's got standard tow links on the front gear, and it weighs about a hundred and fifty thousand pounds right now, but we'll have to tow it backward down the runway. We haven't got room to turn it around. Runway's only about a hundred feet wide."

"What's the clearance under that Orbiter?" asked Hubbard.

"Five feet at the nose gear," came Joe Marvin's voice from the audience.

"I don't think our Air Force tugs can get underneath," Hubbard replied.

"We'll have to lease a low tug from an airline at Houston International," Joe added.

"Okay, then, the first C-130 will be carrying a skeleton crew and a tow tug," Red Richardson said.

"How about a satellite communications ground station?" Frank put in. "Communications from here aren't the best in the world."

"Okay, we'll check with Western Union or somebody. Dave"—he pointed to a man in the audience—"take care of it."

"You guys are getting me loaded up pretty quick," Matt Hubbard pointed out.

"That isn't the whole story." It was Joyce Fisher. "I just talked with my boss at State who's handling things through the Chilean Embassy. He tells me they face the following problems: (a) not enough water for an additional hundred or more people; (b) not enough food for them; (c) not enough electrical power to handle much more than another kilowatt of load; (d) no jet fuel available on the island; (e) no harbor available to off-load ships, so everything has to come in by air; and, finally, if that's not enough, there's no way they can provide beds for a hundred people."

"I had some of that data," Matt Hubbard broke in, "but you've made my job one whole hell of a lot tougher. We'll have to airlift a complete community in there—and, Red, we'll have to get some support from the Army to provide it."

"Matt, can you handle that?"

"Negative."

"Headquarters, are you listening?" Red asked.

"Yeah," came the quiet reply.

"Mike," Red said, "have the Administrator get us some Army support on this. Can I count on you?"

"We'll get to work on it right away. We'll also ask the Navy if they can stand by offshore in case we need additional help in any way. Maybe they can get a boat ashore if there's no port facilities. Or maybe we can get an aircraft carrier so the Navy can fly stuff into Mataveri, too."

"Okay, Mike, coordinate with Joe Marvin here at Mission Control. I'll assume we're going to have food, water, shelter, and electricity courtesy of somebody in DOD."

"We'll get something," the voice from Headquarters promised.

"Another problem." Joyce Fisher again. "The Chilean government's being as cooperative as it can. It isn't averse to the United States coming in there to pick up our Space Shuttle. But the Embassy has to check with Santiago on letting us bring in so many people and so much equipment. They're worried about the environmental and social impacts on Isla de Pascua, and they won't like the extensive U.S. Air Force presence on the island during the rescue operation."

"Tell them we've got several thousand pounds of poisonous rocket propellant sitting down here," Frank pointed out, his voice fading into static and then booming over the long radio link. "One leak, and the wind's blowing right toward Hangaroa. The military governor's very upset about it. And Dr. Esteban has absolutely no means of coping with mass exposure of the population to nitrogen tetroxide fumes."

"Excuse me," Joyce Fisher said. "Let me find a phone and call State." She left the auditorium.

"Tell the young lady from State she can add a couple more items to that list," Matt Hubbard broke in. "We'll have to fly in some runway construction equipment—and I may be able to work this through the Air Force. But otherwise somebody may have to convince the Navy to let the Seabees do it in order to build some turnarounds at the end of the runway. No way can we get a C-5 Galaxy turned around on a hundred-foot-runway width."

"And we'll need the turnarounds for NASA Nine-Oh-Five," came Hank Hoffman's voice from Dryden.

"Any concrete on the island?" It was George Tunney from Marshall. "We've got to pour footings for the stiffleg derrick and the tag-line masts."

"No concrete," Frank replied from Easter Island. "The military governor says there's none on the island, and no equipment to mix or pour it."

"Okay, then we'll have to bring that in, too. George, the stiffleg is Marshall's show. You find us the concrete mixing and pouring equipment, along with the Manitowock crane and cherry pickers you need. Check with Colonel Hubbard on sizes and weights so he knows what he's got to airlift."

"This is getting out of hand." It was Duke Kellogg, sitting in the front row of seats and watching his subordinate run the show. "Our budget won't handle all this."

"Any estimate on costs?" the voice from NASA Headquarters asked.

"Hell, no," Red shot back. "We're just beginning to find out what all the problems are. Until we know how much this is going to deviate from the standard contingency plan, we won't have the slightest idea what it'll cost."

"Where are the funds?" Kellogg asked.

"I don't know," Red admitted, "but consider the alternative. What would it cost to replace the *Atlantis* now that the production line's shut down and the jigs are dismantled? And could we maintain our commitments with only three-quarters of our launch capability? I doubt it. Until I hear otherwise, I'm going to get the *Atlantis* back from

Easter Island. The effort is bound to be cheaper than a new Orbiter."

"Uh, Red," came the hesitant voice of Hank Hoffman, the man who would pilot the Boeing 747 Shuttle carrier aircraft, "I hate to bring this up, but I looked into the flight planning after Joe called me earlier. I can get Nine-Oh-Five to Easter Island with no sweat. But Nine-Oh-Five hasn't got the range to reach Santiago or Tahiti with the *Atlantis* on her back."

"What?"

"I can stretch the mated range to about fifteen hundred nautical miles," Hoffman replied. "The closest landing spot—and I mean the closest dry land, man—is Santiago, almost two thousand nautical miles *east* against the southeast trade winds and prevailing easterlies. Remember, the winds blow in the opposite direction in the southern hemisphere."

"Damn. Hank, that's a problem. Okay, now you've got the responsibility of solving it. You've some of the best engineers and mechanics in the world there at Edwards and Dryden. If you can't figure out some way to cobble-up a midair refueling rig on the Nine-Oh-Five, then work out *something* to squeeze more range out of that bird. Matt, any problem along that line with your operation?"

"Negative. I'm using a C-130 as a tanker to fly JP-4 into Easter Island to refuel the others. When we get the *Atlantis* off that runway and build some turnarounds, I can fly in KC-135s or even KC-10s. We're just going to have to plan every flight very carefully. But, Red, we looked into the possibility of flying boom air-to-air refueling of our MAC Seven-Forty-Sevens a couple of years ago, and it's a major modification that could take months."

Joyce Fisher came back into the room looking very distressed. Red saw her and asked, "Okay, where do we stand, Miss Fisher? Can we get under way from Ellington with an initial crew and a tug to get the *Atlantis* off the runway at Easter Island?"

Joyce Fisher was shaking her head. "No, I wouldn't advise it," she said, her voice shaking. "We have other problems, Mr. Richardson . . . and I must talk to you in private about them . . ."

"Hold it," thundered the strident voice of Alice Arnold

from the back of the auditorium. "What's so important that the news media can't know about it, too?"

Joyce Fisher sighed. This was one of the times she wished she had gone to work for the Peace Corps instead of the Department of State. But the State Department job had seemed so much more challenging. Well, she found herself thinking, isn't this the challenge she always wanted? "You can make a telephone call and find out anyway. Besides, the story will be in the papers and on TV tonight—if it isn't already. Both *Pravda* and Radio Moscow are demanding that the Chilean government intern the *Atlantis* and her crew."

"What?" Red exploded. And the room burst into an uproar.

When things finally quieted down, Joyce stepped onto the low stage, took the mike, and proceeded to explain. "I just talked with my supervisor at the State Department in Washington, and things are somewhat confused. The Soviet Union claims that the *Atlantis* is a military launch vehicle with a nuclear-powered antisatellite weapon in her cargo bay."

"That's ridiculous," Frank said from Easter Island. "Why, I'll let Governor Obregon look into the payload bay and verify for himself that we're carrying Landsat-XIII, a civilian Earth-resources satellite."

"The Soviets are going before the UN Security Council to demand that the United Nations send a commission to verify their claims by having the crew open the payload doors so the commission can inspect the entire cargo," Joyce continued.

"But that's impossible," Red Richardson broke in. "Those payload doors can be opened only in the weightlessness of orbit. We would have to fly in the special strongbacks and supporting jigs to permit them to be opened on the ground."

"The Soviets insist that nobody from the United States goes near the *Atlantis* until a UN commission's had the chance to inspect it and verify the Soviet claims," Joyce said.

There was dead silence in the room for a long moment, until Herb Haynes of UPI asked from the back, "Okay, so what are you going to do?"

Red Richardson knew he had to take the bull by the horns. He had, after all, been put in charge of Shuttle Down by Duke Kellogg. He wasn't aware of all the niceties of international diplomatic protocol or of the big game of world-power politics. But he knew what was really involved here. "As the person in full charge of the recovery of the *Atlantis* under NASA's contingency landing program, I categorically deny the Soviet claims. Anyone in the news media may look at the payload documents, plans, and so forth. You can convince yourself that I'm telling you the truth when I say the *Atlantis* is carrying Landsat-XIII in her payload bay. There's *no* antisatellite weapon or any military space vehicle aboard the *Atlantis*. True, she was launched out of Vandenberg Air Force Base in California, where military space launches take place, but we use Vandenberg for a lot of civilian launches, just as military space launches take place at Cape Kennedy. We've used Vandenberg many times for Shuttle missions into polar or high-inclination orbits, so this is nothing new."

"Okay, Richardson, so what are you going to do?" Alice Arnold's strident voice cut in.

Someday I'll manage to put it to that broad! Richardson thought. He reminded himself to have a word with Casey Laskewitz. But he answered, "We have a situation caused by an in-flight emergency. We don't know what prompted the malfunction, but that's not the prime issue. The safety of the twelve hundred inhabitants of Easter Island demands we get down there as quickly as possible with the expert technicians and special equipment necessary to off-load that nitrogen tetroxide and place it in safe storage containers. I trust that the Chilean government will permit us to do this to insure the safety of its citizens. That'll be the first flight leaving from Ellington Air Force Base. The rest of the Shuttle Down operation will be geared up and ready to go upon approval of the Chilean government. When we get to Santiago, we'll see what's happened in the meantime. Right now, I consider this an emergency, with the lives of more than a thousand people at stake—and I'm not going to sit around on my butt and wait! I'll be on that plane, and I'll coordinate this operation from Santiago and Easter Island."

Richardson, pausing to catch his breath, let his eyes

glance about the room. "All of you involved in the operation know what's expected of you. Don't come to me and hope I'll solve your problems. If you have problems, solve them yourselves. Or call upon the best expertise you can find to get an answer. Just do what you're supposed to do. Joe Marvin, set up a communications center here at Mission Control to keep everybody in touch with everybody else. I'll check in with you en route to Santiago and also when we get there. In the meantime, I want the propellant-unloading crew to get their equipment over to Ellington right now. Frank, hang in there, and we'll get your ship home yet."

And without waiting for questions from the press, Richardson strode off the low stage, saying to Joyce as he went, "Come along, Miss Fisher. I think we're going to need you badly." His stomach was giving him hell again, and he was fighting back the tension hiccups that would have demolished him during the final planning meeting.

Casey stepped onto the low stage and spoke into the microphone. "I know I promised the media a press conference following this meeting, but Red Richardson's got his hands full . . . as you can plainly see. We've got the *Atlantis* crew on the net here, and I'll do the best I can to help you out by running a press conference here and now with the crew. Frank, are you still on the horn there?"

"Roger, Casey. We'll do the best we can to answer all the questions we have answers for right now," Frank's garbled voice came back.

"Okay, if we can get the Shuttle Down people on their way, there'll be room for the news media to come down front and set up mikes and cameras," Laskewitz went on. "Frank, hang in there for a minute until we can get things organized here. Then I'll field questions for you."

"Obregon says we're using up a lot of electricity," Frank remarked.

"Tell him we're going to bring him plenty. Chances are, we'll have to leave a lot of our equipment there because it'll be too expensive to airlift it back."

"Aren't you wasting taxpayers' money doing that?" It was Alice Arnold, of course.

"No, Alice, look at it this way," Casey told her, knowing her particular prejudices and philosophy. "Those people on

Easter Island haven't got a lot of things we call necessities here. They've *always* had an energy shortage. Is it so terrible for us to leave them a couple of electrical generators in exchange for their hospitality in permitting the *Atlantis* to land there? Know what a Shuttle Orbiter costs these days? We're getting off cheap, thanks to Frank King's skill in being able to land the *Atlantis* there without *any* of the ordinary landing equipment."

Back on Isla de Pascua, Frank King was listening to the noisy radio loudspeaker and feeling a bit embarrassed in front of the other three members of his crew. He picked up the old astatic crystal microphone and said, "Casey, don't forget there were four of us aboard the *Atlantis*. I just happened to have the sidearm controller in my hand."

Hap grinned. "Yeah, Jackie and I sat there and took care of the white-knuckle and sweaty-palm department."

"Speak for yourself, Hap," Jackie snapped.

"You mean you weren't even scared just a little bit?" Hap replied sarcastically.

Frank realized he was going to have trouble with these two. So he assumed his bird-colonel personality and ordered, "Hold it down, both of you."

Obregon, Father Francisco, and Dr. Esteban merely watched. And they remained quiet because, although they wouldn't admit it, they were a bit stunned by the fact that their little island and its radio station were part of a meeting taking place thousands of miles away. They listened.

Casey finally got things arranged in Houston, and his voice came through. "Frank, are you still on the line down there on Easter Island?"

Frank keyed the mike. "Roger. But please call it Isla de Pascua or by its native name, Rapa Nui."

"Yeah, but nobody in America knows it by those names," remarked a thin-voiced reporter in the audience.

"Okay, we'll take questions one at a time for the crew of the *Atlantis*," Casey broke in.

"Colonel King," another reporter from Houston asked, using the pilot's military title, which Frank wished hadn't been mentioned at this point, "why did you pick Easter Island as a landing point? Why not the Hawaiian Islands?"

Frank sighed. "Look at a map or a globe. We launched due south out of Vandenberg. When the emergency occurred, it was too late to fly back to the launch site, and we didn't have enough velocity to go all the way around the world back to the United States. Casey Laskewitz will show you the landing footprint of the *Atlantis*. We had a choice: Isla de Pascua or the Pacific Ocean. We're extremely fortunate that Isla de Pascua has a suitable airfield."

"How are you being treated by the Chileans?" another reporter asked.

"With the most gracious hospitality," Frank replied.

"Even considering the current problems with the government of Chile?"

"I don't know anything about that," Frank snapped.

"I have a question for the military governor of Isla de Pascua." It was Alice Arnold of AP, although Frank didn't know her. "Governor, are you going to accede to the demands of the Soviet Union and intern the *Atlantis* and her crew until a United Nations commission can inspect the payload?"

Obregon picked up the microphone. "This is Governor Ernesto Obregon. I heard some reference to a complaint by the Soviet Union a few minutes ago during the conference, but I know nothing more than that. I've been in touch with Santiago, and I've received no instructions concerning that matter. I want you to know we've welcomed the American crew of the *Atlantis* to Isla de Pascua, and unless I receive orders to the contrary from my government in Santiago, we'll adhere to the United Nations treaty on rescue and return of astronauts and space vehicles."

"But will you imprison the crew if your government bends to the demands of the Soviet Union?"

Obregon laughed. The laugh was obviously heard in Houston. "My dear señorita, there are no prisons on Isla de Pascua. Where could one escape to? Our island is only eighteen kilometers long and twenty-four kilometers wide. We're almost four thousand kilometers from Chile or anywhere else, for that matter. No, I don't intend to imprison our guests. Chile is a democracy."

Casey's voice cut in. "Herb, you had a question?"

"Herb Haynes, UPI. Colonel King, is there really any danger from the nitrogen tetroxide rocket propellants still left aboard the *Atlantis*?"

"Yes, sir, if there's a leak in the system," Frank told him honestly. "We don't know what brought on the premature shutdown of our main engines, and we don't know if the cause of the shutdown was something that had an effect on the Orbital Maneuvering System rocket motors. None of the four of us is equipped to look into the matter. If there were fumes or a leak back there, we don't have the protective gear to survive such an inspection. There *is* a danger associated with the OMS propellants. But we've detected no leaks thus far, and every minute that goes by without a problem means that the danger lessens."

"Do you anticipate any problems in getting the *Atlantis* off Easter Island?" came the voice of another reporter.

"Technically, no. We'll get the equipment down here to do the job properly and safely. We may have to make a few additions to the airfield in order to handle the equipment."

"How about the political side of things?"

"That's not my concern, and I'm not qualified to talk about it," Frank said flatly. "I'm the command pilot of the *Atlantis.* I can answer your technical questions, but not the political or diplomatic ones."

"Colonel King, if the Easter Islanders could move all those stone statues around down there, why don't you ask them to use their psychic powers to get the *Atlantis* back to Vandenberg?"

"I have to assume you're trying to be funny," Frank snapped.

"Colonel, would you tell us what—" The voice coming through the ancient loudspeaker suddenly faded into cascades of static and whistles. The young Chilean radio operator sprang to the dials of the receiver and began to work with them. Nothing came from the loudspeaker except more static, interrupted occasionally by bursts of Morse code.

There was a rapid exchange of Spanish between Obregon and the technician.

The military governor sighed. "It appears that an important radio tube's gone bad," he explained. "We've had a replacement on order for months from Santiago, but it must come from Great Britain, where the radio was originally made in 1942 for the Royal Air Force. It seems that we're out of communication with anyone until we can get the reserve transmitter tuned up and on the air."

"How long will that take?" Frank asked. "Any chance of restoring contact with Houston in the next few minutes?"

Obregon queried his radio operator in Spanish. The Chilean naval technician replied, and Obregon turned to Frank. "He says it'll take about two hours to get it warmed up and adjusted. It's even older than this surplus World War Two RAF equipment. I think it was given to us by your Navy in the 1930s, and it isn't simple to use."

"Does this happen very often?" Lew inquired.

"Unfortunately, yes."

"You need a satellite ground station here," Hap remarked.

"We need many things on Isla de Pascua," Father Francisco observed. "But we manage to live reasonably well, in peace, without them."

"But suppose you had an epidemic?" Jackie put in. "How would Dr. Esteban handle it?"

"Where would the epidemic come from?" was Esteban's reply.

"If it were serious, we'd have the proper medicines here within a week," Obregon explained. "After all, we have a jet plane flying between here and Santiago once a week. If all our long-range radio communications broke down, there'd be a Seven-Oh-Seven here in a few days."

"Well, it seems we're out of contact with Houston for a while," Lew commented. "What do we do, boss?"

Frank had already made his evaluation of the situation. "For once in our highly scheduled lives, we'll just have to sit tight and wait. Will you keep the radio station manned for incoming messages, Governor?"

"In this situation, yes, even though it may mean cutting off electricity for another part of Hangaroa to do it. In the meantime, you're our guests, and we'll do our best to make your wait pleasant. It's not often that we have guests here. We're so very far away from everywhere. Now, my friends, we'll get in my jeep, and I'll take you to the Hotel Hangaroa. Dr. Esteban has informed me that there'll be a dinner tonight to celebrate your arrival on Isla de Pascua." He smiled broadly and offered his arm chivalrously to Jackie. "Shall we go?"

CHAPTER FIVE

The Hangaroa Hotel was far from being a Holiday Inn as
far as Frank King was concerned. The government had
built it to accommodate an anticipated increase in tourism
that was a goal of Chile's foreign policy, but Lew thought
they could have used help from one of the American hotel
chains with respect to designing a modern place.

"Welcome to beautiful downtown Hangaroa," Jackie
muttered as they rode down the unpaved street—there was
only one path that could be called a street—of Hangaroa,
the only habitation on Isla de Pascua and the home of more
than a thousand Pascuans and the garrison of the Armada
de Chile. It wasn't quite what the crew of the *Atlantis* had
been exposed to in motion pictures of South Pacific islands, but Isla de Pascua couldn't exactly be termed a
South Sea island in the same league as Tahiti.

The hotel manager, Juan Hey, was also the clerk and, as
the crew of the *Atlantis* learned, the mayor of Hangaroa.
"We are honored to have you on Isla de Pascua," he bubbled eagerly as he welcomed them and the military governor into the lobby-patio of the Hangaroa Hotel. He was a
small man, shorter than Lew or Jackie. His jet-black hair
was trimmed closely, and his features were a strange cross
between Amerindian and Asiatic. Frank thought the man
looked a little like some of the native Hawaiians he had
known.

"Thank you, Mr. Mayor," Frank replied courteously.
"Under the circumstances, you don't know how pleased we
are to be here. I've heard this island's very unusual."

"If there is anything about Isla de Pascua you want to
know, I am the man to ask," Hey boasted. "I am the most
important man on Isla de Pascua. People have come from
all over the world to see me—anthropologists to ask me

questions about how we live, archaeologists to find out about the long ears and Hotu Matu'a, and doctors to take samples of my ear wax and blood."

"We'll be certain to keep that in mind, Señor Hey. Looks like we'll be here for a few days at least, or until we get some help to remove the *Atlantis*." Inside, Frank was profoundly disturbed that communications with Houston had been temporarily cut off, forcing him to twiddle his thumbs and wait for others to take action.

As they walked together through a sunlit portion of the lobby, Juan Hey suddenly stopped in his tracks, his mouth hanging open. "Makemake!" he exclaimed.

"*Qué pasa*, Juan?" Captain Obregon asked.

"Look at the four of them," the Pascuan breathed.

The bright sunlight was backlighting the white nomex coveralls worn by all four members of the crew of the *Atlantis*, making the fabric shine and shimmer. At its edges, the synthetic fabric—whose threads were not white but transparent—caught the sunlight and broke it into little multicolored spectra.

"The legend," Juan Hey whispered, "talks of Makemake and the *akuaku* descending from the skies with clothes as white as a cloud and edged with rainbows . . ."

"Juan," Obregon reminded him gently, "what will Father Francisco think? The stories of Makemake are gone with the old religion."

"Then perhaps these four are *tangata-manu*, the bird-men, come to bring new life to Rapa Nui and those of us who live here."

"Señor Hey," Frank broke in, "I assure you, we're people just like you, regardless of what your old legends say. Sorry, but gods we're not."

Hey was undaunted. "We will see, Miti King. You must have a very powerful and benevolent *akuaku*—guardian spirit." He walked behind the registration desk and produced a register book. "If you will all sign in, please. And the governor requires that you give me your passports."

"You may forgo requesting their passports, Juan," Obregon told him.

As each of them signed the book, Juan Hey said, "We are planning a big dinner for you tonight. Many of us watched your big plane come silently over the island and land at Mataveri. We have seen nothing like it before. Dr. Esteban tells us you fly it to the Moon, so we must have a big celebration in your honor."

"Well, not exactly to the Moon, Mr. Mayor," Hap Hazard tried to explain.

Frank turned to look at Obregon, who simply nodded. "It's time for a celebration," the military governor said quietly.

The rooms were not those of any American hotel or motel, but they were clean, and the fresh breeze off the South Pacific blew in through windows overlooking the late-afternoon sea, where the Sun was just beginning to edge toward the horizon.

Captain Obregon stayed behind with Frank, and once Juan Hey had left, he confided to the Shuttle crew, "All of you must remember that the Pascuans see and know little of the outside world, in spite of the efforts of the Chilean government to operate schools here. We have a few tourists and occasional teams of scientists who're interested in the *moai* and the *rongaronga*. So your arrival gives me an excellent opportunity to break the routine of everyday living by authorizing people to leave Hangaroa village for a celebration. As my guests, you're all free to move about the island as you wish, but I must ask you to agree to several things."

Frank nodded and replied, "Whatever you wish, Governor."

"Please stay away from the Pascuan women. Guard your valuables and beware of the natives, who are all thieves and liars."

"You can't be serious," Hap said in disbelief.

"I'm afraid I am. The government doesn't encourage fraternization with the native women, which is why those in the garrison have their families with them. Our government has no money for supporting illegitimate children of native women. And as for my remark about theft, the Pascuans manage to steal several hundred sheep every year from the sheep-breeding station of the Armada de Chile, in spite of the fact that no Pascuan can leave Hangaroa village without a permit from me. They have no concept of property."

Frank couldn't believe what he heard the dapper little Chilean say. This was the twentieth century . . .

"How can you treat them as second-class citizens?" Jackie asked.

"Señorita, I was schooled in America," Captain Ernesto Obregon replied deferentially, "and I understand some of your feelings. But this isn't America, and we're dealing with people who don't share our values. I, too, personally deplore some of the regulations I must enforce. But these rules and regulations have come about as the result of decades of trying to work with the Pascuans."

"If the Pascuans are thieves and liars, please get guards around the *Atlantis*, but at least a kilometer away," Frank told him.

"They're already there."

To say that Alfred M. Dewey was working harder than he had ever worked in his life was perhaps an understatement. Quitting time came and went, and he was still at his desk and on the telephone.

"Look, Sullivan," he said to the young subordinate he had sent to New York earlier in the day, "tell the Ambassador that NASA is perfectly willing to provide all the payload documents for the *Atlantis*. They'll prove there's no military payload aboard."

"The documents will help, sir, but I can't seem to convince some of the people on our own UN staff, here, that those payload bay doors can't be opened without special rigging that has to be flown in to Isla de Pascua," Nash Sullivan replied over the phone from the United States delegation's offices at the UN in New York. "I think NASA's going to have to send a team of experts up here. Our staff's working on the possibility of holding a special briefing for those members of the Security Council who wish to attend, but I don't think we stand much chance of getting the Soviets to come at all. They'll boycott the briefing. They know they've got no case, but they'll play it for all it's worth."

"I'll see if NASA will send a briefing team up," Dewey said, making yet another note on a pad that was rapidly being filled. "In the meantime, suggest to the Ambassador that he make an offer before the Security Council to permit an inspection team to accompany the NASA rescue mission to Isla de Pascua. I'm sure NASA can accommodate such a request."

"Excellent idea, sir, but it'd help if I had the NASA briefing group here to provide the necessary technical data. I'm capable of giving the briefing myself, but since I'm with the State Department, I don't have credibility. Even our own UN staff people have questioned my technical expertise."

"Sullivan, keep at it and stay where you can be reached. I've got a call coming in on another line," Dewey said. He broke the connection with Sullivan in New York and punched a flashing button on his phone. "Alfred Dewey, Technology Liaison— Ah, yes, good evening, Señor Prieto!"

"Señor, my government has informed me that it intends to be as cooperative as possible in the rescue and return of the *Atlantis* from Isla de Pascua," the chargé from the Chilean Embassy told Dewey. "However, in view of the charge made by the Soviet Union, my government has asked me to forward to your government a number of requests."

"We'll be most happy to comply if we can, Señor Prieto."

"Good. Actually, they are not requests. They are conditions that are attached to my government's permission for your government to send military equipment to Isla de Pascua, along with a very large number of American technicians."

"What are your conditions, señor?" Dewey tried not to permit wariness to creep into his voice, but he had done business with people from Latin American countries for a long time, and he knew there was going to be some sort of expensive condition involved—one that was, of course, perfectly legal if ethically questionable.

"My government is concerned that the Soviet claims may cause certain . . . entities . . . to attempt to create problems. Isla de Pascua is very important to the Armada de Chile because of the large number of sheep that are raised there. A United States military presence on the island, even for the avowed purpose of reclaiming the downed spacecraft, might be viewed as a preliminary step toward a more permanent United States military presence on the island and in my government's strategically important zone of defense in the South Pacific Ocean." Whatever the chargé was getting at, he was certainly prefacing it with prolific preambles and justifying rationales. "Therefore, my government's military and naval forces will participate and assist you in any way possible."

"That's very kind of your government," Dewey replied. But Prieto hadn't come to the hooker yet, so Dewey remained wary, trying not to let it show. "I'm certain that the details can be worked out between our respective operating personnel."

"I am certain they can," Prieto agreed. "I am certain also that your government realizes it is going to cost my government a considerable sum of money to provide the necessary assistance."

"What did your government have in mind, Señor Prieto?" Here comes the kicker, Dewey told himself.

"I am certain that your government would be willing to reimburse my government for expenses entailed in this operation."

"I'll look into the matter and have a reply for you shortly."

"Good. But there are other conditions we must discuss, Señor Dewey. It is my understanding that NASA and your Air Force will be moving a great deal of equipment onto Isla de Pascua for use in this recovery activity. It would greatly simplify the Customs operations if the equipment could be consigned to the government of Chile. This would not tax the Customs facilities or personnel at Santiago or Isla de Pascua, since the equipment would belong to my government and would not require clearance through Customs," Prieto stated. "I'm sure you realize that Customs regulations require a great deal of time and effort to clear large and expensive pieces of equipment for entry and later for departure. This suggestion from my government would permit a rapid transfer of the equipment to Isla de Pascua with a minimum of red tape and delay."

It was quite clear what the chargé had in mind. "I'm not sure that the aircraft involved can be consigned to your government, Señor Prieto. All pertinent aircraft will be required to bring out the spacecraft, the very special equipment, and the people involved."

"The aircraft are quite properly registered to the United States," the chargé put in. "We would hardly expect *them* to be consigned. There will, however, be the matter of landing fees, along with ground-service charges and other costs at Santiago and Mataveri."

Things were obviously going to become expensive. Dewey didn't know where the funds would come from. State would have to find them somewhere—from NASA, DOD, somewhere. But that wasn't his problem.

"Señor Prieto, I can state that my government will certainly be willing to take care of whatever costs are involved, but I'll have to check into the matter of consigning the equipment."

"You have no idea how it would simplify the Customs procedures, Señor Dewey."

"Oh, I do indeed, Senor Prieto."

"It would also simplify the issuance of visas and work permits if Chilean organizations were contracted to make the necessary alterations to the airfield and to perform the other construction tasks needed for the operation of your equipment—such as concrete pads and so forth . . . I have a list of approved contractors."

"May I get back to you this evening on some of these points, señor? Our people are very anxious to reach that spacecraft because of the nature of the rocket propellants that are still in it."

"I am aware of the need for expedient action. But I must also discuss one final matter with you."

My God, weren't they asking for enough under the table as it was? Dewey asked himself. "And that is?"

"My government must be allowed to send a commission, with members of its choice, to Isla de Pascua with your initial aircraft in order to inspect the payload of the *Atlantis* and thus protect itself in view of the claims of the Soviet Union."

"No problem, señor. I can already vouch for that."

"Excellent. If you can get back to me concerning these matters, I will see to it that the necessary protocol and clearances are arranged at once."

Alfred M. Dewey hung up the telephone and put his

head in his hands. Why did this have to happen to him? He had been sixteen years with State, interfacing between the Department of Commerce and various South American governments on trade shows, technology exports, and international marketing problems that Commerce couldn't handle itself. The job had rarely been easy; there had always been a great deal of paper work as well as contact with embassies in Washington. There had been a certain amount of quiet *baksheesh,* as there always was in any sort of international trade, and there were always "import agents" who happened to be relatives of whoever was in power at the time. There were tacit and unwritten contracts involving "consultants" in other countries. That was the way international trade had been carried out for centuries; only the titles of the middlemen had changed.

Dewey himself had been extremely careful not to become involved in such affairs. In the first place, Department regulations stipulated that he couldn't, and Alfred M. Dewey really liked his job.

"Four years left, and this happens!" he moaned to himself. He had to hang on only another four years to qualify for "twenty and out" retirement. Now, when his goal was almost in sight, he discovered himself right in the middle of the very things he had tried so assiduously to avoid for sixteen years. With almost savage ferocity, he grabbed the telephone and dialed Johnson Space Center on the FTS.

Joe Marvin answered. He sounded harried. "Shuttle Mission Control. Marvin here. Wait one, please." Then his voice was muffled as he called to someone in the room: "Pete, try to raise them on one of the international ARTC frequencies that they're supposed to be monitoring." His voice came back loudly. "Sorry about that. Go ahead, please."

"This is Alfred Dewey at State. Is Joyce Fisher available?"

"Oh, the gal from State? Sorry, she departed with the initial group from Ellington a few minutes ago."

"I've got to talk with her," Dewey insisted.

"Hang on, sir. We'll try for an air-to-ground patch through Ellington. Let me turn this over to my communications specialist, Jeff Landers."

The line went dead as Marvin put him on hold. Sitting

there with the phone to his ear, Dewey began feeling worse and worse. When he looked at the wall clock, he realized he had missed dinner. It was the first time that had ever happened to him.

The Lockheed C-130 Hercules was designed and built as an all-around, medium-duty, military transport plane. But because of the intended universality of its function, passenger comfort wasn't one of its features. Though Red Richardson knew that this C-130 ride would be no VIP flight, Joyce Fisher found it to be a totally new experience. But the relative paucity of creature comforts didn't make Casey Laskewitz's job easier with one of his special passengers, Alice Arnold, who *really* wasn't prepared for the Spartan conditions of the flight. Herb Haynes, on the other hand, seemed to be taking everything in stride.

The Hercules is a hauler, but it took three Herks to get the initial operation under way. The eight men of the hypergolic-propellant-handling crew aboard the first C-130 were complacent; they were doing their job, they were drawing hazard pay, and they were earning it per diem with no place to spend it, a very unusual situation regarding government travel. The load of that first C-130 was mostly people, plus the propellant-handling gear.

Richardson was fretting about the second Hercules. It had runway construction equipment aboard that would give the Mataveri runway turnarounds and extend its parking ramps. But the Herk wasn't with the formation yet; it had to fly to Houston International to pick up a low-slung tow tug from Eastern Airlines. No word had been received yet from the flight deck to indicate the second ship had taken off.

The third ship could be seen off to the left if you knew where to look for its lights through one of the little round portholes. The third Hercules was a flying fuel tank. In addition to the almost 10,000 gallons of jet fuel it carried in its regular tanks, the cavernous cargo hold was filled with several fuel bladders holding an extra 6,500 gallons. Number Three was the insurance policy; it could carry enough fuel to insure that the other two could return from Isla de Pascua to Santiago.

The first stop was planned at Panama for topping off.

The planes had more range than that, but Colonel Matt Hubbard hadn't managed to make all the arrangements at Lima and Santiago for landing and fueling when the flight took off from Houston. "We'll have the situation in hand by the time you reach Panama," Matt had promised Red. "If not, at least you'll be on the ground and partway there, and you'll have enough fuel to get all the way to Santiago if you have to bypass Lima."

Red hoped so. There were glitches showing up in the plans now, not the least of which were the Soviet claims at the UN.

Although conversation wasn't easy—the C-130 was noisy from the slipstream rushing past the fat fuselage and from the beat of the huge props being turned by the turbine engines—Red decided to use the opportunity to learn something about the other side of the house from Joyce Fisher. Besides, Joyce was not an unattractive young woman. Something about her, something in the way she looked or moved or spoke, both disturbed and fascinated Red Richardson, one of the legendary NASA bachelors who seemed married only to his job, the agency, and space-flight.

"Joyce," he said, starting out on a first-name basis right away because he was, after all, the boss of this operation, "I'm going to be counting on you heavily from here on. You're my connection with State, and this affair seems to be getting more involved with international diplomacy all the time. What's the latest word on that, by the way?"

Joyce edged over in the passenger seat so she could be closer to Red and therefore not have to speak as loudly. These were typical, universal Air Force tactical transport seats, built for ruggedness, capable of being installed and removed from various aircraft quickly, able to hold an armed paratrooper with his pack and weapons—and totally uncomfortable for anyone else. "I haven't heard a thing from my boss in Washington since I last talked to him during the meeting in Houston," she replied. "I don't expect to hear from him until we reach Panama later tonight, if he's still in his office. I'll try to call him when we land."

"Do you think this Soviet claim will cause us any trouble in Santiago?" Red asked.

She shrugged. "Perhaps. Perhaps not. I don't mean to

give you a wishy-washy State Department diplomatic answer, but I just can't figure all the angles. Chile's a big question mark right now. I'll be able to tell you more once we get there and I can talk to some of my friends privately."

"You've been in the foreign service there?"

She shook her head. The fact that the noise level of the Hercules was so high that she had to lean over quite close to Red didn't bother him at all. Her pug nose was kind of cute, he decided. "My father was in the foreign service in Chile before they transferred him back to Washington and put him on a Latin American desk. I was a teen-ager when I left, but I still have lots of friends there."

"I'm glad. You speak the language. I never had time to learn a language," Red told her. He had to lean very close to where her ear was covered by her dark hair; it wasn't an unpleasant way to conduct a conversation. "Took two semesters of German to satisfy the language requirement, but don't speak or read it any more."

"We're going to be working together on this thing for a couple of months," she said. "May I call you Red?"

"By all means." He grinned at her, the first smile he had managed in more than a day. "Let's keep protocol to a minimum—even with the Chileans. We've got a tremendous job to do. Isla de Pascua isn't the easiest place in the world to run an Orbiter contingency recovery."

She shook her head. "Perhaps we can maintain the usual informality among Americans, but not with the Chileans," she warned him, "or with the Pascuans. You're going into a totally different culture, Red, and it's my guess that it'll drive you bats."

"Why do you say that?"

"Unlike a lot of the government types I have to deal with in Washington, you're task-oriented," she observed. "You're determined to get the *Atlantis* off Pascua as quickly as possible, and you'll move mountains to do it."

"Damned right," he told her firmly. "That's one-quarter of our manned space capability sitting idle and useless— and we're not going to be able to get any additional space-flight capability until and unless we can show that everything we've got is working steadily and scheduled up tight. We've already been told this by several administrations. Nobody in the Oval Office or on the Hill is going to push for more space activity until we demonstrate what we can do out there, things that mean something to them and that they can use to their benefit or for their profit."

Joyce looked at him carefully for a moment, then leaned over. "You're pretty evangelistic about the space program, aren't you?"

"Nobody's ever put it that way before, but yes, I guess I am. I'd have to be to put up with the sort of stuff I have to take in this job."

"Tell me something. What's the space program going to do for people of the Third World, people I know—the people of Chile or Isla de Pascua, for example?"

Red had a ready answer for that. "All sorts of earthly benefits and spinoffs. Instant communications. Worldwide television. Well, we've already got that, to some extent."

"We do? Why can't we talk with the *Atlantis* right now?"

"Because we've just started *using* space, and not everyone's involved yet. But they will be. In the next few years we'll be making products up there. We'll be tapping the Sun for energy to beam to Earth. We'll be moving industry off Earth and into space to help stop pollution. We'll eventually be getting all our raw materials from the Solar System, so that we'll no longer have to tear up this planet."

Joyce Fisher shook her head sadly. "You're a dreamer."

"That's right."

"You haven't got the foggiest notion how the rest of the world lives and thinks."

"Wait until we get to Isla de Pascua and set up the satellite ground station," Red promised. "You'll see what space can do for people."

"Don't be so sure," she warned him. "Remember, we're stepping into a totally different culture. And *that's* the prime reason I'm along, not as a translator, but to act as a buffer between our cultures."

The crew of the *Atlantis* had no such cultural buffer.

But Hap Hazard turned out to be the closest thing to it. There was no way any of them could change their flight suits. The survival kit from the *Atlantis* held no fresh clothing. Frank considered the alternatives and managed a quick bath, although the water that dribbled from the taps over the tub was so hard that the bar of rough soap could barely work up a lather for him. The water wasn't very hot, either. Nor was its tinge of sulfur odor pleasant. After drying himself with an amazingly soft towel, he put his flight-worn clothing back on. He wished he had some deodorant and hoped that the Pascuans wouldn't notice. The landing had caused him to sweat considerably more than had been apparent to the other crew members.

Hap knocked on the door to Frank's room as the pilot finished climbing back into his flight suit. The payload specialist had his arms full of emergency survival rations from his part of the contingency landing kit. "Hi, just thought I'd suggest we all bring along some things from the survival kits as gifts and presents—which would be helpful to us if a dinner here is anything like a luau in some of the Polynesian islands."

"Where did you pick up all this background data? You been to the South Pacific before?"

"No, Frank. But cripes, there's books in the library at JSC."

"I don't know," Frank began. "Maybe we shouldn't give away our survival rations."

"You think they're not going to feed us? They don't look like they're starving here. Why not give some of it away to them? Makes us look good, and gives them something they've probably never had before."

"Sure, like my dad told me it was in Europe, with Hershey bars and nylons and cigarettes—" Lew had walked up behind Hap. "Why not?

"Come on in," Frank urged. "Lew, this isn't NASA Road One or the strip at Mohave. Remember what Obregon told us about the native women."

The warning didn't faze the copilot. "Frank, just because you're a happily married man, don't begrudge us bachelors our hobbies."

"What about your hobbies?" Jackie had appeared in the doorway. Somehow she had managed to arrange her short-cropped blonde hair attractively, and she had put on some lipstick, which caused Frank to wonder where she had packed cosmetics for a Shuttle flight. Maybe it was like her rope ladder.

"Come in, Jackie. Hap suggests we take along some of

the food and goodies out of the contingency kit as gifts at the celebration," Frank told her.

"Government property," Jackie pointed out.

"That it is," Hap agreed, "but we're still on government time."

"And Lew was thinking he might use it as bait, right?" she asked rhetorically.

"Speaking of that, Jackie," Frank put in, looking levelly at her, "what the military governor had to say about the native women probably also applies to the native men."

Jackie snorted. "Who needs them? On the other hand, the military governor's pretty cute."

Hey came for them shortly thereafter, and Obregon was waiting in front of the hotel with his jeep. The trim captain in the Armada de Chile stared at the cans and plastic sacks that all four Shuttle crew members carried and dumped into the jeep; then he looked at Frank.

"Gifts," Frank said, "from our survival kit, which we won't need now, thanks to your hospitality."

Obregon nodded. "These will be welcome. There's little variation in our diet here. But you shouldn't give them to the Pascuans."

"Why, Governor, are you afraid they might get a taste of modern food and begin demanding more of it?" Jackie asked sarcastically.

"Jackie, shut up," Frank snapped. "Sorry, Governor, that was uncalled for, and I apologize."

"No offense," the officer replied. "I went to military school in America. I'm familiar with American women."

The primitive road led north about a mile out of Hangaroa to where a large crowd had gathered. Dominating the grassy plain was a small volcanic cone to the east. But the gaze of the crew of the *Atlantis* was fixed on the seven huge statues standing in a line to the northeast, the stoic stone faces looking westward into the rays of the setting Sun.

"The famous Easter Island statues," Hap mused.

"No, Miti Hazard," Hey said, "those are only seven of the *moai* that we have managed to put upright again on this *ahu*."

"Only seven? How many are there?" Lew asked.

"Hundreds," Obregon remarked.

"Why so many?" Jackie wondered.

"Each *moai* looks out upon that part of the world for which it is responsible," Hey explained quietly, "because Rapa Nui is *te Pito o te Henua*, the Island at the Center of the World."

Hap nodded. "Yes, I guess you're right. It's the center of the world. Depends on how you look at it."

There must have been a thousand people gathered in the dusk. Fires were burning in several locations. Sheep that had been slaughtered only that afternoon were now roasting in the midst of volcanic rocks made hot by the fires.

"Where'd you get the wood?" Frank asked Hey. "I haven't seen a tree on this island."

"The fires are made from dried *totora* reeds that grow in the crater lakes of Rano Roi, Rano Raraku, and Rano Kao," Juan Hey told him. "Because of your arrival, the governor authorized the slaughtering of many sheep for the festivities—so we will all eat well tonight, thanks to you."

As they were guided by Obregon to an obvious place of honor in the assemblage—it was getting hard to see what was going on now that the Sun had dipped below the horizon, bringing with it the rapid semitropical night with its short twilight—Hap asked the mayor of Hangaroa, "You don't go hungry here, do you?"

"No, there are *taro* and *ti*, but few fish now," Hey replied. "Mutton is a treat."

"But isn't sheep raising one of the major activities of Isla de Pascua?"

It was the military governor who explained tonelessly, "The sheep belong to the Armada de Chile, and we export seven tons of wool per year from Isla de Pascua. Therefore, the sheep are not to eat. But no one goes hungry. By government regulation, each family gets three kilograms of meat per week. If all is well, there's one free sheep for every two people every month."

Lew whistled. "Boy, I knew we'd landed out in the boonies, but I didn't think it would be the end of the world and the beginning of time, too."

Hey, the mayor of Hangaroa, smiled as he sat down on the reed mat and indicated places for the honored guests to seat themselves. "No, Miti Clay, you are at *te Pito o te Henua*."

CHAPTER SIX

The navigator clambered down the aluminum ladder from the flight deck and made his way through the dimly lit rows of seats to where Joyce and Red were sitting. "We've sure got popular people aboard this flight," he told them. "Miss Fisher, there's a call for you from Washington, and then Joe Marvin in Houston wants to talk to you, Mr. Richardson."

Red started to get up to let Joyce out into the aisle, but the navigator—a young man in shiny green nomex flight coveralls and with *Air Force* written all over him from his bushy mustache to his black-laced flight boots—added, "Where's Casey Laskewitz? Somebody wants to talk with him, too."

Richardson pointed to Casey three rows back, sitting next to Herb Haynes. Both men reclined in their seats, dead to the world. "Unless the world's coming apart and Casey's the only one who can fix it," Red said to the navigator, "let him sleep. He's with NASA Public Affairs, and there isn't a whole hell of a lot he can report on right now."

"Okay, I won't wake him up until you two are finished. Never disturb a guy when he's logging sack time. But his boss in Washington wants to talk with him, and he says it's urgent."

"For Casey, it's always urgent," Red observed.

Up on the flight deck of the Hercules, the navigator motioned Joyce toward the empty jump seat behind the pilot. The constant drone of the big props was quieter here, but the noise level from the boundary layer of air moving past the nose at 380 miles per hour actually made the flight deck noisier.

"Better use this," the navigator told her, and handed her a headset with earphones and boom mike attached and a long cord with a push-to-talk switch. "You won't be able to hear anything otherwise. You've got to push this switch to talk. Got it?"

Joyce nodded.

As she suspected, her caller was Alfred M. Dewey in Washington. The telephone link had been routed from the Space Center through Ellington Air Force Base to the Naval Air Station at Corpus Christi and thence via military UHF link to the Hercules. In spite of all these interconnections, she could hear her boss quite well.

"Miss Fisher, the Chilean government has agreed to permit us to conduct our operations on Isla de Pascua under certain conditions."

"What's it going to cost, Mr. Dewey?"

"Miss Fisher"—Dewey's voice betrayed the fact that he was somewhat sensitive about the matter—"I don't intend to discuss all the details over an open communications line. However, suitable arrangements and accommodations have been made."

"I understand."

"The Embassy in Santiago will be fully briefed on the matter, and our chargé there will be coordinating activities with you and the Chilean authorities. As I requested, you're to proceed to Isla de Pascua, where, in effect, you'll be our Ambassador Without Portfolio."

Joyce shook her head as she listened. The Chilean government officials knew they had the mighty United States right where they wanted it, and they were probably exacting the maximum toll possible.

"Provided I can get this matter staffed here in State tomorrow morning, when the proper people are around to approve the accommodations and arrangements, I don't anticipate there'll be any problems in clearing your flight through Santiago to Isla de Pascua or in obtaining whatever's necessary from the Chileans. You're responsible, Miss Fisher, for all United States diplomatic affairs on Pascua, including the necessary protocol for the Chilean inspection commission that will join your flight in Santiago."

"Do I report to our Ambassador in Santiago or to you?" she asked.

"To me, please."

"Listen," Joyce said, "I need full details of the

agreed-on arrangements and conditions. I'll probably have to slap a few hands that shouldn't be in the till. If I don't monitor things closely and make sure everything is done according to agreement, this operation could triple the federal budget."

"The Santiago Embassy will have the full details in a cable that will be there by the time you arrive tomorrow. Tell the NASA head of operations—Reed Richardson, is it?—tell him not to dicker prices or costs. That sort of thing is to be referred through the Embassy in Santiago. I'm not certain just whose budget these funds will come out of, but I've been told we shouldn't worry. So we'll let GAO or OMB keep score."

"Mr. Dewey, you sound awfully tired."

She could hear the sigh over the headphones all the way from Washington. "It's been a long day, Miss Fisher. And it may be a long night, too."

"I agree. It's been the same for me. How's Nash Sullivan doing in New York?"

"He got there too late today to do much, but we'll be sending a NASA briefing team up to the United Nations to present the full details to those on the Security Council who'll listen."

Joyce sighed. "Sullivan's got his hands full, too."

"Miss Fisher, in addition to that cable waiting for you when you get to Santiago, the chargé will have the proper documents ready to take to Isla de Pascua for the crew and for the *Atlantis*."

"Documents?"

"The crew wasn't provided with passports, so the Embassy in Santiago is preparing them and obtaining Chilean visas. And the *Atlantis* didn't carry a Certificate of Airworthiness or the FCC licenses for the radio transmitters aboard, as required by international law. There's always been some question regarding whether the Shuttle Orbiter is a spacecraft or an aircraft. The best answer I've been able to get is that back in the early 1970s, NASA and the FAA got together about it, and the FAA didn't have the slightest notion how to grant a Certificate of Airworthiness to a spacecraft and didn't want to spend the time and effort developing the standards for what was considered a single type of specialized vehicle, the Space Shuttle. Apparently nobody bothered to consider all the international protocol that would be required in a contingency landing." Dewey's voice was growing weak now, often disappearing in white noise.

"It's difficult to hear you. Shall I call you from Panama?"

"Very well. I presume I'll be here. Never had to sleep on my office sofa before, but there's always a first time."

"You should try these airlift seats," Joyce remarked. But the connection was so bad by then that she wasn't sure he had heard her. She stripped off the headset and handed it to the navigator. "Lost him."

"Yeah, we're getting out of range of the Corpus UHF transmitter," the navigator replied.

The Hercules pilot turned around. "Paul, try Selcal or VHF. Houston wanted to talk to Richardson. There must be some frequency we can get through on."

"Roger. Stand by, Mr. Richardson. I'll try on another channel."

Although there was constant radio contact between the Hercules and Mexican air traffic controllers, working special communications channels through United States facilities was a different matter. The navigator and the pilot both set to the task of establishing contact with the Federal Telephone Service through the MAC radio communications system. Finally, the navigator handed the headset to Red, who put it on, adjusted the boom mike, pushed the "talk" switch, and said tentatively, "Testing, testing, testing."

"That must be Red Richardson. He's always testing," the voice of Joe Marvin said from Houston.

"Are you still on the board there, Joe?" Red asked.

"Yeah, but I'm going to turn it over to the next shift and get some sleep once I pass some hot skinny along to you. Listen, the second Herk got off Houston International without a hitch. It's got one of Eastern's low-boy JG75 tugs. And we dug up a satellite ground station for you. One of the old ones that was used on the recovery carriers during Apollo. GE and Western Union both volunteered some of their people from here to dust it off, set it up, and operate it. They took it out of storage and we packed it aboard the Herk in place of the runway construction gear, which'll be coming on a *fourth* Herk that Matt Hubbard managed to find for us. The satellite boys'll get the ground station set up and working for you on Isla de Pascua, so you'll have constant communications with us."

"If we have the electrical power to run it. Did anybody consider that?"

"Red, we may work for Mission Control, but we ain't stupid. Ellington loaned us a 10-KVA generator unit, one of their auxiliary power units that's run by a gas turbine and uses JP-4 for fuel—and we'll have plenty of that on Pascua. The fourth Herk will leave Ellington tomorrow with a lot of goodies aboard, including that APU."

"Good work. Looks like we're going to have to bring in just about everything we need."

"Not quite. Talk to Joyce Fisher. I'm sure her boss in State just gave her the same good news and bad news he passed along to us. Guess what, Red? The Chileans are going to help us!"

"Yeah?"

"Yeah. Whether we want it or not—and at our expense."

"Just what I needed. I'm going to have enough trouble handling an American crew under these circumstances. Who the hell saddled me with two crews, neither speaking the other's language?" Red Richardson was clearly upset. "Okay, Joe, make sure that Herk full of goodies has the equivalent of lots of junk jewelry for the natives. Sounds like I'm going to have to buy our way through this."

"According to State, good old Uncle Sam is already paying through the nose for these so-called accommodations. That's the word the guy from State used." Marvin's voice held a note of disgust. "It's cheaper than paying for a new Orbiter. At any rate, I'll stick a lot of goodies in the fourth Herk. But don't go hog wild. State says to talk to Joyce who apparently knows her way around down there."

"I'll do that. But remind State this is my show, and it's my responsibility to get the *Atlantis* off Easter Island as fast as possible. I'm not going to put up with any *mañana* stuff from the Chileans. Make sure State understands. The first time the Chilean helpers get in the way, they're off the job."

"Uh, okay, but better work through Joyce Fisher. According to the man from State, that's why she's there, Red.

And apparently she's got the full delegated authority from State to act in the interests of the United States."

"I'll talk to her about it, Joe, but this job can have only one boss—and that's me!"

He had known from the start it would be a difficult job, involving the interplay of two cultures. But Red Richardson was beginning to realize this interplay was becoming more complicated by the minute.

"Comrade, the Chilean government has acceded to the American request to recover its spacecraft in spite of our efforts at the UN and in Santiago."

"Do you think I am not aware of that? Since the junta took power and installed lackeys of the imperialistic capitalists in government positions, the usual greed of capitalism has overcome revolutionary fervor."

"Our agent on Pascua informs us he will act when the time is right."

"I do not intend to depend on that. We have detached the *Kharkov* and the *Sverdlov* from the Vladivostok command and ordered them to the vicinity of Isla de Pascua. A show of force in the area will do much to deter any American plans to establish a base on Pascua."

"And it will also cover well for the other operation."

"*Da*, a diversion may be necessary if the Americans dispatch naval forces to the area in response to our move."

"Casey, sorry to bother you in the middle of the night." Roger Service's voice from Washington was not quite conciliatory over the long telephone-and-radio link to the Hercules cruising southeastward beyond Yucatán. "But I've got a problem here, and you've handled it in the past."

"What's up, Roger?" Casey had a foul taste in his mouth. In spite of Air Force coffee—which never managed to measure up to Navy coffee, especially on MAC flights— he had been sleeping deeply, lulled by the constant throb of the Herk's turboprops. He wasn't sure he was awake, but he tried to talk intelligently to his boss.

"It's Marty Soloman."

"Oh? What's Marty Baby want this time?" Casey replied caustically.

"He's madder than hell he wasn't included in the initial team to Easter Island with you."

"Look, Roger, Herb Haynes is the pool reporter for the initial segment. That was agreed to by the Washington bureaus of all the wire services and networks," Casey explained.

"He won't buy it. He knows Alice Arnold's with you."

"How come you saddled me with Alice Arnold anyway, Roger?"

"She knows where all the bodies are buried."

"Who and where?"

"How can I put it? Basically, she knows who's doing what to whom and who's getting paid for it over in the Executive Office Building. I had two options. One, I could've let her turn the thumb screws at sixteen hundred Pennsylvania, whereupon there would've been calls to the Administrator that might have upset him. Or, two, I could get her aboard because she's a woman, Jackie Hart's the mission specialist on this flight, and I was simply responding to the latest directive about equal opportunity news coverage. You might say I did it so Alice could cover the women's angle."

"Okay, I'll buy that."

"Now, what can I do about Marty?"

"Get him on the Pan Am press charter, and I'll take care of his tantrums once I get him on Easter Island a couple of thousand miles away from network headquarters," Casey promised.

"He wants to bring his own cameraman, and he demands time on the satellite link."

"Good old Marty Baby. Tell him sure. Give him what he wants as long as he's in New York with immediate access to the network. Once he gets to Easter Island, it's a different matter . . ."

God damn it! Casey thought as he took off the headset after the conversation ended. Am I going to have to hold his little hand all the way from Easter Island? Well, it was either that or let Roger Service screw up four years of careful bridge building to the right people in the media, people who would give the Shuttle the right sort of coverage, thanks to Casey Laskewitz.

At that point, he was beginning to wish he had stayed in

Washington to handle things from there. But standard operating procedure stipulated he was the first to go to wherever an Orbiter had made a contingency landing. He wondered why he hadn't had the foresight somehow to insist home base be adequately covered by someone of his choice whom he had trained. Why had he been so stupid as to forget that Roger Service would be the one sitting on home plate and fretting, possibly even messing up forever the careful structure of relationships built by Casey Laskewitz?

"How we doin'?" he asked the pilot, peering out at the darkness beyond the red-lit instrument panel and the windshield.

"Oh, another nine-five minutes and we should be starting to let down for Panama," the pilot replied with bored professionalism.

"About a five-hour flight, then?"

"Yup."

"How much total time to Santiago?"

The pilot riffled through the papers of his flight-planning documents. "We figure about fifteen hours total, not counting ground time and if the winds hold the way they are."

Jeez, that's forever and a day! Casey thought. Service couldn't hold off the media that long, much less the additional time it would take to fly the 2000 miles from Santiago to Easter Island. He would have to write a release about the initial phase of the rescue flight and dispatch it from Panama when they landed. He figured he would have to do the same for both Lima and Santiago. That meant he had better get busy. No typewriter, so he would have to do it the hard way: longhand on a paper tablet. Damn! Should have brought a typewriter! he told himself savagely. Why hadn't he remembered such a simple thing? Well, maybe he could "borrow" one from somebody in Panama with a promise to return it on his way back from Easter Island at some indeterminate time months in the future.

Meanwhile, the interplay between cultures was moving along just fine on Rapa Nui. It was, Frank reflected through a slightly alcoholic haze created by something Captain Ernesto Obregon had brought along, one hell of a good party.

A full Moon had risen over Rapa Nui in an absolutely

clear sky. The southeast trade wind wafted across the island, blowing out to sea the smoke from the multitude of fires. The brilliant light of the Moon actually threw shadows from the volcanic cones of Rano Roi and Rano Kao. And standing enigmatically on the crest of the hill to the north as if watching yet another incursion of strange peoples meet the unearthly surroundings of Rapa Nui, the Island at the Center of the World, were the *moai*, the huge stone statues.

Yet another clan of terrestrial people had come to the Center of the World.

Like most Americans, Frank had never eaten mutton. At first taste, it seemed greasy and fatty. But, cooked as the Pascuans did it, by the heat of volcanic rocks warmed by flames from burning *totora*, it had a delicious taste.

Frank suddenly realized he hadn't had anything to eat since the prelaunch breakfast back at Vandenberg that morning. It seemed like a long time ago, and it had been in a totally different world. The food tasted good, even if it wasn't something he was used to. He soon found himself unwinding from the events of the day. The incredible stress of landing the *Atlantis* on Mataveri had hyped him up considerably. The adrenalin was still flowing through his system, and he felt horny, the way he had when returning from a combat mission with lots of SAMs and MiGs and flak. But he remembered what Obregon had told him, and he held himself in check, as he had learned to at Bien Hoa and other faraway places where the women were either off limits or looked like one of his daughters. Nevertheless, he began to feel pretty good.

Obregon was feeling good, too. Obviously he was under the sort of stress that was unusual for his culture. As the military governor, the man in charge, he was trying to run a tiny, isolated island under rules and regulations not only decades old but often created by bureaucrats in Santiago who had never been to Isla de Pascua.

But Obregon's early education had been in the United States at various military schools, where he had picked up ideas and concepts alien to his responsibilities as the military governor of Isla de Pascua. As a result, it was obvious to Frank that Obregon deliberately turned his back on sev-

eral quiet infractions of the rules he had laid out to the
Shuttle crew earlier.

The military governor took quite a few belts from the
bottle during the evening. Though he never reached the
point where he began to act drunk, his very professional,
businesslike manner mellowed considerably, and he became increasingly convivial. "You don't know what a pleasure it is, Colonel, to be able to hold a conversation with
an educated military man such as yourself," Obregon confided to Frank. "We get many scientists and tourists here,
but seldom any military men except for my fellow naval
officers on the ship that comes once each year."

"Uh, Governor," Frank replied cautiously, "in my capacity as commander of the *Atlantis*, which is a spacecraft
of our nation's civilian space agency, I'd prefer my military
rank not be used. As a matter of fact, may I ask how you
learned of it?"

"I listened when the reporters were questioning you on
the radio from Houston. And I suspect that Lewis Clay
was also a military pilot before joining your space agency.
However, even though your Air Force now has women pilots, I don't imagine that Señorita Hart is one of them.
With no insult intended, she doesn't exhibit the knowledge
of military courtesy one *always* finds among professionals
such as ourselves the world over."

"You're a very astute observer, Governor."

Obregon unscrewed the cap from the bottle and poured
some liquid into Frank's now-empty cup. "Since you object
to the use of your rank, perhaps we should dispense with
such protocol altogether. We'll undoubtedly be working
closely together in the weeks to come. The use of titles
should probably be continued in public, of course. But between men of similar responsibilities and backgrounds, the
use of titles to convey respect can be cumbersome in private conversations and dealings. I'm aware of American
ways, and I like the informality that signifies basic respect
for one another as competent individuals." He filled his
own cup, screwed the top back on the bottle, and looked
directly at Frank. "I'd be pleased if you'd know me as Ernesto."

Frank looked him straight in the eye also, the two of

them by now oblivious to the raucous party, to the throb of drums, to the spontaneous dancing in the light of the *totora* fires. "What did they call you when you were going to school in America?"

Obregon laughed. "At VMI, my nickname was Chilidog!"

Frank guffawed and raised his cup. "Well, here's to Chili-dog—but I'll call you Ernesto."

The military governor raised his own cup to the Shuttle pilot. "And here's to Colonel King—Frank."

"I'll drink to that."

The celebration was indeed smoothing off a lot of rough edges between two groups of people who were culturally as different as night and day. Hap had been talked into rising shakily to his feet and dancing with an attractive Pascuan girl. She was trying to get Hap to hula, but the NASA payload specialist would have none of it. He started to teach her to disco to the beat of the drums. It was good disco on Hap's part; he knew what he was doing. After watching Hap for a few minutes, the Chilean naval personnel caught the spirit of the thing. As for the Pascuans, they treated it like one of their native dances, adding their own unique motions and steps to what Hap was doing in his bare feet with his white nomex NASA coveralls rolled up to his knees. A combination of Polynesian hula and American disco turned out to be a wild and unusual dance.

"How about that, Jackie?" Lew asked as the two of them watched, sitting side by side on the reed mat that was their place of honor for the evening. "Want to give it a try?"

"Why don't you cut in on Hap?"

"Well, let's not create any problems," Lew replied smoothly. "I'm taking to heart what Obregon said we shouldn't do."

"I didn't think you'd pay any attention to the warning about the women, Lew."

He laughed. "Jackie, don't worry about it. They don't know about Lew Clay, hot pilot, yet. But I think Frank was worried about you and the Pascuan men, although Obregon didn't say anything about *that*."

Jackie looked at the dancing forms. "Hadn't entered my mind, but now that you mention it, he *didn't* say anything about the men, and some of them are attractive."

"What have they got that I haven't got?"

"I don't know. What've you got?"

"Come on, let's dance. Maybe you'll find out."

"All right. I've never really gotten to know any Navy brown-shoe types."

"No shoes tonight. Come on, take off those flight boots, Jackie. You figure we'll ever have another opportunity to dance barefoot in the sand on a South Sea island with no communications and no boss to look over our shoulders?" Lew rapidly shucked his boots and rolled up his flight-coverall legs.

"You know," Jackie said, pausing for a moment, "you're right. And judging from what Hot Pilot King's drinking over there with Obregon, neither of them gives a damn tonight, either." She not only pulled off her flight boots and rolled up her coverall legs, she also rolled up her coverall sleeves and zipped down the front of the coveralls quite a good deal more than she would have done even in a disco along NASA Road One.

Lew obviously noticed. "What, no NASA-issue lingerie?"

"Listen, when you fall outside the ninety-percentile standard that all NASA stuff is designed for, it's too damned tight," Jackie said as she bounced to her feet. "One of my ambitions is to design decent spaceflight fashions for women." She began to move to the music.

Jackie may have been tough, but Lew noticed for the first time—why hadn't he seen it earlier?—that she was basically all female and probably capable of about Mach Three. He decided right then and there he had paid too much attention to the stories in the Astronaut Office, and damned himself for having placed too much credence in them. He got to his feet and began to move to the rhythm of the drums. A time and a place like Rapa Nui might not come along for quite a while, he told himself.

It was apparent that Jackie was thinking the same thing. And he thought it a very good time to check out those rumors.

Nobody noticed the two of them walking slowly up the hill toward the seven huge statues, their arms around one another and their white coveralls gleaming in the bright moonlight. Other couples were doing the same thing. In this time and place, nobody cared. They disappeared into the deep shadows at the base of the enigmatic statues.

In the bright light of a full Moon in a cloudless sky—a Moon once walked by humans and awaiting the next booted imprint on its ancient surface—the black and white shape of the Space Shuttle *Atlantis* sat quietly on the runway, while only a few miles away, near seven huge stone statues with impassive faces, a group of people danced and cavorted and ate and drank by the flickering light of fires and made love to one another with joy and pleasure, as human beings had done for millions of years.

Not even the four space farers in their shimmering white flight suits could help being caught up and lost in the ancient celebration of people coming together to enjoy each other—because, in spite of themselves and what they were trained to do, they were humans, too.

CHAPTER SEVEN

Alfred M. Dewey rose from the sofa in his office, where he had spent the night after long telephone conversations with many people. For the first time in his life, he watched the Sun rise over Washington, D.C.

Because the west coast of South America is an hour ahead of Washington's time, sunrise came earlier to the three Air Force C-130 Hercules transport planes winging their way southeastward. Red Richardson was awakened from a fitful slumber as the light from the rising Sun poured through one of the three small portholes on the left side of the plane, throwing columns of brilliance through the otherwise dark cargo hold. Lima, Peru, was now behind them. Fatigued as he was, he was still running on the momentum of the previous day, which, with the landings in Panama and Lima in the middle of the night, hadn't really been separated from this morning by the usual night of sleep. He went to the john, decided it was useless to try to shave in the cramped and Spartan facilities of the cargo plane's single tiny lavatory, and elected to clamber up to the flight deck so he wouldn't disturb Joyce, who was still blissfully sound asleep in the reclined seat. Thinking of the crew, he grabbed one of the stainless-steel Thermos bottles of coffee that had been refilled in Panama.

The flight crew were still on station, but Red could see fatigue beginning to show on their faces. Each man exhibited the dull and emotionless expression that betrayed he had managed to catnap as the Herk flew on autopilot.

Red waved the Thermos. "Coffee?"

The pilot stretched, then fumbled for the paper cup in the holder on his left. "For the dawn patrol, always. Thanks. Chuck, you'd better go to the john first," he told his copilot. "I'll check it out after you come back."

The copilot pointed to his cup. "Fill 'er up, and thanks. It'll be cool enough for me by the time I get back." He crawled out of the right-hand seat and disappeared down the ladder into the darkness of the cargo hold.

Making a minute adjustment to one of the multitude of controls on his panel, the flight engineer told Red, "Thanks, but I've got some hot tea. Can't take coffee. My system confuses caffeine with uric acid, and I can't always leave my post."

The pilot chuckled and sipped the hot coffee Red had poured. "Santiago about sixteen hundred Zulu time," he remarked. "Noon local."

"Long flight. Will you be able to get some rest in Santiago before the haul to Pascua?" Red asked, worried that the critical flight crew might become overtired and therefore accident-prone.

"I'll hack the six-hour flight to Pascua okay if I can get a good, hot meal and spend an hour or so in peace and quiet walking around," the pilot replied. "On an overwater flight the navigator's the one who sweats."

"We've got to get to Pascua fast with this propellant-handling equipment," Red explained, perhaps unnecessarily. "That Orbiter's loaded with nitrogen tetroxide."

"How much room on that runway with the Shuttle on it?"

"The *Atlantis* rolled out about eight hundred feet from the end of a runway almost nine thousand feet long and a hundred wide."

"No sweat," the pilot said with a grin. "We can drop this bird in fully loaded on an eight-hundred-foot strip. Uh, Pete, see what they put aboard in the way of breakfast for us, will you?" he asked his flight engineer.

Rising a little later over the volcanic cones of Rapa Nui, that same Sun struck Frank squarely in the face as it streamed through the windows of the Hotel Hangaroa. He rolled over and tried to bury his head in the pillow. No use. So he sat up, and wished he hadn't.

Damn, that had been a good party! Too good. He should have known better than to try to stay drink for drink with Ernesto. Whatever the military governor had had in the bottle was good, but it had also been potent.

His tongue was asleep, and his teeth itched.

No, he decided, his teeth had sweaters on them instead.

He didn't recall when the party had broken up. He hadn't looked at his watch. He remembered trying to find Lew and Jackie, and he recalled trying to get Hap into the jeep. Then there was a vague recollection of a somewhat wild ride over a very rugged road with him and Ernesto driving by the committee system—Ernesto steering by reference to the left side of the road and counting on Frank to keep track of the other side.

Well, he thought as he looked out over the little village of Hangaroa and the volcanic landscape of Rapa Nui, he might have time to get shaped up before the first C-5s landed later in the day. Then he remembered that the *Atlantis* was still sitting on the Mataveri runway. No C-5 Galaxy could take off with the *Atlantis* there. What would they try to do? Although he found it difficult to make the simple mental calculations, he figured that nobody would show up at least until much later that evening. Maybe Obregon's men could get the radio transmitter on the air so he could talk to Red Richardson, if Red had made it to Santiago yet.

That would give Frank time to recover from last night. Red would understand. But Frank didn't know who else would be coming. Sometimes the nonflying side of NASA didn't understand the flying side. Well, the guys with the pocket calculators would never have to land an Orbiter without the microwave landing system, so to hell with what they thought.

He managed to wash and shave with what he could find in the personal survival kit. Quite obviously, the one-shot disposable razor had been obtained from the lowest bidder. And the shaving cream in its little plastic baggie wouldn't lather in the hard water.

Naturally, the survival kit contained nothing for a hangover, just four aspirin. Was NASA telling him, in effect, to take four aspirin and they would call him in a few days? Even in his current physical condition, he couldn't help grinning. Two of the aspirin would help—some. At least they would keep him from dying for a few hours anyway. Beyond that, who could tell?

Breakfast would also help, and he hoped that Juan Hey had a decent kitchen, a good cook, and something more than *taro* to eat.

He remembered where Hap's room was because he had poured the payload specialist into it in the middle of the night. His sharp knock on the door brought a reply that was a moan: "Go 'way and lemme die in peace."

It was the sort of response Frank expected, but the tone of Hap's voice was wrong. In fact, it sounded as if the payload specialist were indeed dying. Frank opened the door to see Hap curled up in a fetal position on the bed, holding his stomach with his arms and sweating profusely.

"Come on, Hap, you'll feel better if you get up and put some food into you," Frank began.

"Like hell! I've been sicker than a dog for the last couple of hours. I've got a god-awful pain in my belly, I've vomited everything that's in me, and I've been running to the crapper like there was no end to it." The payload specialist groaned. "Whatever I ate last night—boy, it sure got to me."

Frank walked over to the bed and laid his hand against Hap's sweating forehead. "Hap, you're running a hellacious fever. Let me see if I can find that doctor."

Juan Hey came running when Frank walked through the lobby-patio of the hotel calling for him. The mayor of Hangaroa looked rather pale but seemed to have survived the party in better shape than the Shuttle pilot. He managed to produce Dr. Esteban within ten minutes.

"Nothing very unusual. I see it occasionally here on Rapa Nui. Bacillary dysentery."

"I didn't think there was any of that left!" Frank exclaimed. "How come I don't have it? Hap, did you eat anything some Pascuan offered you that I didn't get offered, too?"

"I don't know, I don't know . . . I ate the mutton and the *taro* and all with the rest of you."

"What did you drink, Señor Hazard?" Dr. Esteban asked.

"The stuff Obregon had. And you had something, too. While we were dancing, Marina Kehu gave me some kind of real potent stuff they make from goat's milk."

The doctor sighed. "We have outbreaks of dysentery from time to time on Rapa Nui. Most of us have a natural immunity to the majority of the bacteria that cause it. The bacteria can come from milk products. Señor Hazard obviously has no resistance to the particular bacterial strain that's brought on his dysentery."

"What's the diagnosis, Doc?" Hazard managed to groan. "Am I gonna die like I think I'm gonna?"

"You very well may."

"Are you serious, Doctor?"

"I wish I were not, Señor King. I'll try to find out whether it's the Shiga or Flexner-Harris strain, although the Shiga type is most common on Rapa Nui. I hope that it is indeed only dysentery and not amebiasis or cholera, which would be even more serious," Esteban remarked with some concern evident in his voice for the first time. "I will start Señor Hazard on sulfadiazine immediately. But I will also have to see the governor. We may have to get some of the other sulfa drugs flown in from Santiago if he does not respond to the sulfadiazine. Perhaps some streptomycin or Chloromycetin can be flown in as well in case he develops granulocytopenia as a result of sulfa therapy. And I'll want to check that fermented drink—if I can find Marina and if she has any of it left. I don't need an epidemic of dysentery on my hands."

"You implied the possibility of dying from this, Doctor. How real is that possibility?" Frank pressed.

"Highly probable without treatment. The biggest problem is dehydration and an imbalance of electrolytes, because he's not only sweating but passing fluids almost constantly. There is also the problem of the exotoxins of the bacteria, and this is usually very painful, often leading to delirium. If therapy is delayed, it can be fatal within three to four days because of both dehydration and intoxication," Esteban explained. "I'll have Captain Obregon get in touch with Santiago. In the meantime, we must force fluids." He shook his head. "It would help greatly if I had some antibiotics . . ."

Frank knew he had to do something or possibly lose Hap Hazard, Dr. Esteban and all the experience he possessed notwithstanding. "We'd better find Captain Obregon at once, Doctor. Then I'll go back to the *Atlantis* and see what we have in the medical kit aboard. Certainly it must have something in it that'll make him more comfortable, and it may contain both antibiotics and diarrhea medicine."

It would be inexcusable to lose a Space Shuttle payload specialist to a disease that had been a common scourge of the human race for eons and that, in the modern world, was considered to be a primitive affliction no longer of great importance.

But it certainly was of great importance to Hap Hazard.

Frank banged on Lew's door. "Roust it out, buddy. We've got work to do."

"Ahwrr," came a muffled growl.

Frank opened the door, strode over to his copilot's bed, and dumped him unceremoniously on the floor. "Get up. Hap's sick and may damned well die. Get dressed. We're going out to the *Atlantis*."

Lew shook his head. He hadn't bothered to undress before climbing into bed. "What the hell are you talking about?"

"Just what I said. Get up and put your shoes on. We've got to get the medical kit out of the *Atlantis*." Without another word, he strode out and down the hall to Jackie's room. Again he pounded on the door.

"Just a moment," Jackie's voice replied, and Frank could hear noises in the room. Then the door opened, and Jackie peeked through. She was still wearing her flight coveralls. "Frank, either the world must be coming to an end or you're living damned dangerously, waking me up under these conditions, especially after—"

"Put it all together, Jackie," Frank told her. "We've got a very sick Hap Hazard. Dysentery."

Jackie's expression changed immediately, and she became all business again. "What can I do, Frank?"

"Go hold his hand, do what Dr. Esteban tells you, and keep forcing fluids into him until Lew and I get back from the *Atlantis* with the medical kit."

"In other words, you need a nurse?"

"I don't. Hap does." He collected Lew on his way back down the hall. The copilot hadn't shaved, but that could wait. "Where are your boots?" Frank asked.

Lew looked down at his rolled-up coverall legs and bare feet. "Damned if I know. I took them off last night at the hula."

"You'll probably never see them again. Some Pascuan's sporting a pair of NASA-issue Space Shuttle crew boots today, maybe the first shoes he's ever had. Never mind, buddy. You'll just have to go barefoot. Let's find Obregon."

The military governor, dressed in a clean set of khakis with an immaculate, razor-sharp press to them, was having breakfast in his quarters with Father Francisco when the two Shuttle pilots arrived. Upon hearing Frank's report, Obregon nodded. "I'll be in touch with Santiago as quickly as I can get to the radio station."

"Can Lew and I borrow the jeep to go out to the *Atlantis* after we drop you at the radio shack?"

Frank almost didn't have to ask.

"I will go to the Hotel Hangaroa and see if there is anything I may do to help Dr. Esteban and Señor Hazard," Father Francisco said as they parted. "I may not be a doctor, but perhaps I can help in other ways."

Both pilots were extremely cautious as they drove slowly up the runway toward the *Atlantis*. Her tail with its rocket nozzles faced them, but there was no way they could tell whether nitrogen tetroxide vapors hung around her. Fortunately, the breeze was very light, blowing gently out of the northwest. That would help carry fumes away from them as they approached, Frank thought.

"See anything?" Lew asked, peering at the tail section as they neared the craft.

"No. OMS pods look okay to me. In fact, there doesn't seem to be anything obviously wrong with her," Frank remarked, looking closely at the *Atlantis*.

"Except she quit working on us," Lew pointed out. "Wonder what happened?"

"We'll leave that for later. Look, I'll drive us around and park under the hatch. You stay with the jeep. I'll go aboard and get the medical kit. If you hear me yell to get out of here, go—and don't wait for me. Understand?"

"Not leaving without you," Lew said flatly.

"If I say so, you will," Frank told him.

They stopped underneath the open hatch with Jackie's rope ladder dangling from it. After Frank turned the jeep's motor off, there was no sound except the sighing of the wind. The *Atlantis* was quiet, with none of the creaking and groaning of the day before. She had settled down overnight, all her structure stabilizing at ambient temperature.

"Nothing wrong with this bird," Lew observed. "I'll go aboard with you."

"Think you can climb that rope ladder in your bare feet?" Frank asked.

"Uh . . . I'll wait for you." The copilot was already having trouble walking barefoot. Like most Americans, he had always worn shoes, and his feet were not tough enough to walk over sharp stones or even pea gravel without discomfort.

Climbing a rope ladder was not the easiest thing in the world to do, Frank decided. He was out of breath by the time he had pulled himself over the lip of the open hatch. He wasn't out of shape, but still recovering from the night before.

The mid-deck was dark except for where light came through the open hatch. However, as his eyes grew accustomed to the lack of light, he began to see better.

There was still the possibility of toxic fumes, and Frank kept checking himself for the initial symptoms of nitrogen tetroxide inhalation as he began to open and empty lockers on the forward bulkhead. He dropped the first load out the hatch and into the waiting arms of his copilot and called, "Lew, I think we're okay on the OMS propellant. As long as we're here, I'm going to off-load our personal equipment lockers and most of the food on board. And I need some clean socks and shorts."

With considerable relief he clambered back down the rope ladder, having removed all he felt would be important to them. Once back on the runway, he rummaged through the equipment and found the medical kit. A quick check of the contents list produced a shout of joy from the Shuttle pilot. "Hot damn! *Sixty* tetracycline capsules. Twelve Dramamine pills. Twenty-four diarrhea pills. And even some painkillers."

"Let's get the hell out of here," Lew urged. "You'll probably think I'm growing a set of chicken feathers, but I'm pretty damned leery about being around this beast as long as she's still got propellants in her. I'm a rather devout coward at heart." As a Navy pilot, Lew had been thoroughly indoctrinated about the hazards of jet fuel and other fuels aboard carriers. He never really liked having to ride atop several million gallons of liquid oxygen, liquid hydrogen, nitrogen tetroxide, and monomethylhydrazine in the Shuttle missions. But all this was part of the most exciting flying job in the world, and he was willing to compromise with the hazards in normal flight operations. But he wasn't so sure he was willing to cope with those hazards in the emergency situation in which they had found themselves.

As they drove off down the runway from the *Atlantis,* Frank was relieved. He knew that approaching and entering the *Atlantis* at this point had perhaps been foolish, but he had done it because one of his crew might not survive if he hadn't.

Hap Hazard now had a fighting chance.

Things were not proceeding well in Santiago.

"The Prime Minister's office has informed me that the Chilean inspection commission will not be ready to go to Isla de Pascua for perhaps another forty-eight hours, Mr. Richardson." The American chargé d'affaires, Art Phillips, hung up the telephone with a note of frustration in his voice.

"*Forty-eight hours?*" Red Richardson exclaimed in exasperation. "Look, the *Atlantis* is sitting out there like an unexploded bomb. She could endanger the entire populace of Pascua. And in two days so many military transport aircraft will be stacked up here in Santiago that there won't be ramp space at the airport for them." Red wasn't really rested after the long flight to Santiago, and there had been a mix-up with visas at the Santiago airport that had created further confusion. Somebody hadn't gotten the word. And the traffic from the airport to the American Embassy had been atrocious, with many detours through back streets because of the new airport expressway under construction. Now, at the American Embassy, more roadblocks were appearing.

"Is the Chilean government fully aware of the potential hazards?" Joyce Fisher demanded. "Are they aware that a delay could be dangerous?"

"Miss Fisher," the chargé replied with a sigh, thinking this young woman from Washington certainly didn't understand the situation in South American countries in spite of the fact that she apparently worked the technical desk for the region, "things don't move as quickly down here. It takes time to get things done. I've expressed all these concerns to the Prime Minister's secretary, and that's as far as I can go right now."

"Art, who's the Prime Minister's secretary?" Joyce snapped.

The chargé's eyebrows went up at this question. "Why, Señor Carlos Aquirre . . ."

"I thought so," Joyce said with a smile, and reached for the telephone on the chargé's desk, asking rhetorically, "Art, may I use your telephone, please?"

Joyce dialed a number. The chargé merely looked on with astonishment. Nobody from Washington had ever reacted this way before.

She spoke in rapid, fluent Spanish to the listener on the other end, finally saying gaily, "Carlos? Joyce Fisher. Qué pasa, amigo?" Then she continued, obviously talking to someone she knew very well. Red didn't understand a word, but the chargé seemed extremely distressed and surprised at the same time because he understood everything Joyce was saying.

Finally, she hung up. "Art, our three Herks are cleared to go to Pascua as soon as we can lift off. The fueling problem's also been worked out—or will be by the time we get back to the airport. And the Chilean commission will be happy to join the press group on the Pan Am charter. When's that coming, Red?"

"Uh . . . should be lifting off Houston this morning," Richardson replied, trying to keep things straight in his mind. So many details! He knew he would have to get some sort of office set up on Pascua, maybe even work out a schedule board to keep track of everything.

"Good. Carlos said the commission would rather ride comfortably in a commercial jet anyway. That Herk was designed for cargo and soldiers, not people."

"Uh, Miss Fisher," the chargé said in tentative tones, "I didn't realize you knew Señor Aquirre."

Joyce smiled. "Art, I grew up in this Embassy. I probably know more secret passages and rooms than you do. Carlos Aquirre and I went to school together. In fact, he was my first date—" She suddenly became all business. "Please don't stand still for any delays in this operation. It's too important to the United States and Chile. The Chilean government's taking plenty of cut. Carlos Aquirre knows I'm here and will be on Pascua, and he knows I know the system. And I know a lot about him, too. If you run into any more trouble, call me on Pascua. Otherwise, follow through to the letter on the agreements spelled out in this cable from Dewey." She indicated the teletype flimsy in her hand. Thinking a moment, she smiled again knowingly. "Carlos is such a nice guy. I'll have to stop and see him on my way back once this thing is over. It's been a few years."

Red was feeling better. In the first place, he was beginning to have a full measure of respect for this attractive young woman with hints of a Latin background in her dark eyes and hair. She was obviously going to be more than just a pretty face and another bureaucrat underfoot. "Still the only way to get things done, isn't it?"

"Beg pardon?" she asked.

"It's still who you know, not what you know."

Joyce shook her head. "No, not entirely. I know some things about Carlos that he'd just as soon forget. He knows it, too, and that helps when it comes to getting things done.

And he expects to see me only after we finish this job on Pascua." She let the matter drop at that.

"I was beginning to work out options for staging the operation out of Lima," Red remarked.

"Oh, we couldn't do that," Joyce replied, shaking her head in disapproval. "That would be an insult of major proportion to Chile, and we'd have to handle the Peruvians—and I don't have that many friends up there."

"Uh, Joyce, just how *friendly* are you with these Chileans?" Red suddenly wanted to know for a reason he couldn't have explained at the moment.

"Mr. Richardson," she rebuked him softly, "that's *my* business. But, lest you evaluate it by current American moral standards, let me point out that here they're not only quite different, but stricter as well—at least in the area you're thinking about. I never went on a date with Carlos without a *dueña*."

"Forget it. My parochialism's showing. Let's get moving."

The now-respectful chargé arranged for an Embassy car to return them to the airport, and they arrived to find Casey engaged in an argument of massive sound level with Alice Arnold.

"Look, Alice, I'm sorry, but I can't help you," Casey was telling her in a voice barely under control. He, too, was suffering from the lack of a good night's sleep on the Herk.

Obviously, so was Alice Arnold. "But I've got to file a story!" the strident female newsperson complained loudly. "The lousy damned telephone system in this dirty, backward, out-of-the-way country tells me it'll be three hours to get through to the States! Circuits are all busy, they tell me. Hell, I don't speak the language, and half the time I can't make myself understood to the operators. Least you could do is get somebody to set up a direct press line for me and Herb—but I get to use it first!"

"Why don't you call your bureau here or get your stringer on the line? File your story through your normal AP channels?"

"How do I know they'll run it under my byline? These foreign bureaus can't be trusted, especially in these backward Third World countries. As for contacting a stringer, forget it. He'll want a dual byline just for filing."

"Careful, Alice, you're standing right in the middle of one of those backward Third World countries you're criticizing," Casey pointed out.

"So? I've got my press card."

"Just be thankful Chile's still honoring a reasonable freedom of the press on an international basis," Casey said, "because you're drawing a lot of attention from a couple of men over there by the stairway who have *security police* written all over them."

At that point, Joyce stepped into the exchange. "Alice, look, please cool it. Those *are* security police. Casey, can I help out here? I speak the language." When Casey nodded in obvious relief, Joyce continued. "Come on, Alice, let's find a telephone. I'll see what I can do to talk the operator into getting a call through right away."

America's Number One early-morning-TV talk-show host riffled through his papers and went on with the news as he saw it. "Well, NASA still has its problems. The space agency hasn't managed to get its people down to Easter Island to rescue the Space Shuttle *Atlantis* and its crew of four. NASA spokesman Roger Service told us in a late-night briefing that there's absolutely no danger of rocket propellants leaking out of the *Atlantis* and poisoning the twelve hundred people of Easter Island. Apparently the Shuttle commander, astronaut Frank King, reported by radio that he'd detected no leaks. But two big questions remain. Why did NASA design a spaceship that uses poisonous rocket fuel? Why didn't other government agencies responsible for environmental safety step in and insist that NASA use a fuel that was safe, especially if there happened to be an explosion on the launch pad that could send poisonous fumes into innocent spectators?

"In the meantime, the United States government continues to deny the claims of the Soviet Union that the *Atlantis* is a military space vehicle carrying a death-ray satellite capable of zapping Earth targets with deadly radiation. America's UN Ambassador has arranged for a full technical briefing of the UN Security Council by experts from the space agency at noon, and this network will summarize what transpires on the evening news. However, the Soviet Union has already indicated it won't listen to the fabricated stories of American space experts. Special American State Department technology expert Nash Sullivan told me by telephone just minutes ago that the space agency will make available to the public the full details of the cargo—which is supposed to be an Earth-viewing satelite called Landsat-XIII. Our own network science experts will have a look at these. Is America's civilian space agency working in cahoots with the Pentagon to build a military death-ray attack capability in space? Later in this hour we'll talk with Dr. Fred Meadows, Top Of The Morning's science reporter, for his analysis of this situation.

"We have no pictures from Easter Island yet. More than twenty-four hours after the space accident, NASA hasn't been able to get its own people, much less the news media, to Easter Island. But we do expect to have pictures via satellite this evening. They promise the interesting contrast of the spaceship *Atlantis* to the enigmatic stone statues of Easter Island. Maybe the statues themselves will be able to tell us more than the space agency has, because NASA spokesman Roger Service says that NASA's rocket experts have no idea what caused the failure of the rocket engines that resulted in the emergency landing.

"Now for other news of the morning . . ."

CHAPTER EIGHT

"Pascua Tower, this is Hercules Redeemer Zero-One, flight of three aircraft at Ostra intersection, landing Mataveri with clearance," came the voice over the loudspeaker in the control tower.

Frank smiled at his barefoot copilot. "Right on the button," he said in a tone of relief.

"Hercules Redeemer Zero-One, this is Pascua Tower,"

the Chilean tower controller replied into the microphone. "Descend and maintain three thousand feet. Hold flight in line astern southeast over the Pascua VOR on the one-two-eight radial. Report the Pascua VOR. Wind one-one-zero at five knots, temperature two-five Celsius, altimeter one-zero-zero-five millibars. Landing Runway One-Zero. Approximately twenty-four hundred meters of Runway One-Zero available. Caution, Space Shuttle Orbiter *Atlantis* parked on the runway two hundred and fifty meters from the departure end of Runway One-Zero."

"Redeemer Zero-One out of flight level two-one-zero for three thousand. Report Pascua VOR. Roger."

"Can they land on the runway with only twenty-four hundred meters available?" Captain Ernesto Obregon asked nervously.

Frank nodded. "They'll use less than four hundred meters of runway," he explained. "That's why the Herks are the first planes to arrive."

"Incredible," the military governor muttered. "But then, all of this is. In a way, I'm glad you made an emergency landing here. It's certainly livened up our lives."

"You haven't seen anything yet," Lew remarked.

The initial radio reporting point was over a hundred miles east, so it was some time before three specks appeared in the blue sky. It was a great sight to Frank to see the three Hercules transports wheel into line in their holding pattern. True, they wouldn't be able to get much done before sunset today, but at least they would be on the ground.

From the flight deck of the lead Hercules, Red Richardson looked down anxiously at the *Atlantis* sitting on the runway. The long shadows of late afternoon threw the island topography into bold relief. Save for the volcanic cones and large rocks scattered across the grassy landscape of the island, the most prominent feature on Isla de Pascua—at least to Red's eyes—was the black and white *Atlantis* on the asphalt runway.

The overnight wait in Santiago had been both boring and frustrating to Red. Delays in the takeoff from Santiago had frustrated him even more. But Isla de Pascua was now below. They had made it at last. Now he could get to work!

"Redeemer Zero-One, Pascua VOR at three thousand."

"Redeemer Zero-One cleared for visual approach, Runway One-Zero. Redeemer Zero-Two and Zero-Three, remain in the holding pattern. Maintain visual separation."

"Zero-One."

"Zero-Two."

"Zero-Three."

Pros, all of them, Frank thought with pride as the lead Herk broke from the pattern and began to swing northwest of the island, losing altitude as it did so.

"You're going to get a lot of practice in the next few weeks," the Shuttle pilot told the young Chilean tower operator.

There would be a lot of air traffic into Pascua in the next two months with craft coming and going during the Shuttle Down operation. One of the reasons Frank wanted to be in the tower for the approach and landing of the initial flight of Herks was not only to hear their approach and watch them land but also to check out the tower operations. He was glad to learn that the Pascuan tower operators—young Armada de Chile officers and enlisted men—seemed able to handle the job. Their command of aviation English, the international language of air traffic control, was more than adequate. And it would get even better.

Looking through a pair of binoculars Obregon gave him, Frank watched as the big wing flaps extended and the wheels appeared beneath the fat fuselage when the lead Herk turned onto final approach.

From the flight deck, Red Richardson watched the approach from another point of view, thinking what it must have been like for Frank in the *Atlantis*, coming in not at an approach angle of three degrees, as the Herk was doing, but at more than twenty degrees—and with no landing aids, and *no* chance of being able to go around again if he missed that narrow strip of black asphalt ahead. It gave Red a new appreciation not only of all Shuttle pilots but especially of Frank King and Lew Clay.

The Herk soared over Hangaroa, was less than five feet in the air as it crossed the landing threshold of the runway, and touched its four main wheels 200 feet down the strip. The pilot moved the propeller levers forward past a detent notch on the throttle quadrant, and all four props went into reverse pitch with a roar. The sixty-ton airplane came to a smooth but rapid stop about a thousand feet down the runway, just abreast of the tower.

"Redeemer Zero-One, left turn at the intersection and follow the jeep. Redeemer Zero-Two, cleared for visual approach."

"It *does* land in a short space," Obregon observed, "like a naval-carrier airplane."

"The Herk has actually landed and taken off from a carrier," Lew put in. "Damnedest sight in the world."

"You're not going to have much room on the ramp," Frank said. "I hope Richardson's bringing in some construction equipment to expand this airfield."

"According to the messages from Santiago, he is. A great deal of it. In order to prevent a Customs problem, the United States is consigning the equipment to my government, though I don't know what we're possibly going to do with it afterward," the military governor remarked. "We should go down to welcome them."

People began pouring out of the parked Hercules by the time the three of them had descended the tower stairway and walked across the ramp. "How're your feet holding up?" Frank asked his copilot, who had spent the day shoeless.

"Getting so I like it—a little," Lew lied. The bottoms of his feet were almost raw. He was looking forward to being able to borrow a pair of shoes from someone on the recovery team. "Oh, boy, photographers! I didn't think they'd bring the media along on the first plane. I'll bet we look just like a couple of beachcombers."

"Yeah, you're going to blow the image all to hell, Lew," Frank said. He couldn't help smiling.

Two people disembarked with cameras and began shooting pictures almost at once. Neither Herb Haynes nor Alice Arnold was going to miss the great photo of the Shuttle pilots—one barefoot, in the tradition of the old South Sea Islands beachcomber—and the natty little Chilean naval officer walking toward them.

The rear loading door and ramp of the C-130 were already being opened and prepared to disgorge the cargo inside. Whoever the crew was, they were working fast.

"Hi, Frank, glad you're all right." A rather haggard Red

Richardson strode up and grabbed the Shuttle pilot's hand. "You, too, Lew, but don't tell me you've gone native already?"

"*Ia orana oe!*" Lew said to him.

"What's that?" Richardson asked.

"Standard Pascuan greeting. Long story. Tell you more later," Lew replied curtly, eyeing Alice and Herb.

Frank spoke up. "Good to see all of you. It's been a long two days."

"Tell me all about it," Red muttered.

Frank introduced Richardson to Captain Obregon, and the two shook hands in a friendly but formal fashion. Red then reached into the pocket of his jacket while saying, "Well, Governor, you'll want these." He handed Obregon a handful of blue-covered United States passports.

"Thank you, Mr. Richardson. I don't think it's an absolute necessity at this point, but it's a formality I'll have to note in my regular monthly report to Santiago." He looked at the five passports—one for Red Richardson and the other four for the crew of the *Atlantis*. He said nothing as he examined them, then remarked to King, "Frank, you and the other members of your crew had better sign your passports before some immigration officer notices and gives you trouble. We can do that later in my quarters, if you wish." He pocketed the documents and added, "Mr. Richardson, would you have the rest of your people turn in their passports at the Hotel Hangaroa? One of my officers will pick them up there. And I apologize because quarters will be very cramped in the hotel. We're not equipped to handle this many people."

"Governor, let me get the *Atlantis* off the runway, and then I'll get some C-5 Galaxies in here with a tent city for our crews," Red told him. "We knew of your shortage of facilities, so we're bringing our own—and you can keep them here from now on to handle such contingencies."

Obregon nodded. The latest messages from Santiago explained there would be no Customs formalities with the equipment coming in—except for the specialized *Atlantis* handling equipment that was listed in detail—because the United States had graciously consigned the equipment to Chile in return for the hospitality of that government in cooperating so fully with the rescue mission of the *Atlantis*.

The captain knew what had transpired between Washington and Santiago, and he was frankly amazed that Santiago had gotten away with so much and that the United States had conceded.

"I've got to figure out where I can put it all," Red began, looking around.

"Have you had supper yet? Would you care to join me for dinner in my quarters?" Obregon asked the NASA mission manager. He wanted to get to know the compactly built, red-haired, ruddy-complexioned man from Houston with whom he would have to work closely in the ensuing weeks.

"Thanks, I'll take you up on that, Governor. But first I'd like to get my propellant crew up to the *Atlantis* to put the tetroxide into safe containers. I want to eliminate that safety hazard right away."

"Agreed." Obregon turned slightly to face several others who had joined Red on the ramp. "And are these the other members of your team?" he asked.

"Oh, sorry. I've had the *Atlantis* on my mind for the last few days," Red apologized. He introduced Casey Laskewitz first.

"Governor, a pleasure. I'd like to meet with you at your convenience to brief you on the press people who're coming here and what they'll be demanding from you—and how I'll be able to take most of that guff off your shoulders, if you want me to."

"American media people? Ah, yes, I know a little about them," Obregon replied with a slight smile. "Señor Laskewitz, I'll be *delighted* if you'll get that monkey off my back, sir."

Casey peered at the wiry little man. "You were educated in the States, weren't you?" he asked.

Obregon nodded. "VMI."

"I thought so. My folks sent me to The Citadel. It seems to me we trounced VMI in football a couple of times."

"I'll forgive you, Laskewitz," the military governor told him. "Sometime you'll have to tell me why you went into journalism instead of the military."

"Very simple," Casey said. "I was a space buff, but I couldn't pass the physical for a service pilot, so there was no use trying to promote spaceflight among missile generals and submarine admirals."

When Red introduced Joyce Fisher, she spoke to the governor in Spanish. Obregon bowed from the waist and kissed her hand in true Latin style. To some embarrassment from the others, the two of them chatted rapidly for about a minute. Then Obregon said, "I hadn't anticipated that you'd have such a lovely diplomatic representative, Señor Richardson. An attractive young lady who also grew up in Santiago will make my job much easier—and the whole project much smoother, I guarantee you. Señorita Fisher has agreed to join us for dinner once you've taken care of those propellants."

It was going much better than Red had anticipated. Obregon blew away Red's preconceived notion that he would be some paunchy Chilean admiral assigned to Isla de Pascua to get him out of the way politically or to give him a final command before retirement. But Red wondered why the dapper captain, who obviously had the trust of his superiors in Santiago, had been sent to such an isolated outpost with so few resources. Richardson didn't understand the logic behind it, if there was any, and resolved to ask Joyce about it when he had some time—if he ever did.

The first thing to do was to get the tetroxide out of the *Atlantis* and begin organizing things for the explosive influx that would occur during the next few days.

"Governor, here's my plan for this evening," Red began to explain. "First we'll get the propellant-unloading and storage-equipment crew busy up at the other end of the runway. Then, somehow, we've got to park these three Herks temporarily. The second Herk has a tow truck to bring the *Atlantis* back down to the ramp so the runway can be cleared. We have to have a place to park the *Atlantis* until we can get the cranes set up and the carrier aircraft in. The second Herk also has a satellite ground station—which will stay on the island, by the way, so you'll have regular worldwide communications, especially with Santiago. We'll have it set up possibly by tomorrow morning. The third Herk is nothing but a tanker to refuel the first two. We'll fly Number One back to Santiago tomorrow with the tetroxide aboard; I want to get it off the island right away. Then—"

Obregon held up his hand. "I understand the urgency of removing the hazardous propellants, Señor Richardson, and I suggest you do it as quickly as possible. But I doubt that you'll be able to get much more done before dark. We have runway lights, but no ramp floodlights. We don't have the electric power available. Get the propellants out, let's have dinner, and we can spend some time tomorrow morning going over your plans and working out the details."

"Governor," Richardson said, "we'll work all night if we have to. We have other aircraft coming in from Santiago once we report the runway's clear. Unfortunately, we don't have the luxury of being able to make this a leisurely operation. The *Atlantis* represents twenty-five percent of the American space capability, and we've *got* to get her out of here as quickly as possible."

"I fully understand," Obregon replied. "I'm aware of the situation. I'm also aware that Santiago has an inspection commission arriving in the next few days. So I can't let you do anything with the *Atlantis* except park her and wait for the commission to inspect her. Please get the hazardous propellants removed and safely in storage. Then I'll expect you at my quarters for dinner, because you won't be able to do any work after sunset. It gets very dark here very quickly in spite of a nearly full Moon. Most of the other things you mentioned can wait until tomorrow. I want to know and approve those locations where you'll be installing equipment and facilities so Isla de Pascua isn't unduly disturbed. Dinner at nine o'clock?"

While this conversation was going on, both Herb Haynes and Alice Arnold had their tape recorders running and were snapping photos madly.

Red sighed. Well, if the governor wanted to discuss matters over dinner, he would go along, for right now at any rate. It didn't seem he had any other choice. But Red was certainly going to have a word with this military governor later tonight because he had a job to do, and he wasn't going to let anybody slow him down. "We'd better get busy, then," he said. "If you'll excuse me, I'll see you at nine." He turned from the party and began to stride toward where the propellant crew was unloading the Herk.

"Colonel King," Alice Arnold interjected, "I'd like to get

an interview with you and the other three members of the crew."

At that point, Casey stepped in. "Alice, I need to talk with Frank here and find out—"

"What're you going to do? Get your stories straight? Or are you planning to brief them on what to say to us?"

"Neither. I'm tired. You're tired. The crew's been under tremendous stress. Let's get everybody settled and I'll arrange a press conference for you and Herb in a couple of hours. Okay?"

"Hell, no! What's the matter with right now? And what's the matter with an exclusive?"

"Why, nothing at all's wrong, ma'am, if you want to interview us right here," Frank said, shooting a quick glance at Casey to tell him wordlessly that he was going to get this news broad off his back in short order. "We're happy to talk to you or anybody else. We're easy to get along with when it comes to working with people having common decency and respect for us as individuals."

"I'll second that," Lew put in.

Herb Haynes moved forward, determined not to let Alice get an exclusive.

"I notice you've removed your boots, Commander Clay," Alice said into her microphone. "This is the first time I've ever seen a barefoot astronaut. Taking up the native ways of this South Sea island, perhaps?"

"Uh—not exactly. It was just . . . comfortable, that's all. Our contingency landing was kind of stressful, and it just felt good to wiggle my tootsies in the sand."

Casey couldn't suppress a laugh. Lew had spoken so seriously that Alice Arnold was caught completely off guard and had absolutely nothing to say, which was unusual.

"Colonel King," Herb Haynes asked, "what went wrong yesterday?"

"Look, we may both hold military rank," Frank pointed out, "but as NASA Shuttle pilots, we've put our soldier suits in the closet. I'm just plain 'mister' until my NASA Shuttle assignment's over and I go back to wearing a blue suit."

"Sorry. I'll repeat my question. What went wrong yesterday?"

"We don't know," Frank replied, unconsciously using

the accepted first person plural of a NASA man being interviewed by the press. "The main engines simply shut down. We were beyond the point where we could return to Vandenberg, and we didn't have enough velocity to go all the way around the world to Vandenberg in a degraded orbit. We're just fortunate that Pascua's here and that Mataveri has a runway long enough to handle the *Atlantis*."

"And nobody knows what caused the emergency?" Herb Haynes sounded a bit incredulous.

"Herb, Frank and the crew didn't have time to think about why it happened," Casey interjected. "They had their hands full landing the craft. We may get an anwer once the experts have the opportunity to examine the *Atlantis* thoroughly. Then again, we may not, because the fault could lie with the External Tank—and that's under about two thousand feet of water."

"Could this affect operational flights of the other Shuttles?"

"Probably not. The system's well proven now. The only thing that might affect the Shuttle operational schedule is the investigators' finding something when they inspect the *Atlantis* in the States," Frank explained. "But it couldn't be a major glitch, not after years of development and operations and lots of successful Shuttle flights to date."

"Mr. King, was it difficult to land the *Atlantis* without all the special equipment they have at the Cape?" Alice Arnold had finally found her voice again.

Frank shook his head. "We've practiced it time after time in the flight simulators at Houston. We all knew what to do and how to do it."

"In other words, it was easy?"

"I didn't say that. Even with the full automatic system available, landing an Orbiter's like trying to get a streamlined brick to glide."

Alice Arnold looked at the commander of the *Atlantis* as a hawk might look at a prairie dog ready to be grasped and eaten. Casey knew the look; he had seen it on other women, the astronaut groupies who had beaten a well-worn path from Lompoc to Lancaster to Houston to Cocoa Beach. Frank King was, Alice Arnold decided, quite a hunk of man in the quiet, competent, and virile mold of John Wayne. She decided to stay primed for opportunities because, after all, they were a very long way from home.

Casey decided he had better warn Frank—if the Shuttle pilot didn't already recognize the signs. After all, Frank had a wife and two kids back in Seabrook.

Alice continued. "Where are the other two crew members, Mr. King?"

"Hap Hazard, the payload specialist, came down with dysentery, but he'll be all right—"

"How could he possibly get dysentery?"

"Easy. You may end up with it yourself on Isla de Pascua."

"Uh, King," Herb Haynes put in, "what about the Soviet claims that the *Atlantis* is carrying a military beam-weapon satellite?"

Both pilots snorted. "Ridiculous," Frank snapped. "When the Chilean commission gets here, they'll see for themselves."

"Will we be allowed to go aboard and photograph what's in the cargo bay?" Alice asked.

Frank looked at Casey and replied, "Why not? It's just a Landsat. We've got nothing to hide."

"How will we know it's a Landsat and not some military satellite camouflaged to look like a Landsat?"

"Because you can take all the pictures of it you want, and then you can go to GE Valley Forge and take all the photos you want of its backup twin brother there."

"Then what in your opinion is behind the Soviet claims?" This was from Herb.

Casey shrugged. Herb looked at the two pilots, who also shrugged.

"But this is a military crew, isn't it?" Alice said doggedly. "You're a colonel in the Air Force, and Clay's a commander in the Navy—and the *Atlantis* was launched from a military space facility."

"We're both service pilots on assignment to NASA for one simple reason: only service pilots are able to get the necessary flight experience in high-performance aircraft that's required to fly the Shuttle. But Jackie Hart's a civilian, and so's Hap Hazard."

"When can I talk to them—especially to Jackie Hart?" Alice put her question to Casey.

But it was Frank who answered. "As soon as we get off

this ramp and down to the Hotel Hangaroa, where she's helping care for Hap Hazard." He turned to where Captain Ernesto Obregon was standing waiting, and suddenly he felt embarrassed for the Chilean military governor, who was totally ignored by these two reporters. "Governor, your jeep and perhaps one or two other jeeps are the only vehicles I've seen on Pascua. Is there any way we can arrange to get these people to Hangaroa?"

"It's not far to walk," Obregon said. "Less than a kilometer. I don't believe the hotel's station wagon is running now. We didn't have reservations for any tourists for over a month to come, so it gave us an opportunity to get some necessary maintenance done."

"No cars?" Alice was incredulous. "You expect me to *walk* carrying all this equipment?"

It was a good thing, Frank thought, that Obregon had been educated in America and understood Americans such as Alice Arnold. Many officials in other countries would have reacted to Alice by throwing up series after series of impenetrable roadblocks in retaliation. But the governor wasn't just another bureaucrat; he was indeed a Latin gentleman, in spite of Alice Arnold.

"I'd be honored to take the señorita to the hotel in my jeep," he replied, a slight smile playing around the corners of his mouth. "I certainly would never want it said that the military governor of Isla de Pascua didn't treat his guests in a gracious manner."

When they arrived at the Hotel Hangaroa, Alice Arnold insisted on seeing Jackie and Hap, and she turned nasty when Frank told her, "Let me check to see how he's feeling. The doctor recommended he get plenty of rest."

"I'm coming with you," Alice said flatly.

Frank sighed. "You probably will, but that doesn't mean I'm going to let you into Hap's room if he's not feeling well."

Hap was feeling better and said he would talk with the two reporters for a short time. This solved a big problem for both Frank and Casey. Naturally, Alice Arnold's first question was, "How'd you manage to get dysentery?"

"Got hold of some local food that had the bacteria in it," Hap explained simply.

"How come no other crew member got it?" Herb Haynes wondered.

"Dr. Esteban says most people here are immune," Hap told him. "Dysentery's a fairly common tourist disease, mostly in its milder forms."

"And Jackie's been nursing you day and night?" Alice looked at the blonde mission specialist, who wasn't very much older than she. Alice noted that Jackie, as well as Lew and Hap, was barefoot.

"Hell, no!" Jackie exploded. "I'm no nursemaid! Hap was pretty damned sick, and I did what I could to force fluids into him so he wouldn't dehydrate."

"And I imagine you kept his morale up, too, didn't you, dear?" Alice purred.

"Damned right! Except Hap didn't need morale boosting—until you got here." Jackie wasn't going to be pushed around in any interview. She didn't like Alice Arnold, and she didn't mind letting her know it.

That made things difficult after the brief interview was over and Juan Hey approached Alice as she was checking in. "I hope you will not be upset if I ask you to share a room with someone else because we are very crowded with all the people here. We have only two other lady guests, and I hope you will not object to sharing Señorita Hart's room with her and Señorita Fisher."

Alice did. She steamed and stormed, but there was no alternative. Jackie didn't like the idea either, but gave in under the circumstances.

Joyce didn't complain, but struck up a lively conversation with Juan Hey in Spanish—a factor that didn't endear her to Alice.

"Miss Fisher," Alice remarked when they were together in the room, "I'm the prime reporter for AP covering this affair, and I'd appreciate it if you'd speak English rather than conduct secret conversations with the natives in Spanish."

Joyce simply ignored the request without comment.

Red Richardson dragged into the hotel at eight-thirty, looking exhausted. He found himself sharing a room with Frank and Casey. "We got the tetroxide out without any trouble. That must've been a real gentle landing, Frank.

There wasn't a leak in any of the systems. The OMS piping was tight, and so were the vernier systems."

"That's a load off my mind," Frank admitted. "I've been sweating it for the last three days. I didn't think we had any leaks; I couldn't detect anything when I went back aboard yesterday."

"You went back aboard?" Red echoed. "With all that tetroxide still there? Haven't we told you guys to get the hell away from an Orbiter if you make a contingency landing?"

"Had to go back to get the medical kit," Frank explained. "Hap was pretty sick, and he needed the antibiotics and diarrhea pills. Under those conditions, Red, I'll break the rules."

"Yeah, I guess so. But where'd the rope ladder come from?"

"Jackie had it. She wanted some way to get back aboard if we had a contingency landing, and we *did* need to get back in. Red, from now on, put a rope ladder aboard as part of the contingency egress kit, will you?"

"Hell, yes, good idea. Why didn't Jackie bring it to the attention of Duke Kellogg or some of the planning team?"

"She did. I guess they ignored her. Come on, get washed up. We're due at Obregon's in less than twenty minutes."

"Look, fellas, do I really have to go to the governor's dinner? I'm bushed."

"Red, you'd insult Obregon if you didn't show up," Casey remarked. "And we've got to work closely with this man for the next six weeks."

"Well, okay. But I haven't got anything formal to wear—just work clothes."

"On Pascua, 'formal' means clean clothes, period," Frank explained. "Ernesto runs a tight operation, but he's no martinet."

"Sounds to me like you've struck up quite a friendship with the governor," Red observed.

Frank nodded. "We found we have a lot in common. He's a very cooperative guy and he's got rough duty here."

"Rough duty? On a South Sea island?"

"You don't know this place, Red. It *is* rough duty. And it's not your typical South Sea island. That fact may hit you tomorrow."

"What do you mean?" Red asked the Shuttle pilot.

"We have the *Atlantis* sitting out at Mataveri representing the high technology that all of us work with every day and take for granted," Frank pointed out, "but you're going to find that you've stepped back at least a hundred years in time. If you hadn't shown up with a tow tug, Obregon and I had worked out a way to pull the *Atlantis* back down the runway to the ramp, using ropes and a couple of hundred men."

"What?"

"The ancestors of these Pascuans used human muscle power to move those *moai* more then ten miles from the quarry at Rano Raraku," Frank told him. "What makes you think we couldn't move the *Atlantis* on its own wheels along a paved asphalt runway with the same technology?" Then he added, "But I'm glad you brought the tow tug. It's an easier way to do the job."

"I'd heard they used levitation," Casey said.

Frank shook his head. "If they knew how to do that, my friend, I wouldn't be flying a Space Shuttle Orbiter—and we'd all be out of a job."

CHAPTER NINE

Captain Ernesto Obregon flatly refused to discuss anything having to do with the *Atlantis* during the dinner he hosted for the three crew members, Red Richardson, Casey Laskewitz, Joyce Fisher, and the two reporters. Father Francisco, Dr. Esteban, and Juan Hey were also there.

The setting was outdoors, in a small patio of the garrison's casern. It was, as usual, a lovely evening, with the southeast trade winds blowing and a gibbous Moon rising over Rano Raraku's quiescent volcanic cone. While the dinner wasn't lavish, the food was good.

Obregon changed the subject every time Red tried to

discuss the work that needed to be done to recover the *Atlantis*. So the conversation turned to small talk and personal subjects. If the others didn't understand what was going on, Joyce did. She knew this was a social affair, both to permit the military governor to get to know the newcomers better—and to allow the Americans to get to know those with whom they would be dealing on Isla de Pascua.

It served its purpose magnificently.

Obregon must have had a fine collection of wines and liqueurs, because the wines served with the meal—something Red called lamb shish kebab and the few vegetables grown on the island—and the liqueur served afterward definitely were not native to Isla de Pascua. They were, Joyce decided, either Peruvian or Spanish in origin. Captain Ernesto Obregon was obviously a connoisseur.

The grace and dignity of the simple dinner, plus Obregon's persistent refusal to permit it to turn into a business discussion, had their effect upon the Americans.

Red Richardson discovered at the end of the meal that he had somehow managed to relax. Getting the *Atlantis* off the runway didn't seem so pressing a task. What the hell, he thought, let the rest of the group have a night in Santiago to relax. Twelve hours' delay in his unofficial and unannounced schedule didn't appear to be a matter of life and death right then.

When Alice Arnold learned she wouldn't be able to use the island's radio station to file her report through Santiago—the radio station was monitoring transmissions that might come in from Santiago, and Obregon refused to permit it to be used for other purposes—she started to throw a media tantrum, realized it wouldn't do her any good, and finally began to relax, too.

By the time they were sipping liqueur after the meal, all the Americans concluded that they were, for all intents and purposes, almost on another planet. Once the satellite ground station was set up and functioning, they would become part of Planet Earth again. In the meantime, there seemed nothing better to do than to relax and enjoy themselves.

"A wonderful dinner, Captain, and a most gracious welcome to Easter Island for us," Casey remarked.

"This is Isla de Pascua," Father Francisco reminded the

Public Affairs man. "Or, to be more exact, the native name is Rapa Nui."

"What would you prefer we call it, Father?" Casey asked.

"It is correct to use either name," the priest replied.

"The ancient name given it by the original settlers from the coast of South America is unknown," Juan Hey noted, "but Rapa Nui was the name given to it by the second wave of settlers who arrived eastbound out of the Polynesian Islands."

"The Europeans called it Easter Island, or Isla de Pascua, because the Dutch captain Roggeveen first sighted it on Easter Sunday in 1722. We Chileans call it Isla de Pascua," Obregon added.

"That's what it's called on the aeronautical charts, too," Frank pointed out.

"I'm going to have to call it Easter Island in my reports," Alice Arnold said. "Most Americans won't recognize it otherwise. They don't even have any idea where the hell it is."

"I've often wondered why your reporting style is different, Alice," Herb Haynes remarked. "I'm beginning to understand it now. To you, readers are stupid, right?"

"Damned right! Most of them didn't pay any attention to what they were told in school, and they don't pay too much attention to anything now except what's splashed all over the wall in front of them in big fluorescent letters," the woman reporter shot back. "And they'll forget it all the next day. I report the news on that basis. If I didn't, I'd only get a sidebar on page ninety—and I'd be looking for another job."

"I recall Hugh Downs once suggested we were 'overcommunicated,' which meant we were being bombarded by so much information all the time that we couldn't assimilate it, so we treated it as entertainment," Herb Haynes observed quietly.

"Well, that isn't the case on Pascua—at least not tonight," Casey said with a sigh. "But the minute we get that ground station set up, it's going to hit the fan as usual."

"Señor Richardson," Father Francisco commented, "I noticed it at first in Frank King before he and the other members of his crew grasped the reality of Isla de Pascua.

And I have noticed it in all the people who flew in this afternoon. Why are you so anxious to work twenty-four hours a day to get the *Atlantis* back to the United States?"

Red Richardson had an immediate answer. "Because the whole future of our space program depends upon the Space Shuttle's being a big success in this decade."

"More than that," Frank added, injecting his own viewpoint on a subject he had put a lot of thought into, "the future of the whole human race rides on the *Atlantis* and her sister ships. Our future is *out there*." He waved his hand toward the gibbous Moon and the strange southern constellations in the sky. "With space, as with every other frontier, pioneers have to go out and prove its worth to the rest of the human race."

"If we don't do it *now*, while we have the capability to get started," Casey said quietly, "we may not get another chance. Not if we're stuck on this planet and running out of raw materials and energy—plus continuing to breed far more people than the planet can afford to feed. This is a closed system, and the Shuttle is the first step in opening things up so that we can begin to work with the whole Solar System."

Father Francisco sipped his liqueur thoughtfully for a moment. Then he suggested, "Look around Pascua while you are here, my friends. I do not claim that Pascua and its people are generally representative of the rest of the world. Probably not. But look around and ask yourselves this simple question: what can space do for the Pascuans that they need to have done, that they could not do for themselves, and that would not merely change but improve their lives? Do not give me a hasty answer, because there can be no answer until you have observed this island closely."

"The technology we're developing in our space program can make the lives of people everywhere better and easier," Red said.

"With no insult intended, I have generally found that Americans simply do not understand the world," Dr. Esteban interjected. "The world—and Pascua—has problems that need technology to provide the solutions. But not just high-technology answers like the data that can come from the Landsat, but real and—if I may be permitted to use the term—down-to-Earth answers that can be used on the personal level. The rest of the world is not the United States and would perhaps take centuries to reach your level, if indeed your level is a desirable and attainable goal for many peoples, which it probably isn't."

"Those are very difficult questions you've asked us," Casey observed. "Even in the United States, we have trouble trying to get the basic realization of the potential of the Shuttle and space across to people who're living with high technology every day. Your questions are a lot tougher."

"But when you have found answers, you will have no trouble getting anybody to support your pioneering efforts," the doctor stated. "You may be able to find some answers here."

"Here? On Isla de Pascua?" Red asked in disbelief.

"I would like to point out," Father Francisco said quietly, "that the Pascuans call this island *te Pito o te Henua*, the Navel of the World."

"Ernesto, your fine wines and liqueurs have mellowed me to the point where I find myself wallowing in philosophy, which is certainly well beyond the accepted mental capabilities of a mere Air Force officer and NASA Shuttle pilot," Frank remarked. "But if this is the Navel of the World, permit me to quote a Russian who also viewed space travel from the viewpoint of childhood: 'The Earth is the cradle of reason, but one cannot live in the cradle forever.' If answers to these questions can be found here at the Navel of the World, maybe we can cut the umbilical cord more quickly."

The military governor raised his glass. "Here's to space and to your search for answers—although I still don't understand your relentless desire to accomplish such an expensive and difficult task."

"To space. We're doing it because it's there," Frank responded.

"And because it's our job," Red added.

"And because if we don't do it, either it won't get done or somebody else will do it in a way we don't like," Casey said.

"Like the Soviets with their orbital weapons," Frank noted.

"Ah, but you have them, too!" Dr. Esteban pointed out.

"Reconnaissance and communications satellites, yes. But not orbital weapons," Frank told him. "At least, not to my knowledge."

"With only four Orbiters, we haven't got the lift capability to do anything like that," Red explained with a touch of disgust in his voice. "If we had, I'd hear some scuttlebutt about it or could make some shrewd guesses based on the published NASA mission schedules. No, the Soviets are the people who have the lift capability for orbital weapons systems—which leads me to believe their claims may be part of a cover-up."

"That's not the root of the Soviet matter." Joyce spoke up for the first time in many long minutes. "True, we know the Soviets are interested in the military utilization of space, but they've also got a significant industrial processing capability that they're developing quickly with their Salyut space stations. I handle a lot of technology export matters, and I can tell you that the Soviet Union's rapidly growing into a strong international competitor with the United States in high technology, especially high technology derived from space."

"What's behind the Soviet move, then, Joyce?" Red asked.

"Frankly, I think their move in the UN is designed to blunt any possibility that we'll evolve competition to them in space manufacturing. We walked away with space communications, but the Soviets want to lock up space processing for themselves. The best way to do it is to discredit our Shuttle program and force us to curtail it in the face of international criticism."

Casey shook his head. "I never thought about it that way."

"That's the way I have to approach most of the problems my boss tosses in my lap," Joyce pointed out. "*Never* believe the rationale that's on the surface. You've got to dig beneath the headlines and the official announcements and ask yourself who's doing what to whom and who's going to profit from it, monetarily or otherwise."

"Damn! I left my cassette recorder at the hotel," Alice remarked suddenly.

"You mean you can't remember things without it?" Herb taunted.

"Who remembers anything any more? The only thing you have to remember is whether it's stored on tape or film," Alice snapped.

"Except when you're in a place like Pascua, where there are no microfilm or videotape libraries," Casey observed. He thought for a moment, then exclaimed as if it were a sudden realization, "We're a long way from home!"

"Are you so certain of that, Miti Laskewitz?" Juan Hey inquired.

"Huh?"

"This is, after all, my home," the Pascuan pointed out. "*Y mi casa es su casa.*"

Obregon added, "Here you're probably closer to the 'home' situation of generations of your ancestors than in the United States."

"That's going to change very rapidly," Red said. "To get the *Atlantis* out of here, we're bringing in a lot of equipment and more than a hundred people. That can't help but change things, even though we'll be here less than two months."

"Quite possibly. In fact, very probably," the wiry little military governor agreed. "I don't know whether or not the effects will be helpful to the Pascuans or to Chile's situation here on Pascua."

"Governor," Herb Haynes put in, "you were curious about the NASA people's apparent obsession with the Shuttle and space. I'm wondering what an educated and diplomatic man such as yourself is doing here as the military governor of Isla de Pascua, two thousand miles away from Santiago."

Obregon looked him right in the eye and replied levelly, "Because it is my job."

"*Touché*, Ernesto!" Frank said.

"Can we go where there's some light?" Red asked, unconsciously slipping back into his role model as a NASA manager. "We need to talk about our schedules, where we're going to put things, and what we have to do."

Obregon looked up at the sky. The Southern Cross rode in the meridian. "It's a lovely night, and the hour is late," he observed. "It's been a difficult and trying several days for all of us. You've traveled far."

"Everyone who comes to Isla de Pascua has to travel

far," Father Francisco added. "It is probably the farthest place on Earth these days."

"It is also capable of providing enjoyable moments such as this, which can be few and far between elsewhere," Dr. Esteban put in.

"I'd rather see this evening end on a pleasant and restful note, because tomorrow we'll have to face the realities of the *Atlantis* and the consequences of her landing here. I agree with Señor Richardson: we must discuss what's to be done and where we're going to put things. In the interim, let's leave them where they are tonight. Shall we meet at my quarters tomorrow morning at, say, nine o'clock?"

That was all there was to it. Red couldn't bring any pressure to bear on Obregon. The Chilean naval captain was the boss, period, and he had driven home that point with the dinner that evening. It had been a subtle and mannered assertion of the governor's ultimate authority, and Obregon had done it with such diplomacy that Joyce was forced to admit to herself the man was well chosen as Pascua's military authority—and that the international diplomatic world would undoubtedly see more of Captain Ernesto Obregon in the years to come.

As the American party walked through the streets of Hangaroa back to the hotel, Red remarked, "I'm relaxed as an old rag, but I don't think I'm going to sleep very well tonight. I keep thinking of everything we've got to do tomorrow and the next day." Obviously, he wasn't accepting Obregon's assertion of power and control.

"Red," Frank admitted to him, "I was the same way two nights ago. I'll bet you'll sleep like a baby—like you haven't slept in years."

"Maybe so."

As they strolled through the dimly lit lobby of the hotel, Frank noticed for the first time that two of the group were missing. He didn't say anything about it. But in the absence of the two reporters, he might tactfully ask Lew tomorrow where he and Jackie had gone after the dinner party had broken up. He didn't want to know the details, but he *did* need to know the broad outlines in case, as command pilot, he might have to handle any problems as a result. Lew could be a problem; Jackie was and had been a problem for a lot of people for a long time. And the environment was conducive to creating further problems.

It's never the technical problems, he told himself. It's the problems created by people that are the biggest headaches.

"Sullivan, how did it go today?" Alfred M. Dewey was putting in another late evening.

"The NASA briefing team did very well," Nash Sullivan reported from the United States' UN office in New York. "Most of the Security Council members were convinced that we've got a Landsat aboard the *Atlantis.*"

"Were the Soviets there?"

"No. They weren't expected—officially, that is. But they had people observing for them."

"What's your assessment of the possible Security Council vote on the Soviet resolution to send in a commission?"

"I think the Security Council will be willing to accept a report from the Chilean commission. So it probably won't come up for a vote until after the Council hears what the Chileans have to say. If the commission confirms our documentary evidence, the Soviets'll undoubtedly press for a UN commission. The staff here doesn't know whether to abstain or to exercise the veto."

"Neither do I, but I'll try to get some answers tomorrow," Dewey replied, making further notes. He had already used up three yellow ruled pads.

"When's the Chilean commission due to land at Pascua?"

"Tomorrow, once the NASA team gets the *Atlantis* cleared off the runway so the chartered jet can land. We may have a preliminary report from them by tomorrow night or the day after at the latest. According to the Chilean chargé here, the matter's very sensitive and potentially embarrassing to the Chilean government."

"I'd suspect so if the payload were indeed an orbiting beam-weapon satellite," Nash Sullivan remarked.

"Incidentally, the Secretary has advised the Chilean Ambassador in Washington of the Pentagon's detection of two Soviet naval vessels proceeding across the Pacific from Vladivostok toward Isla de Pascua," Dewey said quietly. "You may be asked by the Chilean UN delegation to confirm this, and you may do so."

"Aha! That's a new wrinkle. Will we respond?"

"I suspect the Armada de Chile may do something."
Dewey dodged the question. He had discovered through
his own underground network that the U.S. Navy was
planning to dispatch the aircraft carrier *Kitty Hawk*, the
guided-missile cruiser *Halsey*, and the guided-missile destroyer *Cochrane* in the direction of Isla de Pascua as soon
as they could be made ready for sea at Pearl Harbor and
San Diego. The Soviets would learn this soon enough
through their own recon satellites as well as from espio-
nage agents. "But keep it in mind, because we may wish to
initiate some action in the Security Council if the Soviet
ships begin to pose a problem to our efforts to recover the
Atlantis."

At six A.M., Red was at Mataveri Aerodrome, supervising the attachment of the tow tug to the nose landing gear
of the *Atlantis*. He had already instructed the satellite communications ground-station team to begin setting up on a
corner of the ramp below the control tower. He wanted
communications with Houston as rapidly as possible.

Towing the *Atlantis* backward down the long, narrow
asphalt runway was no easy job. The tug driver was experienced from similar situations at the Cape, but the Cape's
runway was wider. Therefore, it was nearly eight-thirty
A.M. before they had moved the *Atlantis* more than half-
way back along the runway.

At that point, Captain Ernesto Obregon wheeled up in
his jeep. He looked at what was going on, offered no comment, then suggested that Red ride with him to his quarters
for the scheduled planning conference. Red glanced at his
watch, realized it was almost time for the meeting, and
accepted the offer.

As they drove off down the runway, Obregon said
firmly, "You've moved the *Atlantis* without my permission,
Señor Richardson."

This remark surprised Red. "What the hell, Governor?
We've got to get it off the runway. You know that's the
first order of business."

Obregon nodded. "Indeed I do. But I don't know where
we're going to put it. And I notice that you've instructed
the satellite ground-station crew to begin erection of the

station next to the control tower. I'll stop there on our way so that you can tell them to cease work immediately."

"Governor, we've got to get our communications link established—the quicker the better," Red complained.

Obregon brought the jeep to a halt alongside the runway, set the parking brake, and turned in the driver's seat to face Red. "Señor Richardson, apparently I didn't make myself clear last night. I'm the military governor of Isla de Pascua. I'm in charge of the island, and I'm responsible for what happens here." The Chilean's command of colloquial American English was fluent, which was an important element right then because he was trying very hard to communicate with a job-oriented American.

"I know that."

"There's very little room on the two ramps available," Obegron told him. "I want to know where you intend to place various pieces of equipment and where you intend to park the aircraft. I must insure there'll be room available for the regular LAN-Chile flights. In addition, I have a government commission arriving later today to inspect the *Atlantis* and her cargo. I thought I'd made it abundantly clear last night that nothing was to be done this morning until we'd had our meeting."

"I saw no need to wait to clear your runway . . . or to set up the ground station—"

"There is indeed a need to wait."

"Oh? Why?"

"Because I believe there is a need, and I'm the highest military and civil authority on this island."

"You mean I've got to come to you before I do *anything*?"

"No, not once we've discussed what you intend to do and it's met with my approval," Obregon said simply.

Red was not accustomed to dealing diplomatically with people other than Americans. He saw the conversation as a confrontation between himself and Obregon for control of the recovery of the *Atlantis*, and he reacted accordingly. "Governor, you may be head honcho on this island, but I'm in charge of recovering the *Atlantis* and I'm responsible to my superiors back in the United States."

"Understood. But in the meantime, you're on Chilean soil, and this is not the United States of America. *I am the government here!* Señor Richardson, I've no desire to run your operation, but I cannot and will not permit you to run it as you see fit without regard to some of the unique characteristics of this island and the way people live here— factors that probably aren't apparent to you but which are of the utmost importance to me. Therefore, to eliminate problems and prevent troubles, you must check with me first. I don't want to be a little tin god, but you *must* cooperate with me and I *must* know what's going on. You and your people will be gone from Pascua in two months or less, but I'll be here for several more years. I will have to deal with the legacy you leave."

"I don't get it."

"Let me put it bluntly, then: I'll not permit you Americans to come in and take over Isla de Pascua, doing what you please, putting your equipment where you wish, setting up your living facilities where both water and sanitation may cause problems for the rest of us on this island, and generally using the island for your immediate needs regardless of the long-range changes you may be creating," Obregon explained firmly.

"Oh, so you want an environmental impact statement, then?"

"I'm not certain what that is."

"Never mind. American bureaucratic terminology. I don't want to create any long-term changes either. I just want to get the *Atlantis* out of here as quickly as possible. King didn't land here deliberately; it was an emergency."

"I realize the landing of the *Atlantis* happened purely by chance. But it's already creating problems on the island. I know there will inevitably be other problems while you and your people are here. I want to insure that the two of us will be able to work out the problems together. And, when you finally do leave, I want this island to suffer as little as possible as a result of your having been here. I have to live on and govern an isolated island with one airplane a week and one ship a year. I can't call for help to get me out of a bind on Pascua as a result of some problem you've left behind."

"Okay, Governor, I understand what you're trying to tell me," Red replied. "But you and your government are getting a hell of a lot of expensive equipment from us for free in this deal. You'll end up with a ground station to put you in touch with the rest of the world via satellite, plus additional electrical-generating capability, plus an improved water and sewage system, plus an improved airport. Don't tell me those things are going to create problems for you."

"Yes, some of them will. This island and its people have been totally isolated from the rest of the world for longer than they can remember," Obregon pointed out. "The coming of the LAN-Chile jets ended a lot of our isolation, and the coming of your communications satellite ground station will probably complete our transition from being the island at the end of the world to a place that's just another island."

"Governor, are you afraid to let the Pascuans know how the rest of the world lives and thinks?"

"To some extent, yes, because I'm not at all certain—knowing the Pascuans—that they can handle the shock of the end of their isolation. And I'm ill-equipped to handle it."

Red shook his head. He was in beyond his depth. "Governor, I'm just an engineer who's been given the damned difficult job of getting an expensive piece of hardware out of a place where nobody ever thought it would land. I can't do anything about some of the problems you're going to have because the *Atlantis* landed here. But if I have to work with you as the local government in order to get my job done, I'll do it. I don't have to like it, but I'll do it. But you've got to understand something, too."

"And that is?"

"You went to school in America, and you said you understand the American obsession with getting a job done. Okay, I've got a job to do here. The quicker I get it done, the less problems for you in the long run. I'll cooperate with you until the minute you try to slow me down with any *mañana* crap. If I run into any of that, we'll find out who's the meaner and nastier."

"You have my word that I'll neither cause nor tolerate any delays that can be avoided." Obregon thought for a moment before continuing. "And, Señor Richardson, I'll do my best to avoid another eyeball-to-eyeball confrontation, if you will. But if it comes to that, please remember that I am the *military* governor of Isla de Pascua, with all of the capabilities the title implies."

"I think I understand you, Governor. Sometimes I have to do a job under conditions that aren't to my exact liking, but that's the way the game is played. Okay, I'll play ball if I know what the rules are."

CHAPTER TEN

There was hardly room for everyone in the office of the military governor. Obregon had spread a large topographical map of Isla de Pascua on the table. Crowded around were the Shuttle crew—including Hap Hazard, who refused to miss the meeting—and Joyce Fisher, Red Richardson, Casey Laskewitz, Father Francisco, Juan Hey, and Dr. Esteban.

"Okay, here's what I'd like to do," Red started off once Obregon had nodded at him. "I'll get the *Atlantis* clear of the runway this morning and park it temporarily here on the south ramp—if that's all right, Governor."

Obregon nodded.

"But," Red continued, "I can't bring in C-5 Galaxy transports until I get turnarounds built at both ends of the runway; a C-5 Galaxy can't turn around on a thirty-meter runway. So I'm sending all three C-130s back to Santiago to pick up as much of the construction equipment as they can carry. The fourth Herk arrived there yesterday with additional equipment aboard. My first priority is to build those turnarounds. Governor, any problem with building them about two hundred meters square on both sides of the runway ends?"

"I don't believe so," Obregon admitted. "But how are you going to feed and house the people you're bringing in until you get the tent city set up? It seems to me you won't be able to do one thing without doing the other."

"I'll do it with C-130 Herks. I'll run them back and forth between here and Santiago, bringing in as much of the tent city and the other facilities as they can carry on each trip in addition to construction equipment and workers. When I get enough of the tent city put up, then I can bring in more construction workers. And once I get the turnarounds built, I can really haul stuff in here—a hundred tons or more at a crack in a single C-5 Galaxy. Joyce, has the Embassy arranged for the Chilean contractors, and are they standing by for airlift?"

"When we left Santiago, our chargé was making those arrangements," Joyce replied, "but until we have good communications—perhaps later today when the ground station's set up—I can't give you an answer to your question, Red."

"Okay, but please let me know when you find out, because the rest of my operation depends on those construction crews," Red told her. He turned to Obregon. "Governor, I'm going to run out of ramp area at Mataveri very quickly, so I'll have to lay more asphalt ramps. Can I extend both parking ramps out to the runway as well as to the northwest, where they'll become part of the turnarounds? Will it disturb anything to have those ramps extended?"

Obregon and Father Francisco both leaned over the map and peered at the pencil lines Richardson had sketched.

"It will bring the north ramp very close to Hangaroa," the priest pointed out.

"Any problem, Father?" Red asked.

"No, not on a temporary basis."

"Will it affect any archaeological areas?" Joyce Fisher inquired diplomatically.

"Probably," Dr. Esteban observed. "The whole island is an archaeological area."

"Why not build temporary ramps and turnarounds so you can tear them up and restore everything once we get the *Atlantis* out of here?"

"Good idea, Casey," Joyce remarked. "Can it be done, Red?"

"Yeah, but it'll mean keeping the airlift operating for a few more days after I get the *Atlantis* out." This whole operation was already costing a small fortune, Red thought. What difference would another couple of days make at this point if it would keep the Chileans and the Pascuans happy?

"Where had you considered putting your living facilities?" Obregon asked.

"Governor, we'll put up some forty U.S. Army tents to house a hundred and fifty people," Red explained. "Since I haven't got time to drill test wells for water, I'm flying in a small desalinization plant. It'll be located near the tent city, with a pipeline drawing ocean water to the site. I'll be flying in our food. Electricity will be provided by three ten-kilowatt, gas-turbine generator units, parked where convenient. The big problem's waste disposal; if I have to, I'll put it all in honey tanks and ship it back to Santiago for ultimate disposal."

"Could the sewage be treated for use as a fertilizer here on Pascua?" Dr. Esteban wondered.

"If you're short of fertilizer, why not? But the source won't last forever, only until we get the *Atlantis* and the extra people off the island," Red pointed out.

"I was thinking of installing the treatment facility for the use of Hangaroa residents afterward," the doctor explained.

"Why not? It belongs to you," Joyce said. "The same holds true of the electrical generators, if you can fly in enough fuel to keep them running. And the sea-water desalinization plant will be yours, too."

"We will use it all," Esteban asserted. "We need modern facilities."

"Spares?" The single word came from Obregon.

Joyce sighed. "And maintenance. Come see me after the meeting, Your Excellency. We'll iron out those details."

"Your tent city will require adequate drainage, even though this isn't the rainy season," Obregon remarked. "However, it's best not to take chances. I'd suggest locating it on the southwest slopes of Mount Ororito, just off the runway. A narrow road leads into that area, and you can pump sea water from Ovahi, which is less than two kilometers from the site."

Red jabbed at the map with a pencil. "Okay, that's where the tent city goes. I'll have part of it here by tomorrow night. Now: communications. I'd like to set up the satellite ground station near the control tower and radio shack, where I started to early this morning."

Obregon shook his head. "We can't provide you with any electricity. Our radios and other facilities have taxed our generating equipment almost to its limits."

"How about on a temporary basis, for two days, until I can get another generating plant here?" Red asked.

"It'll be difficult, but we can do it."

"Thank you. Now, I'll have to pour some concrete pads for the stiffleg derrick so I can eventually lift the *Atlantis* aboard NASA Nine-Oh-Five, plus some smaller pads for the tag-line masts. Where do you want some nice concrete pads for future use, Governor?"

"How big are they and what do they look like?"

Richardson drew out a set of blueprints, and Obregon studied them for a moment. "Can you put the mating facility out here, on the ramp northwest of the control tower where you'll extend the ramp? We'll put some buildings on those pads later," Obregon suggested.

"No problem, Governor. I'm happy to put anything anywhere you want me to as long as it doesn't conflict with getting the job done." Richardson rolled up the drawings. "That covers most of the big problems. What else?"

"Have the Chilean inspection commission and the press taken off from Santiago yet?" Joyce asked.

"No. They won't leave until they receive word the runway's clear here," Obregon replied.

"Then please delay them until tomorrow, Governor," Joyce said.

"Tomorrow? Why?"

"How many people are on that Pan Am charter? Casey, how many press people?"

"I don't have an exact head count. No communications."

"Your Excellency, how many members of the commission and their staff?"

Obregon shook his head, indicating he didn't know either.

"All right. To get an estimate, how many people can a Boeing Seven-Oh-Seven carry?"

"About a hundred and ninety," Jackie Hart volunteered. "I used to fly 707-331s for TWA before I joined NASA."

"Let's assume it isn't quite full," Joyce continued. "How can we handle another hundred and fifty people on this island tonight without the tent city set up and operating? We're already three and four to a room in the hotel."

"You're right, Joyce. The media gang will scream bloody murder if they don't have what they consider *civilized* facilities. We can't doss them down with blankets under the stars," Casey said in agreement. "Hold that Pan Am charter, Governor."

"I can certainly ask the commission to delay its departure under these conditions," Obregon observed. "No problem there."

"What excuse can we give the media people?"

"Simple: no room on the island for them," Casey replied, then looked at Father Francisco with a grin and added, "Or, to make the media people feel that we're treating them in accordance with their own evaluations of their importance—pardon my blasphemy, Father—we could tell them there's no room at the inn . . ."

To everyone's surprise, it was Father Francisco who roared the loudest.

When the room had quieted down, Obregon continued the discussion. "We have a few more matters to settle. First of all, I'm told by Santiago that you'll use Pascuan workers wherever possible, Señor Richardson."

"That's what I'm told, too, Governor."

"Let me know how many workers you need, how long you'll need them, and if you require any special skills. The size and duration of this job is such that I won't issue daily permits to leave Hangaroa, although I'll insist that workers return to the village when their shift is over."

"What's this?" Red was rather astounded at the military governor's apparently absolute control over the Pascuans. "Exit permits from the village?"

"The Pascuans aren't allowed to leave Hangaroa without a written permit from me," Obregon announced. "Before you ask why, let me explain. The Pascuans have no concept of property. Therefore, they'll take anything that catches their fancy. All of them are thieves. Isla de Pascua's a sheep-raising station for the Chilean navy, and in spite of everything we do, the Pascuans manage to steal several hundred sheep every year. So I must control them.

Señor Richardson, you'll detain and turn over to my military police any off-shift Pascuan you find who doesn't carry a permit from me. Understood?"

Red nodded.

Father Francisco added, "Please do not think harshly of the governor. He is correct. Despite attempts by my predecessors and myself to teach the Pascuans, it is true that they have no concept of property. They cannot help but be thieves, according to our definition."

"Our language," Juan Hey noted, "does not have a word for personal possessions. I feel bad my people are considered thieves. Perhaps someday the old language and the old ways will pass, and we will change."

"Maybe," Casey said quietly, "what you and your people learn from satellites will help."

"Three other absolute requirements," Obregon resumed. "None of your people is to give the Pascuans any of your alcoholic beverages. They have their own drinks that serve them well."

"And we'd better be careful of *those,* good buddies," Hap Hazard reminded them. "They can knock you right on your can."

"As I explained to Frank King," the governor continued, "there will be no fraternization between your people and the Pascuan women. He can explain why to you at a later time. There are many reasons, but the first one is that it can lead to trouble between your people and the Pascuans."

"I'll do my best, Governor," Red commented, "but some of the workers assigned to me are Chilean, and I don't know if I can enforce that prohibition with them. I'm not even sure who's responsible for them. As a matter of fact, I don't have enough control over the NASA and Air Force people to prevent *them* from sneaking off in the middle of the night."

"Simply tell them, Red, that if they're caught and aren't shipped off to jail in Santiago, they'll be sent home at once and suspended or court-martialed—whichever applies," Joyce said.

"Okay, I'll tell them I'll try to come see them on visiting days. What's the third hooker, Governor?"

"Merely a reminder of what I said previously: guard

your property and equipment, or things will turn up missing very quickly."

Frank coughed and looked at Jackie, Hap, and Lew. Lew had found new shoes now, which, although not NASA flight boots, at least protected his feet.

"If any of your people get dysentery," Dr. Esteban injected, "please let me know immediately. You can reduce the possibility by not drinking Pascuan milk products. You should have no trouble with meats or vegetables that are well cooked. You will have your own food, so that will eliminate a great deal of potential risk. However, many bacteria cause dysentery, and you will probably have some people who are susceptible. With so many people coming to this island, we will have to be very careful about public health measures. Cholera is not unknown in this part of the world, and leprosy is still a problem because the specifics to treat it are not yet generally available. I will continue to inspect all incoming airplanes for public health purposes. Beyond that, please consider that my modest medical facilities are available if needed."

"Thanks, we'll keep that in mind," Red said. "Let me know what drugs and other pharmaceutical items you'd like to have on hand to handle about a hundred and fifty visitors, and I'll get them flown in."

He turned to Frank. "Since we're short of accommodations here, you and the crew climb aboard the first Herk to leave and get yourselves back to Houston. We're short of flight crews and—"

Obregon and Esteban raised their voices together, then the doctor deferred to the military governor. "I'm afraid the crew of the *Atlantis* can't leave Isla de Pascua," Obregon stated.

Frank kept quiet. This was news to him. Joyce started to say something, but Red broke in. "Well, why not, Governor? We *are* short of accommodations, and that'll mean four fewer people to feed and sleep."

"The inspection commission may want to speak with them," Obregon explained carefully.

"Has the commission specifically requested this?" Joyce asked.

"No, but as military governor, I shouldn't permit them to leave Pascua until the commission clears their exit. They were the ones who landed the *Atlantis* here. If I were to allow them to leave and thereby become unavailable to the commission, I'd be quite derelict in my duty."

"You're right, Your Excellency," Joyce admitted.

"If you're not permitting the crew to leave, are you interning them, Governor?" Red's tone turned defensive.

Obregon shook his head. "Of course not. But they should be available for the commission to question concerning the landing. If I let them go, they'd probably be detained in Santiago and sent back here."

"Look, Governor, they're an expensively trained spaceflight crew. NASA can't afford to have them down here on Pascua doing nothing." Red continued to object. "We're desperately short of flight crews. I've got to get them back to Houston for that alone. In addition, engineers are waiting in Houston to debrief them so we can find out exactly what went wrong. It's just as important the crew gets back quickly as it is for the *Atlantis* to be returned.

Obregon looked sternly at Richardson, who was at least a head taller than the Chilean naval officer. With an edge to his voice, he said, "Mr. Richardson, I will not permit the crew of the *Atlantis* to leave Isla de Pascua until the commission approves."

"You just said you're not interning the crew. Well, I'd like to know exactly what you *are* doing to them, Governor!" Red exploded. "You have, in effect, imprisoned them here on this island. They're all American citizens; I brought you their passports. As American citizens, they can come and go as they damned well please! How about the rest of us? Are we going to have to get your permission to leave, too? In fact, are you going to require us to get permits from you to leave the hotel or the tent city every day—as the natives do under your control?"

"Excuse me, Your Excellency," Joyce broke in. "May I speak with Red and the crew of the *Atlantis* in private for a moment?"

"Of course. I think you'd better."

Joyce beckoned the crew members and Casey to join her and Red, then led them outside, where she lit into Red Richardson. "Look, I don't know what's between you and Obregon, but you've got to realize that he's Lord High Everything on this island."

"He's already told me that in no uncertain terms," Red fired back. "But who's running this show? Do I have to ask him for a permit every time I have to go to the bathroom?"

"No, but when he says you can or can't do something, you'd better not argue," she told him firmly.

"So what do I do? Let *you* hold my hand instead?"

"Precisely. That's what I'm here for. You may be a good manager for NASA, Red, but the methods you use to get things done in Houston are not—repeat, *not*—the ones that'll get the job done here."

"Well, I'm not going to let this little tin god stand in the way of getting the job done, and I've told him as much."

"Oh, you have, have you? Ever seen the inside of a jail in any South American country?"

"What's that got to do with it?"

"You may get the chance. Obregon has full power to put you in the slammer for any reason he deems suitable," Joyce snapped. "You're not on American soil now. You're not subject to American laws. If you or anybody else on the recovery team gets in trouble with Obregon, there isn't *anything* the State Department can legally do to help you. Do you understand that, Red?"

"Aw, hell, do you mean to tell me my employer isn't going to stick by me and protect me?"

"The United States government *can't*." She sighed. "Granted, I'd go to bat with Obregon and get in touch with people I know in Santiago. We'd manage to get you or your people released. But, Red, I'm going to have enough problems without that, too. I just might decide to let you stay in stir a couple of days to learn your lesson. Understand?"

"Okay, yeah, I understand. So you want me to work through you with Obregon?" the NASA mission manager asked.

"At least until we get things running smoothly, yes, please do so," Joyce replied.

Frank spoke up. "Red, you've just gotten off on the wrong foot with Obregon. He isn't such a bad guy. If you think of him as you would anybody from the Air Force or the Navy who's working with NASA, you'll find he's mellow."

Red looked at the Shuttle pilot. "I sensed a bond of friendship between you and Obregon, Frank."

"Yeah. Don't ask me why, but there is," Frank said.

"Come to think of it, it wasn't such a sharp idea to send any of you back to Houston right away," Red admitted. "Frank, we can use your friendly relationship with Obregon. I'd like you to stick around and work with Joyce here." Richardson's impetuous-redhead's anger evaporated once he again started thinking about getting his job accomplished.

"Why not? This is going to be interesting," Frank noted.

"The same goes for the rest of you," Red said. "Hap, you're probably not feeling well enough yet to travel, are you?"

"Not really, Red," the payload specialist told him. "Besides, that baby in the payload bay is my responsibility. I know it inside and out. I'd really like to stick around just in case you need somebody who knows the Landsat—and you might, depending on what the Chilean commission decides to do."

"I'd like you to take them through the payload bay, Hap."

"No problem. I'd planned to."

"How about you, Jackie?" Red asked. "You can stick around and help out, or you can go once Obregon says so. I wasn't thinking when I said something about the shortage of flight crews. With the *Atlantis* on the deck here, we're not short of flight crews—we're short of Orbiters."

"I'll stick," Jackie said. "Casey's going to need help with that bitch Arnold—and I can handle her because I can be bitchier."

"Aw, don't approach the matter that way, Jackie," Casey put in with a pleading tone. "I'd much prefer it if you'd figure out a way to get along with her. After all, you're the prime female interest in this news story, kid."

Jackie thought a moment. "You're right," she said simply. And she also told herself that a lot of press coverage from Pascua wouldn't hurt her a bit when it came to bucking for that pilot's rating with Duke Kellogg. In fact, a lot of good media exposure might be just the thing.

"Lew?"

The former Navy fighter jock grinned. "Ever know a brown-shoe Navy type to turn down a long liberty on a South Pacific island, Red? Just give me a cot in a tent where I can throw the body occasionally, and I'll be a happy and helpful staff man. Matter of fact, I'm the world's best supervisor, and I figure you've got a lot of jobs to do—and Every Job Needs A Supervisor."

"You're on."

"Okay, Red, have we got it square now?" Joyce asked.

"Yeah. No problems, Joyce, once I know what the score is. I was working under the assumption I was supposed to run the whole show," Red admitted. "Now I realize it's got to be a team effort, so that's the way I'll operate. No skin off my nose. In fact, it's a load off my shoulders because now I can worry only about keeping Duke Kellogg happy and getting the *Atlantis* on top of Nine-Oh-Five and out of here. However . . ." He paused for a moment, then said, "I strongly suggest we try to put our heads together at least daily, maybe at breakfast. We'll iron out sticky problems, straighten out assignments and responsibilities, and yell at each other. Only way to get a big project done."

"You must have a difficult time in NASA," Joyce observed.

"Yeah, I do. And from what I know of everybody here, we all do." A note of disgust crept into Red's voice. "None of us would be standing here now if we weren't the kind who gets the job done, regardless of what the book says about doing it."

When they returned to the meeting room, Joyce said something in Spanish to Obregon, who smiled and replied to her. The diplomatic protocol was in Joyce Fisher's hands now, as far as Red was concerned—and he was content to leave it that way.

There wasn't anything left to discuss, so the meeting broke up. Obregon and Red drove the jeep down the runway to where the *Atlantis* sat, waiting to be towed, while the rest took the short walk up the hill to the airfield. The Herk crews were sitting or lying on the ramp in the shade of their aircraft. The place had an attitude of expectant waiting.

When Red reached the site, the General Electric people

got busy setting up the ground station. Early in the afternoon, they completed their tests and were linked in with the telecommunications network of the United States through a Westar satellite in geosynchronous orbit. Suddenly, Isla de Pascua had two voice channels, a teletype channel, and two television channels linking it with the rest of the world on the low-noise, high-reliability basis that only satellite communications can provide.

The Herks took off for Santiago after refueling from the tanker. And Red Richardson sat down in the ground-station trailer and began to work with Houston again. He found himself talking to another world. He realized only then what less than twenty-four hours disconnected from the rest of the world on Isla de Pascua had done to him.

Duke Kellogg seized the phone from Joe Marvin. "What took so long getting the ground station set up?" Kellogg demanded. "We've been standing by here for more than a day. What's the reason for the delay, Red?"

"Well, we sure as hell haven't been lying in the sun on the beach," Red told him. "Duke, we got the Herks in here last night, but couldn't unload because there aren't any ramp lights. When we started to get things out of the Herks this morning, I discovered I hadn't touched second base with the military governor."

"So?"

"Protocol, Duke."

"That was supposed to be handled by State. What's the matter? The woman they sent along can't hack it?"

"Far from it. I'd be in jail without her. Joyce knows her way around. We had to spend a couple of hours this morning meeting with the governor, bringing him up to speed on our plans and getting his permission on where to locate things."

"Why couldn't you have done that last night, Red?"

"Because Governor Obregon wouldn't let us. Duke, this place works differently."

"Listen, Red, if you run into any of that *mañana* stuff, you let me know and I'll get on the horn to the State Department."

"Don't worry, it's worked out. Has the tent city left yet?"

Duke Kellogg had to explain to Red that it hadn't, because of a red-tape jam-up with both the Army and the Air Force.

"Duke, don't you ever say one damned word to me again about any *mañana* stuff down here," Red growled. "I can't bring in the Chilean commission or the press until I get that tent city and all its facilities—and I don't know how long Obregon can keep that commission cooling its heels in Santiago."

Joyce, who had been listening in on another headset, spoke up. "This is Joyce Fisher from State. Sorry, but I've been listening to the conversation. Mr. Kellogg, I'll talk to my boss at State about this as soon as I can get through to him. If the Chileans think we're trying to delay the arrival of their commission, they could get nasty—and we're sitting down here on Chilean soil." She also had come to the conclusion that if the commission were kept waiting too long, the Soviets would certainly redouble their efforts in the Security Council for a full-dress UN commission—and that would hold up the recovery of the *Atlantis* for weeks or even months.

"I'm serious, Duke," Red broke in. "We've got to have those facilities here—and fast!"

"Okay, we'll figure out something."

Like hell! Red told himself. If it isn't in the book, Duke won't know what to do. So Red would work it out with Joe Marvin, and they would ram it through and cover it with paper work later.

Joyce used the other voice channel to connect her to Alfred M. Dewey in Washington. While Red worked with Houston on the mundane technical details of the airlift, she finally reached her boss.

"Thank heaven I've contact with you again." Dewey's voice reflected his relief. "I hope things are under control there, because everything's breaking loose up here."

"Our only problem is housing for the Chilean inspection commission, Mr. Dewey," she told him. "Otherwise, we've worked out all the protocol and arrangements with the military governor—his name is Captain Ernesto Obregon, by the way, and he was educated in the States—and everything's running along smoothly on that front. Incidentally, it's Obregon who's delaying the Chilean commission in

Santiago, not me. There's no place to put them if they try to come to Pascua right now."

"No accommodations? That's hard to believe."

"You'd have trouble believing this place," she told him. "We're stacked up three and four to a room in the little hotel, and the flight crews of the aircraft and some of the other technicians are sleeping in the airplanes or wherever they can find a place to stretch out."

"The Chilean chargé informed me earlier today that the inspection team had only three people."

"Only *three?* Well, that's the first word we've gotten on that, Mr. Dewey. I thought for certain there'd be at least a dozen, plus staff people of equal number. Maybe we can handle three more people."

"I don't see why not. Have NASA send the crew of the *Atlantis* home on the next plane. That'll give you room—"

"Governor Obregon doesn't want the crew to leave until the commissioners have had an opportunity to talk to them, if they wish."

"Oh, very well. But advise the governor the commission's only three people—he may know them." Dewey repeated their names to Joyce, who wrote them down. "It's being headed up by the commander of the Chilean Navy, Admiral Montero. The other members are Colonel Amaldo Ríos of the Chilean air force and its top astronautics expert, Professor José Pérez."

Not only was it possible that Obregon knew them, but Joyce knew two of them herself—Ríos and Pérez.

She was becoming a bit upset. Why hadn't they been told by the Chileans that their inspection commission consisted of only three people? Had somebody withheld that information deliberately, knowing that living space on Pascua would be saturated and that Obregon would have to request a delay on that basis? "Mr. Dewey, I'll get this information to Governor Obregon immediately."

"Good. Now, I have other information that has reached me through channels that must remain nameless at this point. And I must ask you to treat this information in a most prudent manner. You may pass it on to the military governor at your discretion. I don't know the man and I can't anticipate his reaction. I'll rely on your judgment." Dewey paused, then continued. "Two Soviet naval vessels are proceeding in the general direction of Isla de Pascua, which is believed to be their destination. One of them is the *Sverdlov*, a guided-missile cruiser. The other is the *Kharkov*, an aircraft carrier of the *Kiev* class with a squadron of Yak-36 Forger aircraft. The intentions of these two ships are unknown, but our analysts suspect they may show the flag in the vicinity of Pascua, rather a subtle hint by the Soviets that they don't intend to accept blithely any report from the Chilean inspection commission. They may demand to conduct their own inspection."

"But that would be an open violation of Chilean sovereignty!" Joyce exclaimed.

"Yes, it would, wouldn't it? It has us worried here in Washington. We're not sure, under the circumstances, which way the Chilean government might bend."

"I am," Joyce said flatly.

CHAPTER ELEVEN

Joyce, Frank, and Governor Obregon awaited the arrival of the Chilean inspection commission with some trepidation, each of them concerned in a different way.

They sat in Obregon's jeep at the base of the tower, where a loudspeaker had been rigged to permit broadcasting of all tower–air radio conversations. Redeemer Zero-One had reported the formation of four Herks inbound at Ostra intersection, as required by protocol, but it would be about a half hour before the big four-engined craft appeared in the eastern skies of Isla de Pascua.

"You look worried, Frank."

Frank shook his head. "I'm not, Joyce. I know what we've got in the *Atlantis*. But I don't know if we'll be able to explain it to them."

"They all speak English very well," Joyce told him.

"That's not it," Frank admitted. "I don't know what sort

of people they are, so I can't figure out whether or not they're a hangin' jury."

"Hardly," Obregon put in quietly.

"Then why do you look worried, Ernesto?" the Shuttle pilot asked.

"Because I know them and because they are very powerful men in Chilean affairs—and because one of them is my superior officer in the Armada de Chile."

"You said you knew them, Joyce. Who are they?" Frank asked her.

"The commission is headed by Almirante Eduardo Miguel Montero, the Commander-in-Chief of the Armada de Chile," Joyce explained. "That's why the governor's nervous. I know the other two—Coronel Amaldo Carlos Ríos of the Fuerzas Aéreas de Chile, the air force, and Profesor José Ricardo Pérez, who's president of the Sociedad Interplanetaria Chilena."

"The big guns," Frank observed.

Joyce nodded. "I told you this was a sensitive situation for the government of Chile and that it would put the biggest names in the country on the job. The small size of the commission means Chile's seriously concerned about getting a report off to its UN delegation fast, in view of the movements of the Soviet vessels in the Pacific."

Obregon turned quickly to her. "You know about the Soviet ship movements?"

Joyce nodded. "Yes, but I don't know whether or not it affects us, Your Excellency. The Soviet guided-missile cruiser *Sverdlov* and the new aircraft carrier *Kharkov* left the Vladivostok area three days ago. I don't have any information concerning their course, but I understand it's extremely rare to find Soviet ships in the South Pacific."

"It has a bearing on this situation—particularly if they are indeed headed in this direction," Obregon observed. "After all, Joyce, Isla de Pascua is Chile's western point of defense."

It didn't escape Joyce's attention that the governor had addressed her familiarly by her first name, uncharacteristic not only in a Latin American country but in diplomatic circles as well. "If I get more information on the matter, I'll tell you immediately, Your Excellency."

Obregon looked at her, not totally unaware of her subtle, attractive sensuality. "As I told Frank, we're going to be working together closely on Pascua for a long time. I acknowledge your fine technical education and diplomatic training as well as your knowledge and understanding of my country. But between ourselves, privately, I think it'd work better if we dispensed with the protocol of titles. If you don't object, I'd like to call you Joyce. And 'Your Excellency' sounds terribly formal coming from such an unexpectedly attractive diplomatic representative. 'Ernesto' would sound better. There's much to be said for the women's liberation movement in your country."

Joyce broke forth in a radiant smile. "Why, thank you, Ernesto!" Then she spoke in Spanish until Frank held up his hand.

"Uh, look, a linguist I'm not," he pointed out.

"Sorry, we'll keep it in English," Joyce said.

"Thanks."

Obregon chuckled, obviously still under stress about the coming inspection, but grateful for the momentary relief of tension.

"Pascua Tower, Redeemer Zero-One, flight of four. I have the airport in sight," a voice rasped over the tower loudspeaker.

Four specks had appeared in the eastern sky above the cone of Mount Ororito.

Obregon stepped out of the jeep and smoothed his khaki uniform. "Time to get to work." A detachment of naval troops from the Pascua garrison moved into position on the ramp at Obregon's signal.

The three members of the Chilean inspection commission were the first to disembark from the Herk that taxied up to the ramp at the base of the tower.

Both Joyce and Frank discovered that Obregon had arranged for full military honors—nineteen-gun salute from an old U.S. Army thirty-seven-millimeter antitank gun that Obregon's contingent must have had stored somewhere for such occasions, a small drum-and-bugle group that played four ruffles and flourishes, eight uniformed side boys who lined up on either side of the Herk's forward passenger hatch, and a formation from the Isla de Pascua garrison.

"Full protocol," Joyce remarked in an aside to Frank. "That means we've got to accompany Ernesto. Come on."

Frank was impressed, and the complete meaning of his emergency landing on Pascua began to dawn on him. He wished Red were present, but the NASA mission manager was supervising construction of the runway turnarounds. Casey hovered in the background with Alice Arnold and Herb Haynes, both of whom had their recorders going and their cameras clicking.

At the very last moment, Frank remembered that he was a civilian for all intents and purposes, and suppressed the impulse to salute both the Chilean admiral and the air force colonel. Instead, he simply shook their hands formally upon introduction. All three commission members gallantly kissed Joyce's hand, and Colonel Ríos and Professor Pérez greeted her familiarly in Spanish.

After the members reviewed the honor guard with Obregon, they were led to the jeep by the military governor. Much to Frank's relief, all three men spoke good but accented English.

Admiral Montero was all business. "Governor Obregon, Señor King, let us get to the matter at hand."

"What is your pleasure, sir?" Obregon asked in English, taking his cue from the admiral that this was to be the official language of the occasion. "I've arranged quarters for you at the garrison because our facilities at the Hotel Hangaroa are very crowded. Would you care to be shown to your quarters first?"

"No. I am under direct orders from the President of Chile to conduct an inspection and make a full report as quickly as possible," the admiral snapped. "We wish to be taken to the *Atlantis* immediately. Señor King, is your crew available to accompany us on our inspection and to explain matters?"

"Yes, sir. They're waiting right here." He beckoned to his three compatriots, who were standing by a few yards away, all still attired in their flight coveralls, which had been washed by the hotel staff. Carefully, Frank introduced Lew, Hap, and Jackie to the commission members.

Colonel Ríos was obviously highly impressed that Jackie Hart was a crew member of a space vehicle. "Are you a pilot?" he asked her.

She nodded. "I was a fully rated Air Transport Pilot

with about two thousand hours before I joined NASA," she explained.

"Then you also fly the Space Shuttle?"

"Someday," Jackie promised loudly for the benefit of the tape recorders of Alice and Herb.

A short walk across the ramp brought them to the *Atlantis*, gleaming black and white in the noon sunlight. Her name was written boldly in black on her sides, the words *United States* and the flag emblazoned on the fuselage near the tail. Obviously the Orbiter had seen many flights; smudges of black and brown flowed back along her fuselage where the thermal protection tiles had ablated after atmospheric entries and deposited their heated material in the airflow paths along the Orbiter's surfaces. The hatch still hung horizontally open, but Obregon had allowed Red to position the LAN-Chile boarding stairs so the commission wouldn't have to rely on Jackie's rope ladder.

Admiral Montero looked up at the *Atlantis*, obvious admiration for her technology and capabilities revealed on his face. The first things he asked for were the spaceship's papers.

Frank handed over a vinyl-bound packet containing an airworthiness certificate, the registration certificate, an international cachet obtained from the National Aeronautic Association, the proper FCC radio transmitter licenses, a list of crew members with their passport numbers, and a cargo manifest. None of these had been aboard when the *Atlantis* had landed on Pascua.

Frank resolved to have a chat with somebody in Headquarters about the necessity of carrying required international papers aboard every Shuttle that flew henceforth. Obviously, in their drive to perfect and operate the Shuttle space transportation system, a whole series of NASA managers had simply overlooked everyday international protocols.

Thank God we were able to put the staff together in a hurry and get it here before the authorities came! Frank thought as the commission carefully scrutinized the documents packet. Obregon had gone out on a limb for them, but Joyce had managed to save his neck—as well as to bail out the crew of the *Atlantis*.

The commission chatted among themselves in Spanish as

they went through the packet, nodding as they examined each document. Finally, Admiral Montero remarked, "The papers appear to be in order. Captain, do you have the passports of the crew?"

Obregon nodded.

"I presume they have the proper visas?"

"Since their landing on Isla de Pascua was an emergency, I used my authority as governor to grant them visas of sixty days' duration," Obregon said quietly. "Their personal documents are in order, sir, and you may view their passports and visas in my office at your convenience if you wish."

"Later, perhaps, if we deem it necessary," the admiral responded curtly. "Señor King, because of the . . . unusual nature of your flight, we have been charged by the President of Chile to inspect your spacecraft to insure that the cargo manifest is correct. Do you have any objection?"

"Not at all, Admiral," Frank replied easily. "It would be my privilege as commander of the *Atlantis* to escort you on a tour of the ship. Since you're particularly interested in the payload, Mr. Hazard will accompany us because he's the mission's payload specialist directly responsible for Landsat-XIII."

No mention had been made of the Soviet claim. However, Montero went on to ask, "How can we know that the payload is Landsat-XIII, as the ship's documents claim?"

Professor Pérez pointed out, "Admiral, I know a Landsat when I see one. I have the documents from NASA. We've built a ground station to receive the Landsat transmissions at the university in Santiago."

"Well, then," Frank said, indicating the LAN-Chile boarding stairs leading to the open hatch of the *Atlantis*, "welcome aboard. If each of you will take a flashlight from the governor, we'll go aboard. There's no electric power because everything's been shut down, so it's dark inside. Please watch your heads—the *Atlantis* isn't designed as a passenger transport. It's a space truck."

"Would it be easier for you to open the cargo bay doors and let us look directly at the cargo?" Colonel Ríos inquired.

Frank shook his head. "As Professor Pérez must know, to save weight the doors were designed and built to be opened only in the weightlessness of orbit. It takes special equipment to open them on the ground—and that equipment's back in the United States. We'll just have to take you into the payload bay itself."

The tour wasn't comfortable, but crawling around inside a Space Shuttle Orbiter on the ground isn't supposed to be comfortable. Frank remarked that there was a lot more room in the weightlessness of orbit. The first order of business was the huge, dark payload bay. Admiral Montero had some trouble negotiating his portly form through the restricted openings of the air-lock hatches. Colonel Ríos and Professor Pérez, both younger men, found the going much easier.

There really wasn't too much to see in the payload bay. It was quiet, dark, and surprisingly cool inside because of the insulation of the tiles on the external surface of the *Atlantis* and the Shuttle's grayish-white color. Four Quick Getaway Specials were bolted to the side of the bay forward. The rest of the huge bay—fifteen feet in diameter and sixty feet long—was empty except for the middle, where Landsat-XIII rested in its cradle, iridescent blue solar panels folded around its spindly tubular frame. Montero obviously didn't know what he was looking at. Ríos, on the other hand, didn't either, but was looking for military payloads. Pérez knew what a Landsat looked like and spent considerable time with his flashlight inspecting what he could view of the satellite. Although it was somewhat difficult to see into the payload-bay area behind the Landsat, both Ríos and Pérez shone their flashlights carefully into every nook and cranny they could.

Frank and Hap didn't try to rush them. The object of the inspection was, after all, to let the Chileans see for themselves that there was only a Landsat aboard, not a military satellite and definitely not an orbital beam-weapon system—though Frank wondered how they would be able to recognize a particle beam weapon. He had seen only two Top Secret photos of such a satellite.

Hap was good at answering the commission's questions using simple terminology. Frank thought the man would have made a very good teacher. Hap's natural enthusiasm for space and its potential got through, especially to Professor Pérez and, to a lesser extent, to Colonel Ríos. Obviously Admiral Montero knew little of space technology and had been appointed as head of the commission because of his position and probably because of his political clout and family reputation as well. Or, Frank thought, Montero might be aiming for or was under consideration for a higher position in the still-influential military junta that officially was no longer in power—but probably had plenty to say about running Chile.

All three commissioners became more attentive and interested when Frank took them up to the flight deck, showed them the controls for unloading the Landsat with the payload arm, and let each of them sit in the pilot's seat. Back down on the mid-deck, he and Hap showed them the living accommodations for the crew in orbit. Admiral Montero had no doubt had some sea duty, because he was most interested in the compact manner in which the life-support consumables were prepared and stored on the mid-deck.

The commission was reluctant to leave the *Atlantis*. After all, they did not often have the opportunity to board a spaceship. Finally, Montero said, "I believe we have seen enough here for now. We may wish to return later."

"No problem," Frank told him. "We have nothing to hide. This is strictly a civilian operation with no military implications whatsoever."

"That, señor, is what we are here to confirm," the admiral reminded him. "It's well past time for lunch, and I'd like to talk to you and your crew during the meal, if you'll join us." The head of the Armada de Chile was still a diplomat despite the pressure being applied to his government by the Soviet Union. *La dignidad de hombre* ran deep in this culture, Frank decided. There were obviously strong class distinctions, and obviously Frank and his crew were being afforded the distinction of being members of the ruling group. The crew of the *Atlantis* comprised a new type of people who didn't yet fit into the old classifications of the culture and were, therefore, being treated first class unless they proved themselves otherwise.

Frank hoped Lew's training as a naval officer would prevail over his normal fighter-jock personality. He wasn't worried about Hap; the payload specialist was so enthusiastic about his job and about space that he had an almost puppylike affability. But Jackie, with her rough-and-ready approach to the world of male domination, worried him the most.

She shouldn't have. During the Spartan meal in Obregon's quarters, Jackie behaved herself. In fact, she was most charming to the three Chileans, who treated her with great respect and deference. For once in her life, Jackie wasn't on the defensive; she was being treated as she thought she should be treated, and she wasn't competing directly with men.

The meal was long and leisurely, lasting well into the afternoon. Only after several hours did Frank realize that the suave Chileans were in fact grilling the crew of the *Atlantis* in a very thorough but unobtrusive manner. Through the skillful use of conversation, they had drawn a great deal out of the normally friendly and gregarious Americans.

Only Colonel Ríos seemed probing and suspicious. "Why is the payload bay not full, Colonel King?" the Chilean air force officer asked, deliberately using Frank's military title.

"Colonel, the *Atlantis* can carry more than thirty-five tons into Earth orbit if it's launched toward the east to take advantage of the Earth's rotation," he explained carefully. "But when we have to launch into an orbit that goes over the Earth's poles, we can't take advantage of that additional velocity. So we have to run the *Atlantis* with less payload than she's capable of carrying. Do you fly your C-131s with all the cargo they'll carry if you have to make a long haul—like from Santiago to Pascua, for example? The same trade-off holds for the *Atlantis*. We traded payload weight for additional velocity. Our Orbiter's running light. That's why most of the payload bay's empty."

"Why did you launch from a military facility?" Ríos persisted.

"Because of safety precautions. Going south of Vandenberg means there's no people under the flight path until orbit's achieved."

"But isn't it possible to launch to the south from Cape Kennedy?"

"Not without flying over the heads of people during a critical portion of the mission. Space flight isn't yet as safe and reliable as aviation—as our emergency landing on Pascua proves."

"I am merely wondering, Colonel, why the United States launched a civilian Landsat mission from a military rocket base."

"Colonel Ríos, as long as I'm working for NASA, which is a civilian government agency, I don't enjoy the privileges of my Air Force rank." Frank's voice wasn't hostile, but there was an edge to it. He didn't like something about Ríos. For one thing, the Chilean air force officer kept boring in, trying to find holes or chinks in the story of the crew of the *Atlantis*. "That may be difficult for you to understand, but it's an American way of doing things. We maintain a definite separation between our civilian and military space programs. That's been our practice since President Eisenhower established the policy back in 1955."

"Then why does your civilian space agency use service pilots?"

"There are lots of civilian Shuttle pilots in NASA, but not enough civilian pilots with enough experience flying very advanced aircraft. So, Colonel, NASA has to borrow pilots from the Air Force, the Navy, and the Marine Corps. As you undoubtedly know, both Lew Clay and I happen to be service pilots on detached duty to NASA."

"I beg your pardon, but I am merely carrying out my assignment of investigating the emergency landing of the *Atlantis* on Isla de Pascua," Colonel Ríos said without a touch of apology in his voice. "A Space Shuttle launched into orbit from a military rocket base with military pilots in command—one can begin to understand the claims of the Soviet Union."

"Colonel!" Admiral Montero admonished his subordinate harshly. "Although it was the claim of the Soviet Union in the United Nations that prompted the President to send this commission to investigate, we are investigating for the President of Chile, *not* for the Soviet Union. We are not here to prove or disprove the Soviet claims. We are here to determine the nature of the situation for the President—nothing else."

"*Perdóneme, almirante.*"

"*No importa,*" Montero muttered, then addressed the crew of the *Atlantis*. "I thank you all very much for your helpful cooperation. We may need to talk with you again later. Now, if you will excuse us, we would like to discuss our business in private." He stood up and took Jackie Hart's hand. "One must certainly admire the American space program for more than its high technology." And he kissed her hand.

Joyce and Casey were waiting patiently for them outside the garrison's casern. "Well, gang, how did it go?" Casey asked.

"Surprisingly, it went very well," Frank said, "and we were thoroughly but discreetly questioned."

Lew cocked his head. "You know, you're right. I thought it was just a social occasion, because these Latins like to mix business and pleasure. But yeah, they did find out a lot about us, didn't they?"

Hap shrugged. "So? Did we have anything to hide?"

Ernesto Obregon emerged from the casern and walked over to them. "They're conducting their discussions in total privacy," he explained. "Not even the governor of Isla de Pascua is permitted to sit in."

"How do you think it went, Governor?" Casey asked. "Alice Arnold and Herb Haynes will want to know. In fact, they want to interview the commission."

Obregon shrugged. "Difficult to tell. The commission certainly has all the facts. I think there's only one conclusion they can come to, because I came to that conclusion myself days ago: there's no military significance to your flight."

"Can I quote you, Governor?" Casey asked quickly.

"No, not as long as my government has an official commission investigating the matter," Obregon declared flatly.

Casey waved his hand. "Okay, I understand. But, Governor, please don't make an offhand remark like that in front of Alice Arnold—or in front of any of the members of the press when they get here. I'll respect a confidence and so will Herb Haynes. But lots of American reporters won't."

"Señor Laskewitz, I'd be very grateful if you'd advise me concerning this when the press plane arrives."

"Be happy to, sir. And speaking of the press, our Embassy tells me they're getting very restless in Santiago," Casey added. "It's been five days since the *Atlantis* landed, and only two reporters have been able to get here to cover the story. I don't know how much longer I'll be able to keep them happy in Santiago with only audio reports from here."

"I thought the matter was up to Richardson," Obregon observed, "and how rapidly the tent accommodations could be prepared."

"It is, but the media people tell me they'd be willing to sleep in the airplane until the tent city's ready."

Obregon sighed. "Sleeping quarters aren't the total problem, Laskewitz. We can't feed a hundred additional people here, and we don't have the water or sanitation facilities. We're on the verge of overtaxing this island's facilities now. I'm sorry if I'm going to become the target for the American press, but circumstances force me to restrict the number of people on the island temporarily. Therefore, I have to order the press plane to stay in Santiago until Red Richardson tells me that the temporary facilities will handle first the NASA recovery team and secondly the media."

Casey knew when he had pushed too hard and too far. "Yes, sir. No problem, sir. I'll handle the press somehow. It would be a lot of help if you'd let me set up a conference via satellite with the media people waiting in Santiago. And if we could get the inspection commission to participate, it would keep those reporters off my back."

"I don't know whether they'll agree to talk to the press, Laskewitz."

"At least we can ask them, Governor." Casey was in a difficult position. Both Herb and Alice had filed stories which had gone into the press pool over loud objections from Alice. Herb's undeveloped thirty-five-millimeter film, which had gone to Santiago with the Herks the day before, was the only photo coverage from Pascua. Still photos and pool reports had given the reporters and TV crews in Santiago something to file, but they were very anxious to get to Pascua and didn't understand why they weren't permitted to do so. Only Casey's familiarity with the media and its people had prevented irreparable harm, but he knew he couldn't hold off the press forever. Questions were being fired his way via the satellite link with Santiago as to why Alice Arnold was along with Herb Haynes, the one who had been selected by the reporters as their initial pool man.

"It would also help, sir, if I could give them some sort of schedule so they'd know when they could expect to come," Casey said. "Right now, they're sitting around the airport or in hotels, not knowing when they'll leave. It doesn't make them any happier. In fact, some of them are beginning to file rather nasty stories about Chile as well as about NASA."

Obregon thought about this for a moment. "Let's talk with Richardson and determine a schedule. Then we can have a radio press conference. If I can convince the commission to participate, all to the better. If not, we'll have to do without."

"I think I can cover in the event the commission doesn't want to participate," Casey replied thoughtfully. "I'll tell the reporters the jury's still out and doesn't want to discuss anything until it's got all the information and had the chance to mull everything over."

Frank and Joyce decided to tag along, but the other three members of the crew said they would like to try for a swim in the ocean off Hangaroa. Frank caught the vibes from Jackie and Lew that they had something else in mind, but he didn't say anything. After all, they were adults.

Red had set up a temporary office in a vacant storeroom in the radio shack at Mataveri. Dr. Esteban and Juan Hey were both with him, and clearly he was having trouble.

"Juan's doing great with the Pascuans we've put to work grading the site for the tent city," Red explained, frustration showing in his voice and mannerisms. "But the Chilean contractors who came in with that last flight don't seem to know what the hell they're doing, and I can't explain it to them through Esteban here."

"*Qué pasa, doctor?*" Obregon asked.

Esteban replied in a stream of rapid Spanish. Obregon nodded and then turned to Richardson. "Dr. Esteban is not completely familiar with engineering terminology. Perhaps I can help, since I understand something about it."

"It's not only my own unfamiliarity with the metric system," Red admitted, "but I can't convince the Chileans that they can't just lay a thin coat of asphalt on the ground for either the turnarounds or the parking ramps—not for a C-5 that weighs more than three hundred tons. Nobody understands how *big* those mothers are! I know a little pidgin Spanish from growing up in Texas, but not enough to run this show."

"I'll talk to them right away," Obregon promised. "But the main reason we're here is to determine your schedule. When do you plan to have the turnarounds completed and the ramps built so that the C-5s can come?"

"The turnarounds should be completed by the day after tomorrow," Red replied, "and that'll allow the C-5s to come in, but they can't stay long because we won't have any place to park them on the ramps. It'll be a matter of arrive, unload, refuel from the tanker plane, and take off for Santiago again."

"How about the tent city?" Casey asked.

"Site grading's under way, and if the Pascuans continue to work as well as they have been, we'll have most of Ororito City erected by the day after tomorrow."

"Then can we bring the press plane in?" Casey wondered anxiously.

"If everything continues to run as it is, yes."

"Thanks, Red. That's what I needed to know," Casey said, then he turned to Obregon. "It's sixteen hundred hours right now. We can't make the deadlines for the afternoon papers in the States. But if I can schedule that press conference for eighteen hundred hours with both Santiago and New York, it'll make the media people happy because they'll be able to hit the six o'clock TV news."

Obregon nodded. "I'll talk to the commission. But you may certainly go ahead, whether they participate or not."

"Will you be available for questions, Governor?"

"Yes, but only on local matters. I'm not in a position to take questions concerning the commission or the Soviet claims."

"Yes, sir, I understand."

Frank went off to round up the rest of the crew and was surprised to find the three of them on the abbreviated beach below Hangaroa. Meanwhile, Casey began to set up his press conference in the satellite ground station. His first step was to contact Roger Service at NASA Headquarters.

"Laskewitz, how long is that Chilean governor going to refuse to let the press plane onto Easter Island?" Roger Service snapped from NASA Headquarters. "We're really under the gun here. We've had all sorts of pressure put on us by the networks and wire services. We've even had some calls from the Hill about it."

"It's not totally the decision of the military governor, Roger," Casey told him. "There's simply no way to handle any more people on this island until Red gets the tent city set up."

"You mean they can't handle eighty media people there?" Roger Service's voice was full of disbelief.

"That's right, Roger. I told you this island's the end of the Earth, and that's no idle metaphor. It can't even handle the seventy-five people of the recovery team, much less another eighty media types. We've got close to thirty people here already. There's no more room—not enough beds, not enough food, not enough water, and not enough sanitary facilities."

"Is Red dropping the ball, Casey? Look, it's been five days now since the *Atlantis* landed there."

"Roger, there's two thousand miles of water between us and everything else in the world. The logistics of this operation have outstripped anything that was ever considered in the contingency landing plans." Casey was well aware that Roger Service had absolutely no accurate conception of conditions on Isla de Pascua. "When the media get here in force, they'll see for themselves. The most important thing we're missing right now is a video camera so we could let the whole world see. As for Red, he's doing a superb job. We'll have the press plane in here the day after tomorrow. In the meantime, to keep the animals quiet, we're going to feed an audio news conference out of here via satellite at seventeen hundred hours your time. Since we've got two audio channels available to us through the satellite, we can have an interactive press conference."

"What do you mean?"

Casey sighed in exasperation. "The media will be able to ask questions. I'll have the crew of the *Atlantis* available, as well as the military governor. I doubt we'll get the inspection commission to participate."

"Why? The Soviet claims are damned important, Casey."

"I know that. I think the commission's on our side, and they've certainly seen that the *Atlantis* carries nothing but the Landsat-XIII. But I doubt we'll be able to get anything out of them until they've made their report to the President of Chile. Look, Roger, this press conference is just for the purpose of taking some of the heat off. You've got about an hour to set it up in Washington, and I've got to get through to Santiago now to get the troops ready there. I'll be with you again about fifteen minutes before the scheduled start. Hang in there."

CHAPTER TWELVE

It was a madhouse when the chartered Pan Am 707 landed at Mataveri two days later.

Casey had tried to work out suitable procedures with Obregon, but the facilities simply weren't up to handling eighty media people with all their equipment and baggage. Obregon decided to forgo visual inspection of their paraphernalia; he just didn't have the manpower.

The more vocal media representatives objected loudly when nobody was permitted to leave the plane until one of Obregon's men collected the passports. Then Dr. Esteban went through, carefully inspecting every International Certificate of Vaccination. At last Obregon himself boarded the plane to speak to the new arrivals. He stood at the head of the aisle and spoke into the microphone of the plane's PA system, repeating all the caveats he had already explained so many times.

Finally, he announced, "Casey Laskewitz, the NASA Public Affairs man here, has asked me to tell you there will be a press conference at the *Atlantis*, here on the ramp, in two hours. The crew will be present. Thank you. You may now disembark."

Casey stood at the bottom of the loading stairs to welcome each of the media people as they disembarked. He knew nearly every one of them with the exception of some of the camera crews and technicians.

Marty Soloman, the crack science reporter for a major network who had covered space activities and general science for years, was a cross that Casey knew he would have to bear. The dark-haired little man who seemed so pleasant and knowledgeable on TV was in real life an obnoxious, biased sensationalist, and an opportunistic little snob. He began exhibiting all those endearing traits as he got off the plane. Casey could see it coming and wondered at that moment what would happen if he ever got Marty together with Alice Arnold. Like bringing two chunks of U-235 together, he mused.

"Casey, what's this crap that I've got to *walk*? Hell, I've got three suitcases of clothes, to say nothing of all the gear my crew brought. Don't tell me there aren't any taxis in this godforsaken place?" the little man complained at the top of his voice.

Casey couldn't help laughing aloud. He was joined by some of Marty's media compatriots who knew him and detested him as well. "Marty, old chap," Casey told him, pointing to the side of Rano Kao's volcanic cone, "tell me what you see up there."

"Looks like a herd of sheep. What's that got to do with it?"

"The naval garrison's the only outfit with vehicles here, and it doesn't have many. Those sheep are the only animals on Isla de Pascua. If you want something to carry your gear, go catch a couple of sheep if you can; maybe you can get them to bear your burdens for you."

"Wise guy!"

"Come on, Marty. Rough it with the rest of us," called Hugh Hucksman, one of the anchors on a very popular weekly TV newsmagazine.

A week had wrought extensive changes on Isla de Pascua. Ororito City, enough tents to house and feed a hundred and fifty people, had been erected north of the runway on the slopes of Mount Ororito. Water was still in short supply because the desalinization plant wasn't scheduled to go on line for another day, and the sewage-treatment facility was barely in operation. Food would consist of canned Army rations until field kitchens and cooks could be flown in and set up. But there was electricity aplenty from the turbogenerators brought in by the fleet of Herks that now numbered six and were making daily round trips to Santiago.

Red had completed the runway turnarounds, and additional Chilean crews were working to expand the parking ramps. Most of the difficult and critical early work was nearing completion.

Casey was not surprised that some of the creative media people had commandeered one of the mess tents and turned it into the Easter Island Press Club, complete with a bar stocked from the ample supplies purchased in Santiago and carried on the press plane.

The press conference in the bright sunlight in front of the *Atlantis* went off well, with the usual questions and the usual responses—not much different from the initial radiolink news conference the day the *Atlantis* had landed. But as far as the media were concerned, it *was* different because they were at last on Isla de Pascua, on the spot, able to talk directly to the crew, to Red Richardson, and to Captain Obregon. And they were able to transmit their individual video or audio reports back to the States via the satellite ground station.

The initial confusion over who got to use the station in what order was settled very easily by Casey; the reporters drew straws for positions in line. By then, most of them understood why it had taken a whole week before anyone could file stories directly from the island. There were exceptions, but Casey handled them with aplomb.

As the news conference was drawing to a close, two C-5 Galaxy transports appeared in the sky and wheeled around Mataveri, their landing made possible by the fact that the runway turnarounds were in place. Even Obregon was visibly impressed as the first Galaxy soared in over Hangaroa to touch its twenty-four main tires on the approach end of Runway One-Zero. The 222-foot wingspan greatly overlapped the 100-foot-wide runway. The four engine pods below the wing weren't over the asphalt strip at all, causing their jet blast to kick up huge clouds of sand and dust when the pilot operated the thrust reversers. Colonel Matt Hubbard was pilot-in-command of that first Galaxy, and after he had parked it on the crowded ramp, he was able to give the reporters a complete rundown of the planned airlift operation. The two Galaxies contained the rest of Oror-ito City, food, additional water to subsidize the Pascua supply until the desalinization plant was operating, and a lot of miscellaneous cargo. All in all, each Galaxy brought in a hundred tons of cargo and still had fuel aboard for the return flight to Santiago.

Joy abounded in network headquarters in New York that evening and in wire-service bureaus and city rooms around America as well. At last there was video from the scene. What they didn't know was that the schedule for the recovery operation wouldn't be very exciting or visual to nontechnical types until NASA 905 arrived—and that was still a problem.

Red discussed the situation with Joe Marvin in Houston later that evening during the daily-progress conference. "Red, Hank says there's no way they can stretch the range of Nine-Oh-Five by installing additional tanks. With the *Atlantis* on her, the Nine-Oh-Five is right at maximum gross weight for a Seven-Forty-Seven's landing gear. Hank won't risk going over max gross, not off an eighty-eight-hundred-foot runway."

"Well, tell them to get busy on the midair refueling mod," Red replied testily. "I told them that was the way a week ago."

"The Air Force says they looked into it for their Seven-Forty-Sevens a couple years ago, and the modifications are extensive."

"So? The sooner Hank gets started, the sooner he can get that bird down here."

"Well, they're working on it, Red. Boeing sent some engineers to Dryden, and Lockheed sent over the team they had used to install the in-flight refueling system in the C-141Bs, and the Air Force has some of their experts over from Edwards next door. It'll be a jury-rig, but they'll figure out something that'll work."

"You know, Joe, it just occurred to me—how the hell did they expect to airlift an Orbiter back from Okinawa or Spain with a range of only nineteen hundred nautical miles max? Why didn't somebody think about this before?"

"Because," Joe Marvin said quietly, "this whole program was planned and scheduled on a no-fail basis right from the day the contract was signed in 1972. Nobody could afford to put much thought into what would happen if it failed. The people who made those early decisions are long gone into retirement—"

"Leaving us to hang in their stead if we don't pull off a miracle."

"You said it. I didn't."

It didn't make Red Richardson feel better.

Alice Arnold was also in a blue funk. For a whole week she had had to share the *Atlantis* story with only Herb Haynes, and he was a pussycat to handle as far as she was concerned. Now she was back in the rat race. Her only compensation was that she managed to hang on to her room with Jackie and Joyce at the Hotel Hangaroa and didn't have to move into Ororito City to share a tent with other female reporters.

She couldn't face the idea of going up to the newly established Press Club at Ororito City. Instead, she walked into the small bar located in one corner of the dining room at the Hotel Hangaroa, where she found Joyce, Frank, and Hap Hazard.

"May I join you?" she asked.

Frank started to say something, but Hap interrupted. "Sure, why not?"

"Thanks. The new Press Club's a little bit far for me to walk tonight."

"I wondered why you were here instead of up with your media friends," Frank said.

"They don't know about this place yet, so I can still come here for some peace and quiet," Alice admitted. "Look, the prices being what they are here, let me buy. I'm on expense account, not per diem like all of you."

"Well, that's mighty friendly of you, Alice," Hap bubbled.

"You look like you've just lost your last friend," Frank observed after Juan Hey—bartender as well as hotel manager—served another round.

"You're a very perceptive man," Alice noted.

"Well, I can understand, too," Joyce put in for the first time since Alice had joined them. "You no longer have a semiexclusive story here."

"Oh, that doesn't bother me," Alice lied. "I've had almost a week to get to know everybody personally, and that gives me a leg up on the ones who arrived today. For example, I can get directly to Obregon—or to you, Frank. The sort of stories I file out of here from now on will be personal-interest stuff."

"What makes you think we're personally interesting?" Frank asked. "I'm just an old fighter jock."

"Aw, don't belittle yourself, Frank," Hap objected. "Don't you know that Headquarters wants us to put on the Big Astronaut Act, just like in the old days with the Apollo Project when astronauts were all supermen instead of what we really are: ordinary, everyday truck drivers with no real hope of going further than delivering space-science stuff to low-Earth orbit—when we could be building space factories and power satellites and space colonies." Hap was becoming full of Johnny Walker Red.

"Speak for yourself, Hap," Frank said. "Better yet, go hit the sack. Looks like you've had a long, hard day."

"Yeah, answering the same old questions from the Chilean inspection commission," Hap continued to complain. "They've been here three days now. When the hell are they going to decide we're telling the truth about our mission and payload?"

"Probably when they get good and ready," Joyce put in. "Look, Hap, they know you're not lying about the payload, and they know the Soviets have thrown out a red herring for political purposes. The commission realizes they've got a real hot issue here, and they're worried about how to handle it. I've talked to them about it."

"How'd you manage that?" Alice asked. "They've been completely secretive, hiding out in Obregon's casern."

"Oh, I've known Colonel Ríos and Professor Pérez for a long time," Joyce admitted.

"Yeah, I forgot you grew up in this dirty, primitive, backwater part of the world," Alice remarked.

Joyce bristled. "You're making the same mistake most Americans do. That's what gets our country into trouble and causes the Department of State a lot of problems dealing with the rest of the world."

"Look, dear, that's what we taxpayers are paying you to do," Alice fired back.

Joyce pushed herself away from the bar and stood up.

"Excuse me, please," she said, and walked out of the room, leaving the three of them staring.

"Got her!" Alice chortled, and upended her glass.

Hap didn't say anything. He was more than slightly embarrassed over the encounter between the two women.

Frank looked at his drink and quietly asked, "Why did you do that, Alice? She's right, you know. Someday you're going to find yourself in deep trouble."

"Not with that good old press card in my wallet!"

"Sure."

Hap stood back from the bar, leaving most of his drink untouched. "Excuse me, I'm still kind of bushed from my bout with that Pascuan saniflush I got hold of. Think I'll turn in." He walked slowly out.

"Hey, Juan Hey!" Alice called. "Set 'em up again, man!" Then she turned to Frank. "Well, at last I've got you alone."

Frank looked at her. "Oh? Well, now that you've got me, what are you going to do with me? Eat me?"

"I might. I've never eaten a Space Shuttle command pilot before. You might taste pretty good. Different, anyway."

Frank sighed. "If you'd been around about fifteen years ago, when I was a hot young captain eager to get his hands on fast airplanes and fast women, we might have found out, Alice. But them days am gone forever, as the old saying goes."

"The old saying may be wrong, you know."

"I don't think this is the time or the place to find out whether it is or not."

"Okay," Alice persisted, "let's check out another old adage that says all bets are off when a pilot's more than fifty miles from home. Christ, Frank, you're half a world away from Seabrook, Texas!"

"No, I'm not. In terms of miles, maybe, but not inside, where it counts. Thanks for the drink, Alice. Maybe the Easter Island Press Club won't seem so far away now." He got up and started to walk away.

"God damn you!"

He turned. "Quite possibly. You know, Alice, you've changed my mind about a lot of things. For example, I once thought that Jackie was a tough bitch. Good night."

But Frank didn't go upstairs to the room he shared with Casey and Red. Not just yet. He wandered out into Hangaroa and began walking slowly northward to where he could see the seven huge *moai* standing on the *ahu* in the moonlight, gazing forever westward toward the sea.

He was more than a little upset over the brash encounter with Alice Arnold. In his time he had met many brash women on the make for jet jocks. And before marrying Ellie, he had played the role of the hot jet jock. But for the last twelve years Frank had tried to play fair with Ellie, not out of religious conviction, but for one simple reason: he loved her and couldn't even imagine going to bed with another woman. He had grown expert at handling the young groupies and some of the older ones as well.

He was walking faster than usual, his mind preoccupied with the anger of the encounter with Alice. His anger at himself or his anger at Alice—he couldn't separate them in his mind. So distracted was he that he almost walked right over somebody else going in the same direction, but at a slower pace.

"Oops! Sorry. Uh—Joyce! What the hell are you doing out here at this time of night?" he asked as he helped her to her feet after practically running over her.

"Wow, you're sure heading somewhere at full bore, Frank," she replied, dusting off her slacks. "I was going to ask you the same question."

"I asked you first," he reminded her.

"Let's keep walking. I might even tell you," she remarked, resuming her leisurely amble along the dirt track toward the seven *moai*.

They walked in silence for several minutes until the huge stone statues loomed tall before them. Frank finally said, "Well?"

Joyce sighed. "I can't afford to lose my temper or argue in public. My training's been too strict for that."

"I didn't think the State Department conducted such training."

"They don't. My father pounded it into me. According to him, it's better to step out of an argument, whether you think you can win or not. If you lose, you've irreparably damaged whatever cause you've championed; if you win, you never stand a chance of really making a friend or a convert of your opponent. So I just had to stroll out here and cool off after the incident in the bar."

Frank chuckled. "Hap was the smart one."

"What do you mean?"

"He excused himself and left right after you did. He avoided both an argument and being left alone with Alice Arnold."

Joyce looked up at him. "So you were left alone with her, huh?"

Frank nodded.

"And?"

"I don't like pushy bitches."

"You seem to get along fine with Jackie."

"Compare the two," Frank suggested, and proceeded to explain. "Jackie's a pussycat in comparison. Jackie just wants to fly the hottest and newest stuff available. She doesn't want to compete with men, but she must, to do what she wants to. Jackie seems pushy and bitchy at times because she's chosen a field that's been almost totally dominated by men."

"Is Jackie good?"

"Jackie's an outstanding pilot and mission specialist. She'll be one of the first women Shuttle pilots, if not *the* first."

Joyce nodded. "I see. I guess I haven't known Jackie long enough. On the other hand, Alice—well, I don't guess we have to analyze Alice, do we?"

"Nope."

"So why did you walk away from her?" Joyce asked. "I thought you pilots were game to try anything, especially away from home."

"That's the image, all right. But it's also a generalization."

"You love her very much, don't you?"

"My wife? Yes, I do, Joyce."

They had reached the site of the seven statues and walked quietly around the level stone *ahu* altar platform until they could look up at them in the moonlight. "Think of all they've seen," Joyce remarked.

"Open canoes, sailing ships, steamships, airplanes, jet planes, and now spaceships," Frank mused.

"Gods, great chiefs, sea captains, slavers, explorers,

conquerors, warriors—and astronauts," she added, "not to mention the women who were usually with them."

"Or waiting at home."

"Where's 'home,' Frank?"

"Seabrook, Texas."

"No, Frank, that's where you're living right now. That's where you get your mail. Where's *home*? Where do you *live*?"

Frank thought about what she had said, then replied, "I'm not sure. Maybe I live 'out there' somewhere. Maybe somewhere in space is my ultimate home. God knows I've spent most of my life trying to get there. Maybe I'm just trying to go home again." He stopped, then asked, "Where do you live, Joyce? Maybe that'll give me a clue."

She spread her hands to indicate their surroundings. "Right here, right now. My past is a memory. My future hasn't become a memory yet. And don't ask me where that future is; I don't really know."

"You're different," Frank told her.

"Of course. So are you."

"And you've loved many people, haven't you? I can tell."

"Certainly. The more I've loved, the more I'm capable of loving. I'm very close to my family; I love them very much," Joyce admitted candidly. Then, almost as an after-thought in case Frank might not fully understand, she said, "You see, I don't have that unfortunate American belief that love's so special it has to be rationed to only a few people exclusively in a person's life. In South America, they know differently; their heritage is Hispanic and Ara-bic, not Puritan and Teutonic. And I grew up in South America, where I've known and loved many people, too."

"Casey told me."

"Told you what?"

"That you knew practically everybody, from the Prime Minister's secretary to two of the members of the inspec-tion commission."

She nodded. "But not everybody."

"You're not married, Joyce?" It was a rhetorical ques-tion.

"No. Getting a Chem-E degree at MIT didn't leave

much time for a roaring social life, even with a skewed male-female ratio in the student body."

"Joyce, you're going to make some lucky man very happy someday."

"How do you know I haven't already—and several, at that?"

"I don't know. Have you? And how many?"

"None of your business! That's my little secret. It will make me seem mysterious and somehow more secretly desirable." She was kidding him, and he knew it.

"I'm flattered," he retorted. "Whatever made you think something would make you more mysterious and secretly desirable to me, a happily married Space Shuttle command pilot only thousands of miles from home and for all intents and purposes completely alone on a South Sea island with you? Aren't you taking a big risk?"

"No. I know you. I think I've known you all my life. Because I know exactly what you're thinking. I know the conflict going on behind those eyes. I know you still ration love because you're an American right down to your NASA nomex flight coveralls."

"Are you so sure you know what's under these NASA-issue nomex flight coveralls, Joyce?"

"Pretty sure."

"I'd like the chance to prove you're wrong."

"You just have. You are one of my loved ones. *Usted es muy hermoso. Venga acá!*"

It was a completely new experience for Frank King, the seasoned fighter jock, test pilot, and Shuttle astronaut.

For the first time, he felt totally enfolded and cherished. Far beyond the joyful physical sharing of each other, Joyce made him an integral part of a union that transcended basic sexual activities and both drew from him and gave him a deeply emotional force of great power that allowed him to exceed his former limits of time and available energy.

Frank felt very strange as they watched the Sun come up on the seven *moai*. He felt absolutely no guilt and no remorse. For the first time in many long years, he had shared something totally and deeply. There was an equally strange glow about the *ahu* and the seven *moai* in the early sunlight, an aura that he felt could not completely be the result of the sunrise light.

A new idea flickered through his mind and was gone.

Even if he went to the end of the Solar System, there was something special about this island that would always be one of the many places he would call home from now on. He didn't know why. He didn't ask why. Perhaps this was a magic place. Maybe the Pascuans knew, or maybe the *moai* could answer his question if they could speak.

Casey and Red were logging heavy sack time as Frank quietly let himself into the room. Ten to one, he thought, Casey had helped inaugurate the Easter Island Press Club last night. And Red had probably been with him. It must have been a wild and raucous party. But up at the seven *moai*, only four miles away, Frank had had the impression nobody but the two of them was within thousands of miles.

He gave a quiet snort as he shaved. Was there something unknown, special, or magic about Rapa Nui after all? Why had ancient people chosen it as the site for huge statues laboriously carved from volcanic rock? Why, after many archaeological expeditions, did Rapa Nui still have an aura of mystery about it? And why did it just happen to be there, right under the orbital ascent path of the *Atlantis*, with a runway conveniently just long enough to accommodate it? Why had Space Shuttle Orbiter OV-104, strangely named the *Atlantis*, malfunctioned so that it could be landed *only* on Rapa Nui?

Frank had never been a superstitious man, in contrast with some of his fighter-jock buddies over the years. He had just done his job by extending his senses into whatever machine he was operating. But he found himself thinking about such things for the first time that morning.

He went to breakfast without his two roommates and was shortly joined by Jackie, Lew, Hap, and Herb Haynes. There was nothing but small talk until Captain Ernesto Obregon appeared, saw them, and walked straight over to where they were eating in the sunlight.

"*Buenos días, mon capitaine,*" Frank greeted him.

"You're mixing your languages," Obregon pointed out. "You'd best stick to one you know a little bit about and speak English. Where're Red Richardson and Casey Laskewitz?"

"Still sleeping off the inaugural ball of the Easter Island Press Club," Frank told him.

"Yes, it was a good party. Casey Laskewitz acquainted me with various members of the American press," Obregon said without batting an eye. "I need to know when the next plane's scheduled to leave for Santiago."

"Did you check with Colonel Matt Hubbard?" Lew asked. "He's command pilot of the lead C-5 Galaxy, and he's handling flight operations."

"Where is he?"

"Probably sleeping in his plane. That bird's a flying hotel," Frank pointed out.

Obregon nodded. "I'll check with him. But I still have to get Casey Laskewitz out of bed. Admiral Montero told me he wants to announce the commission's preliminary report after he talks to Santiago via satellite this morning, and he's agreed to a press conference after he's done so."

Frank stood. "I'll get him, Ernesto. When does the admiral want to make the announcement?"

"Before noon, and he wants to be on the next flight back."

Admiral Eduardo Miguel Montero chose to conduct his preliminary announcement and press conference on the ramp at Mataveri, in the open forward cargo door of a C-5 Galaxy with the cargo-hold floor as a stage. The cream of the world's press managed to stagger out of their cots in Ororito City, get their acts together, and be on hand on the ramp, cameras, recorders, and notebooks ready. Accompanied by the other two members of the commission, the admiral invited Obregon and the four *Atlantis* crew members to join him. Montero was not totally unaware of the need for theatrics in making his announcement. And he did so in English.

The direct TV-satellite link permitted anxious people in Washington, Houston, and New York to watch—as well as others in Moscow and elsewhere who were perhaps not quite so tense.

"Ladies and gentlemen," Montero began, "the President of the Republic of Chile has created this special investigating commission to look into the details of the emergency landing of the United States Space Shuttle *Atlantis* on Isla de Pascua, which is Chilean soil. The commission had consisted of myself as chairman, Colonel Amaldo Carlos Ríos of the Fuerzas Aéreas de Chile—the Chilean air force—and Professor José Ricardo Pérez, the president of the Sociedad Interplanetaria Chilena, the Chilean representative of the International Astronautical Federation.

"We have inspected and confirmed the validity of the necessary international documents relating to the *Atlantis*, her crew, and her cargo. We have personally inspected the interior of the *Atlantis* and directly viewed the cargo. We have questioned the members of the crew. We have discussed privately within the commission all information that has been willingly made available to us, all that we have been able to obtain ourselves, and all that could reasonably be expected to be investigated by a commission such as this.

"On the basis of this timely inspection conducted on Isla de Pascua itself, it is the conclusion of this special investigation commission that the *Atlantis* was launched from a military launch site, Vandenberg Air Force Base, California, a site used for both military *and* civilian space launches by the United States of America. Further, the commission finds that the purpose of the flight of the *Atlantis* was to place in a polar orbit a civilian satellite known as Landsat-XIII, whose mission would have been to monitor nonmilitary Earth activities such as sea conditions, pollution, and so forth. The *Atlantis* was manned by a civilian crew of four qualified NASA astronauts. The *Atlantis* suffered an emergency of unknown cause that prevented it from completing its flight into orbit and required that an emergency landing be made on Isla de Pascua, which was the only landing site available to its pilot.

"There was no military activity connected with the flight or emergency landing of the *Atlantis*. As a representative of the government of the Republic of Chile, I pledge the full efforts and support of the government of Chile in permitting the United States to retrieve the *Atlantis* from Isla de Pascua.

"Colonel Ríos and I will return to Santiago today to make our full report to the President of Chile. Professor

Pérez has elected to remain on Isla de Pascua as an observer to provide incontrovertible witness to the continued nonmilitary nature of this flight, landing, and rescue operation.

"We will accept questions from the press for fifteen minutes. Then we must return in this Galaxy transport to Santiago so that I may make our report to our President this evening."

Fifteen minutes of questions from the press followed. Finally, there was a general hand-shaking all around. The admiral and the colonel clambered up the ladder to the forward flight deck. The crew of the *Atlantis* and Captain Obregon descended to the ramp, whereupon the huge nose door swung down to seal the front of the cavernous cargo hold. The ramp was cleared before the fanjet engines were started.

Colonel Matt Hubbard stepped to Frank's side as the Galaxy taxied out to the runway. "Glad to get it out of here," he remarked.

"I thought you were command pilot for Number One Galaxy," Frank said, watching the C-5 taxi onto the runway.

"I was, but I've got to lay in here, where the action and the problems are. This airlift requires some complex scheduling," Hubbard explained. "I've got two more C-5s due at thirteen hundred local. We won't have ramp room for more than two at a time until Richardson and those Chilean crews get the ramps expanded, and I'm having one hell of a problem scheduling the Herks in between the Galaxies."

"Want some help?" Frank volunteered. "The four of us know something about flight scheduling, and we're about as useful as tits on a boxcar around here for a while. If we don't do something, Red will probably send us back to Houston to get us out from underfoot."

"Hell, yes, I could use your help," Hubbard replied.

The C-5 turned at the end of the runway, threw a huge cloud of dust and sand as its engines came up to speed, then began to move slowly down the runway. Running light, with no cargo and only fuel aboard, it lifted off after using only half the runway, leaving behind it two plumes of dust where its engines had overhung the sides of the asphalt strip. Its twenty-eight wheels retracted into its belly, and it began a long, slow-climbing left turn to the east.

Frank watched it go. "Fascinating," he remarked.

"What is?" Matt Hubbard asked.

"That something that big can fly. I'm strictly an old fighter jock, you know."

"I gotta laugh at that statement coming from a Space Shuttle command pilot," Hubbard told him.

As the C-5 rapidly disappeared to the southeast in a climb, Frank continued to watch.

It suddenly ceased to exist, becoming an expanding yellow ball of flame.

CHAPTER THIRTEEN

Frank was the only one who saw the explosion of the C-5 Galaxy. Typically, though more than a dozen TV cameras stood on the ramp, not a one was following the departing transport. Dozens of cameras, some with long lenses on them, were in place, but not a single photo was taken.

Colonel Matt Hubbard reacted to Frank's sharp intake of breath and explosive expletive. But Hubbard saw only the fireball. Others reacted to the sharp flash of the explosion. And still others didn't notice until the thunder rolled over the airfield long seconds later.

Frank was the only one with the presence of mind to respond to the situation. Not taking his eyes off the expanding cloud of smoke, flame, and debris, he reached over and tore Herb Haynes's portable tape recorder away from the reporter, who was so surprised at the action that he released it without hesitation. Frank noted the position of the explosion with reference to landmarks, pushed the "record" button, and began to dictate what he thought he had seen. He was still talking when the full realization of what had happened spread over the crowd and erupted into shouts, screams, and a panic attempt to capture the aftermath of the explosion on record.

"I don't know which happened first," Frank told the recorder. "The right wing appeared to separate, followed immediately by the left wing inboard of the Number One engine. This may have been the result of the explosion, which appeared to have a brisance quite unlike that of fuel tanks. But all fuel aboard probably burned because of the large, long-lasting fireball. I don't know whether the accident was caused by a bomb aboard the plane, by a malfunction of the fuel system, or by some structural failure."

"That was my C-5!" He turned to find Colonel Matt Hubbard standing beside him, his face as white as a sheet. "I was supposed to be flying the left seat on that plane," he muttered. "I turned it over to Jimmy to fly the round robin to Santiago. Damn it! God damn it!" Matt was shaking.

"Easy, Matt." Frank tried to calm the man. Colonel Frank King had been in similar situations in Vietnam, where pilots had died because they had flown for friends unable to take the fatal mission. That sort of thing was always a shattering experience. "There was no way you could have known that would happen."

Ernesto Obregon was at Frank's right. "Frank, you saw it all?"

He nodded. "I did."

"My admiral was aboard! I'm sending the boats out to search for survivors," the governor said. He crossed himself and muttered something in Spanish. He, too, was shaken. Frank had never seen Obregon shaken before.

"You won't find any," Frank told him bluntly. "That C-5 disintegrated. I didn't see any large parts fall out of the fireball, just little pieces. Nobody aboard could have survived. I'm sorry, Ernesto."

"I'll send boats anyway. They might find something. Was it a bomb?"

"I don't know. It could have been an equipment malfunction."

"We've had wing troubles with the Galaxy since Day One," Hubbard admitted. "We fly it at cruise with the ailerons rigged ten degrees up to unload the outer wing. All C-5s have been back for retrofit on the wing structure, but they're getting near the maximum-design life. And we've had continual fuel-system problems, particularly with vapors in those big wing tanks."

"Have you lost any others in flight lately?" Frank asked.

"No, and I've never seen one blow up in flight. It just can't happen," Colonel Matt Hubbard said shakily.

"It just did," Frank reminded him.

"Governor, I'm posting my armed guards around all these aircraft immediately, and I'd like to have you put the entire airport under tight security," Hubbard told the military governor, reacting at once to the possibility both of sabotage and of terrorism.

Obregon nodded. "I was going to suggest just that, because I suspect sabotage."

"So do I," Hubbard said.

"Ernesto, Matt, who's had ready access to these aircraft on the ramp?" Frank suddenly asked.

"Your people . . . and some of mine," Obregon replied after thinking for a moment. "I think I know which of my people have been aboard."

"Governor, nobody's to come near these planes from now on except my crews," Hubbard snapped. "I've got two more C-5s on their way, and I can't turn them back. But once they're here, nothing moves into or out of Mataveri until a picked team of my men goes over each aircraft. My load masters and cargo masters will handle all unloading and fuel transfer, using my flight crews. And, Governor, please get all the media people off the ramp, not only for the security of the aircraft, but for their own safety. I don't know if there're bombs aboard the planes parked here now!"

The reporters and their crews had clustered around them. Obregon turned and took in the situation. Raising his voice, he shouted, "Clear this ramp immediately! No questions, no interviews, no speculations about what happened! Get off this ramp now for your own safety! We don't know whether or not it was a bomb, but these other planes here may be sapped!" He turned to his Armada de Chile marine detachment, the departure honor guard for the late admiral and Chilean air force colonel. Orders were snapped in Spanish, and the platoon removed twenty-round box magazines from their belts and snapped them into their Swiss SIG510 rifles. The media people moved, some of them still rolling their video cameras and walking backward toward the tower and the satellite ground station.

Casey helped. He was a tall, gangling man who stood a head above most of the crowd. He waved his hands and motioned the media crews back. "Let's go, gang. This ramp may be unhealthy. Come on, don't take chances. Talk and bitch and ask questions later, but not right now."

Joyce fought her way through the throng, looking for Professor Pérez, and found him standing dumbfounded. She put her arms around him. *"José, José . . . He perdido a mi amigo también!"*

"Joyce, I wanted to stay on Pascua to witness the full recovery operation," the scientist said in strained and halting English. "If not for that, I would've been aboard."

"I know. *Cálmate, cálmate.*"

"Creo que estoy muy bien, gracias."

But Joyce sensed that something *was* wrong with the Chilean. She had known him for a long time, and there was something different about his reaction to the loss of his two colleagues. Under the circumstances, she temporarily dismissed the feeling and led Pérez off the ramp to the small building at the base of the tower.

There was a mob scene at the temporary building housing the satellite ground station. Casey was doing his best to keep some of the more aggressive reporters from storming the station to file stories. But the NASA PA man couldn't make much headway and was rapidly losing control of the situation when the crowd suddenly parted.

Governor Obregon strode purposefully toward the door, flanked by rifle-bearing Chilean marines. He stopped in the doorway and told the newsmen, "When I've reported this incident to my government and Miss Fisher has reported it to the United States government, we'll answer what questions we can. Then you'll be permitted to use the ground station in an orderly fashion under whatever arrangement you make with Casey Laskewitz."

"You can't keep us from using this station. It belongs to the United States." As usual, Alice Arnold was stridently speaking up for her concept of freedom of the press.

"On the contrary, it's Chilean property on Chilean soil—and as military governor, I *can* restrict its use until we've completed official business. I don't want our governments to learn of this disaster from the newspapers."

"You're restricting the freedom of the press, Governor." It was little Marty Soloman, vociferous as usual.

Obregon sighed. "As I told all of you when you arrived on Isla de Pascua, you're on Chilean soil and subject to Chilean law. I'm the military governor of this island, and I told you I wouldn't deliberately be arbitrary. In this case, I'm not being arbitrary, but I can't permit the limited communications capability here to be saturated when both the Chilean and the American governments must be informed immediately."

"You're being arbitrary as hell!" Alice Arnold yelped.

"Be careful, Miss Arnold, or I'm likely to become *really* arbitrary, whereupon you'll find yourself on the next plane for Santiago—and I *do* have the authority to make that happen. No, leave your press card in your wallet; it won't do any good. Now, all of you please excuse me. *Profesor Pérez, venga aquí, por favor.*" He disappeared into the ground station.

Joyce sat on the metal treads of the stairway leading up to the control tower. "Oh, God, what an awful thing to happen! And I've got to report it to Dewey when Obregon and Pérez are finished talking to Santiago."

"Joyce, are we becoming involved with Chilean politics here?" Frank asked her.

"You mean, was that C-5 deliberately destroyed by Chileans—Marxists, left-wing radicals, Cuban-inspired revolutionaries, or old Allende supporters—because it carried two members of the junta? Possibly. Quite possibly. But was it a bomb, Frank? Or was it a malfunction of something in the aircraft?"

"I don't know. I don't think we'll ever know unless Ernesto's boats pick up some pieces that'd confirm a bomb explosion when analyzed." He didn't know whether to ask Joyce about something that had occurred to him as he had watched the orange fireball that had once been a graceful C-5 Galaxy. But he had to bring the question up. "Joyce, if we're getting involved in Chilean politics, we've got to do something to bring it to a screeching halt right now. I don't know what either one of us can do about it, but I won't stand by and see the *Atlantis* jeopardized by political machinations."

"We may have no choice, my space-dreamer friend."

"Like hell! One regiment of United States Marines, and Pascua would be secured until we got the *Atlantis* away from here. Then the Chileans could have their volcanic rock back to play whatever games they wanted to!" Frank was angry, and his voice reflected that emotion. "This is costing us billions, and we've lost ten damned fine airmen along with a fifty-million-dollar aircraft. And we've got an Orbiter worth several billions squatting here like a sitting duck. How long do you think Washington's going to stand still for that?"

"Frank, I hate to dash cold water on your idealistic view of the world," Joyce told him gently, "but I'm afraid I've got bad news for you. There'd never be an order from the Oval Office to send the Marines here to protect the *Atlantis*. If it came to a choice between maintaining the existing Latin American foreign policy, such as it is, and saving part of the United States space program in the form of the *Atlantis*, can you guess what the decision might be? Which is more important to the Administration right now? And if it came to a real showdown, what do you think would happen to us?"

Frank thought about that quietly for a long minute. "I think, Joyce, that I'll ask Red or Matt Hubbard to get some M16 rifles in here—just in case."

"Ernesto may not let them on the island. He won't like it."

"He won't know about it."

Obregon and Pérez spent a long time secluded in the ground station shack. When they emerged, Obregon looked around at the crowd. "I wish to apologize if what I said earlier offended any of you. I was and still am under considerable pressure. I'd like to ask a favor of one of the media crews who made a videotape of the admiral's verbal report before he left. I will not and cannot restrict your use of anything you record here, and I won't even consider censorship. But my government would greatly appreciate it if, under the circumstances, one of you would permit them the use of the videotape of the admiral's statement. It would be transmitted to Santiago and retaped there. It would be used with full credit because it's the *only* report that the inspection commission would be able to make as a full commission. It would most certainly lead to refutation of the current charges against the United States in the UN Security Council, and it would be of inestimable value to the security of your country and mine."

"To hell with you, Governor!" somebody shouted from the back of the crowd. "If you want our tape, pay for it, just like your government made the United States taxpayers fork over all that equipment to you!"

Bill Jacobs from NBC raised his hand. "Governor, I apologize for the outburst from my colleague. Small people do petty things. NBC would be proud to have you use our videotape." The tall, handsome newscaster turned to his cameraman, who ejected a video cassette from his recorder and gave it to Jacobs, who in turn handed it to Obregon. "Just give it back when you've transmitted it to Santiago, will you, sir? I've got to send it to New York as quickly as you'll let me."

"Thank you, Mr. Jacobs." Obregon took the cassette and returned to the interior of the ground station shack. A few minutes later he emerged again and returned the cassette to the NBC reporter. "Miss Fisher, now it's your turn."

"Frank, please come with me," she said quietly to the Shuttle command pilot.

"Sure."

"Joyce, do you want to use our tape, too?" Bill Jacobs asked.

Joyce sighed and replied, "Unless somebody else would like me to use his to spread around our thanks to those of you who are being so helpful right now."

"You look distraught, Joyce," observed Walter Bishop of CBS.

"I am. Many of you know my father was in the foreign service in Chile and that I grew up in Santiago. The Chileans may have lost two valuable men, and we may have lost ten fine young airmen and a C-5 transport plane—but I lost a very old and dear friend, Colonel Ríos." Joyce knew that the video cameras were running, and she could hear the click-whine-click-whine of thirty-five-millimeter cameras. She didn't particularly care about the loss of hardware, but she cared very much about the people. And if the world knew about it, so much the better.

"With all deference to my colleague from NBC, please use our videotape in your report to Washington," Bishop offered. "It may help if there're two official records taken from two locations."

"Thanks. It will."

When Joyce got through to Alfred M. Dewey and made her report, Dewey almost came apart. "*Two members* of the inspection commission? *The* Commander-in-Chief of the Chilean navy? The Deputy Chief of Staff of the Chilean air force? Good heavens, Miss Fisher, this is an international incident!"

"No, sir, not if we handle it properly. One member of the commission's still alive and well on Pascua," she told him calmly. "We have several videotapes of Montero's verbal public announcement to the press. If you'll make arrangements, I've received permission from CBS to transmit their videotape to you for the use of the State Department. As soon as I make my report to you, the media will probably be filing their stories, and it'll be all over the evening news. That'll give you and NASA—and probably the White House, too—time to put together a news release expressing our deepest regrets to the President and people of Chile as well as to the families of the Air Force people who were lost. And it gives you a perfect excuse to release the Montero verbal report."

"But will it be believed?"

"It can be confirmed by Professor Pérez."

"Very good, that's what we'll do if I can get clearance. I'll send this information up to the Secretary and over to the White House," Dewey said. "You're doing a fine job there, Miss Fisher. Now, I've got some additional information for you on the Soviet naval vessels. They've been located by Navy Orion patrol planes passing about seven hundred miles south of Hawaii on a course toward Pascua and refueling at sea. The carrier *Kitty Hawk* and the guided-missile destroyer *Cochrane* are paralleling their course and keeping them under air surveillance. The Navy is putting together Task Force Sixty-Nine, and the guided-missile cruiser *Halsey* will leave San Diego tomorrow to join the *Kitty Hawk* and the *Cochrane*. So when those Soviet ships show up at Pascua, you can be sure the Navy's right behind them."

"Mr. Dewey, is a Marine contingent in that task force?"

"Marines? Why?"

"The NASA and Air Force people here are a bit nervous. They're not sure the Chilean naval contingent on the island can provide security against losing more airplanes—or even against a terrorist attack."

"That sounds a bit farfetched, Miss Fisher."

"We don't think so. We may be getting involved in internal Chilean political affairs. After all, Admiral Montero and Colonel Ríos were involved with the junta."

"Miss Fisher, you know Chile, and I'm counting on you to keep this operation out of internal Chilean political affairs."

Joyce could sense Dewey's frustration and indecisiveness just in the tone of his voice. She knew the only thing he wanted to do was play it safe and get out of the affair with as little controversy and as few opportunities for mistakes as possible. He was a career Washington foreign service man, safe in his office from the vagaries and threats of revolutions, demonstrations, terrorism, and day-to-day interfaces with other societies that were the lot of foreign service people in the field. "Mr. Dewey, with all due respect, and knowing the Chileans as I do, I'll tell you flatly right now that under these circumstances on a very vulnerable piece of Chilean soil, we *can't* stay completely out of their affairs! I'll be in touch with the Ambassador in Santiago about it, and I respectfully request that you bring this to the attention of the Secretary. If people are starting to play rough—and it looks as if they are—we're sitting ducks out here on the only land within two thousand miles."

"Miss Fisher, you're overreacting to the situation there. Under the circumstances, I can understand. Try to get a good night's rest, and you'll feel better about it tomorrow once all the anxiety born of this morning's incident has had a chance to dissipate. I really don't believe you're in any danger down there. You know we'll back you up in all possible ways from here."

Joyce knew the history of the United States foreign policy over the past thirty years. She didn't tell her boss, but she didn't believe a word he said.

Frank, who had heard the whole conversation and kept his mouth shut the entire time, didn't believe his reassurances either.

The journalists really put the pressure on Casey, and he quickly relieved it by setting up a cat-and-mouse press conference in a tent in Ororito City, with Obregon, Pérez, Joyce, and the *Atlantis* crew on the spot. The main question couldn't be answered and was, therefore, repeatedly asked: "What was the cause of the Galaxy's explosion?"

Finally, Casey exclaimed in desperation, "Look, gang, you're asking the same question over and over, and you've got the best answers we have right now. Let's break this up. File your stories to make your afternoon deadlines. I'll be up at the Press Club, and if you really want to talk to any of the NASA or Air Force people, I'll see what can be done. Conference adjourned!"

After supper another conference was quietly brought to order on the south slopes of Rano Kao, atop the cliff of the birdmen, *tangata-manu,* only a couple of miles from Hangaroa and completely out of sight of Ororito City. Frank organized the gathering, which was attended by Lew, Jackie, Hap, Joyce, Red, Matt Hubbard, and himself.

"What the hell is so damned important and secret that we've gotta come all the way out to the boonies?" Red demanded. "I've still gotta keep my eyes on those Chilean contractors. We should have the ramps completed tomorrow."

"Just between us chickens," Frank began, looking out over the expanse of the South Pacific Ocean beyond the small islet of Motu Nui, "we're probably going to have a little visit from two Soviet naval vessels in a couple of days. They've been spotted by Navy P3s and our surveillance satellites—seven hundred miles south of Hawaii and headed this way."

"Obregon knows that," Joyce pointed out. "He doesn't seem concerned."

"Well, maybe he knows something we don't," Red said.

"I think it's the other way around," Frank remarked. "Planes from the carrier *Kitty Hawk* are tracking the Soviet ships now, and the Navy's put together Task Force Sixty-Nine—the *Kitty Hawk*, the *Halsey*, and the *Cochrane*. The ocean around here is going to be full of ships pretty soon."

"Well, what the hell are the Soviets doing sending ships down here?"

"I don't know, Red," Joyce said, "but they've got a perfect right to put in here for a diplomatic visit under the international rules of the sea."

"Which means they may want to take a look at the *Atlantis*," Jackie added.

"Why?" Hap asked. "The Chilean report will shoot them down."

"Not necessarily," Joyce replied. "Frank, would you let the Soviet commander inside the *Atlantis* if he pays a social visit to Obregon and asks to see the Orbiter, whose presence on Pascua is, after all, the center of attention in the world press right now?"

"Hell, no," Lew Clay growled.

"Hold it, Lew. Joyce has a point," Frank noted, and then explained. "Yes, I'd take him aboard and show him everything—with all the media people taking pictures to beat hell. Know why?"

"Sure. What have we got to hide?" Hap said.

"Right. If they're playing games with us—and what else are they doing if they're sending two ships more than eight thousand miles from Vladivostok?—we'll play games with them, especially since Task Force Sixty-Nine's hot on their heels, and they know that from their own recon satellites." Frank sat back on a rock, clasped his hands around his knees, and grinned. "We'll get Obregon to take us out to the *Kharkov* in a boat, and *we'll* pay a social visit to *them*, with the U.S. Navy standing by and the media recording it all with long-focus lenses."

"Neat," Red observed, but obviously something was bothering him. "So somebody tell me why they're sending two ships eight thousand miles when we know they're doing it and they know we know. And when we're sending three of our best ships alongside them."

"Cosmetic cover-up," Jackie suddenly said.

"Huh?" Red questioned her.

"Diversion," Colonel Matt Hubbard added. "They're great chess players. I agree with Jackie. It may be a move to cover something else."

"What?"

"Who knows?" Hubbard admitted. "Got any ideas?"

"No, but that's why I wanted to get us all together without Obregon," Frank told them. "Look, we've got our own little problems as Americans if something happens—not that I distrust Obregon. I trust him, but he answers to a different boss than we do. I just want us to be prepared to defend the *Atlantis,* our aircraft, and our people if we have to."

"NASA Nine-Oh-Five will be here eventually, too," Red reminded them. "It's a bitch of a job, but they're cobbling-up a midair refueling system for her. They're going to test it en route to Santiago and here."

"Risky," Jackie said.

"The whole damned operation's risky, except that some of the people who planned it didn't think so," Red complained.

"Matt, can you liberate some M16 rifles or even some Ingram MAC10 submachine guns for us?" Frank asked.

"I've got MAC10s aboard my C-5s," Hubbard answered casually. "Not enough for everybody, but enough to discourage all but the most serious potential hijackers. Let me see what I can do about M16s. I used to run Coors beer from Colorado to some guys at Andrews. I'll call in a few debts."

"I might be able to get some MAC10s from my friends in Santiago," Joyce volunteered.

Frank shook his head. "No, Joyce, that might tip them off that we're suspicious of whatever's cooking. Matt can get weapons out of the Air Police or some of the Army's airborne boys he has to haul around from time to time."

"You're right," she said.

"Did I hear you right, Frank?" Jackie asked. "Are you saying we might have to shoot our way out of this?"

"No, but don't you think it's a good idea to be ready to if we have to? Damned if I know what goes through the twisty minds of the Russians. Who knows what they've got figured out now that we've managed to blow away their claims that this was a military mission?"

"Didn't they expect their claims wouldn't hold water once an inspection commission had a look?" Red asked.

"Maybe they didn't expect the Chileans to react as they did. Maybe they anticipated the UN Security Council would do it instead and that they'd be able to stack the deck a little bit," Joyce pointed out.

"Anybody here not know how to shoot?" Frank looked around the group sitting on the rocks in a semicircle facing the sea. Nobody said a thing. "I figured as much. No one does the sort of things we do without having learned how to use weapons at one time or another—including you, Joyce."

"Why, Frank, whatever made you think that nobody ever taught me how to shoot to kill if I had to?" she replied sweetly in a tone that belied the basic strength Frank knew was part of her. "Maybe Alfred M. Dewey doesn't know how, but he hasn't served in countries where people shoot at each other in the streets from time to time—I know how to hit with a MAC10 on full auto. Will you show me how to use an M16?"

"Gladly."

"Shooting and hitting's on my mind, too," Matt Hubbard admitted. "I don't exactly like the idea of having my airplanes flying around in skies full of Soviet Goblet and Goa antiaircraft missiles and Yak-36 fighter planes. Maybe I should've scheduled fighter cover after all when you first called me about this operation, Red."

"We'll have it anyway from the *Kitty Hawk*," Red commented.

Jackie exclaimed, "Whoever thought a contingency landing would result in an eyeball-to-eyeball confrontation with the Soviets?"

"That doesn't bother me as much as the question *why*," Frank replied.

CHAPTER FOURTEEN

"Well, where's the Soviet navy?" Red asked.

Although there was room for the basic NASA team in Ororito City, they had chosen to remain in the hotel so they could maintain the privacy of their "how-goes-it" breakfasts.

"They should've been hull-down on the northwest horizon last night at sundown—if my navigational calculations are right," Lew remarked. "They weren't."

"Obviously," Red said.

"Joyce, have you heard anything more from your boss at State?" Frank asked.

Joyce shook her head.

"That bothers me," Frank admitted. "What's delayed them?"

Juan Hey, who had been helping serve the food with the assistance of another Pascuan, heard this and remarked, "It is very simple, Miti King."

"Simple?"

Juan smiled and said, in the gentle manner of the Pascuans, "It's strange to me that you seek new worlds and still don't know your own. We know the sea and the sky the way you know the stars." He motioned out the window toward Hangaroa Road. "The heartbeat of the sea is different."

"It is?" Lew wondered. "How? What do you mean?"

"The waves on the beach are normally five per minute," Juan explained. "Yesterday the heartbeat of the sea changed. Today the waves arrive eight every minute. Look at the sky. What do you see?"

Frank looked at the clouds as a pilot. "High cirrus and cirrostratus. Mare's-tails. They seem to be focused in the northwest. I've got it, Juan: there's a low-pressure area out there."

"There is a big storm—a typhoon—a long distance from us, and it will not come to Pascua. It will go far to the north."

"South Pacific typhoon," Lew put in. "It's delayed them. We'd better see if Houston will squirt us some GOES-West pictures. Matt might want to know where the typhoon is and where it's heading."

After breakfast they walked to the ground station, and soon they were examining a picture of the South Pacific taken by the western geosynchronous weather satellite 23,400 miles over the equator. The picture told them that Juan Hey's reading of the sea was correct. Typhoon Bernard was 600 miles northwest of Pascua.

"Right across the course of both the Soviet ships and Task Force Sixty-Nine," Lew pointed out.

"I'm glad to know about it," Matt said with obvious relief. "Nothing between us and Santiago but the usual broken-to-scattered cumulus between three and eight thousand feet. The Air Weather boys were right: that South Pacific high-pressure area just sits out here all year and moves a thousand miles north and south according to the seasons. No wonder the weather's been so good."

"And no wonder they're short of water on Pascua," Hap added.

Because of the good weather, things had moved right along. The concrete pads for the stiffleg derrick and tag-line masts had been poured, and the stiffleg and tag-line masts were now set up. A C-5 had brought in the strong-back that was now being fitted over the *Atlantis*. NASA 905 was due to arrive at noon.

Life on Pascua had settled into the daily routine of preparing Mataveri for the arrival of NASA 905 and the eventual mating of the *Atlantis* to the carrier aircraft. The natives soon became accustomed to the huge C-5 transport aircraft that whined in over their heads on final approach to Mataveri. And because the work grew more highly scheduled and the eventual arrival of Soviet and American naval vessels was still just a matter of waiting, boredom set in. This was most evident among the journalists, some of whom decided that the big news story was over and went back to Santiago and New York, content to get pooled TV coverage from Pascua.

After the Chilean inspection commission's report and the death of two of its members, things became strangely quiet at the UN. The Soviets said nothing. The Chilean report was forwarded to the Security Council, but there was no vote on whether or not to accept it. Alfred M. Dewey told Joyce the United States didn't want to force a vote of acceptance in the Security Council because the Soviets would certainly veto it. The State Department was content to let the matter die of inattention, thereby saving face all around.

Joyce's recommendation that the President of the United States announce the award of the Legion of Merit to Admiral Montero and Colonel Ríos was quietly overlooked. But there were exchanges of diplomatic sympathy notes between Washington and Santiago, and the matter of the C-5 accident was left hanging. The Chileans and the U.S. National Transportation Safety Board announced intentions of investigating the incident.

The planned arrival of NASA 905 was the first big event in days. The operation would become photogenic again.

Frank, Lew, and Hap accompanied Matt into the flight-scheduling room, where they had spent most of their time helping the MAC officer set up and schedule the many flights into and out of Mataveri. Red joined them about nine A.M. in what had become the flight operations room in the radio shack below the tower. "We're all set for Nine-Oh-Five," he told them as he poured a cup of coffee and sat down. "Time for coffee anyway. When the caffeine level in my blood gets low, I get mean; I'm no longer my sweet, lovable self."

"You should've joined the Navy," Lew pointed out. "It runs on coffee."

"The Air Force would like to," Matt put in, "but we've had to stick to milk and Cokes. In general, Air Force coffee's so lousy."

"You can say that again," Lew grumbled.

"Tell me, Red, how did you NASA types finally solve

the range problem with Nine-Oh-Five?" Frank said. "Did you put in an in-flight refueling receptacle from a C-141B or a B-52H?"

"Couldn't. When Hank finally came to that conclusion and the Dryden gang was forced to think their way out of the problem it became relatively simple," Red explained, while he sipped coffee. "Since they didn't need to transfer a lot of fuel in a hurry the way they do with a B-52, they got smart and installed a probe off an old A-7. With the probe-and-drogue system, there's no need for high-pressure fuel piping. Sure, it takes forever and a day to transfer enough fuel, but they're in no hurry as long as they take it aboard faster than the engines burn it off. Boeing installed a series of bladder tanks—the kind they use when they ferry a little Seven-Three-Seven to Europe—on the old passenger deck over the center of gravity, and Hank's got unlimited range now with in-flight refueling."

"All of which goes to prove when you've got good engineers on the job and they've got to perform, they come up with an answer," Hap added.

The door to the room opened and Ernesto Obregon walked in, a broad smile on his lean face. "Gentlemen, good morning. I thought you might like to know two naval vessels are in the territorial waters of Isla de Pascua."

"The Soviet ships?" Frank asked, getting to his feet.

Obregon shook his head and led them outside. He gave Frank a pair of binoculars.

A cruiser and a destroyer were on station about three miles off Hangaroa. From their flagstaffs flew the national colors of Chile.

"Two of our best ships: the cruiser *O'Higgins* and the destroyer *Serrano*," Obregon remarked. "I once served on the *Serrano*."

"Why didn't you tell us they were coming, Ernesto?" Frank asked.

Obregon shrugged. "Did you think the Armada de Chile would ignore the C-5 incident and the Soviet vessels? After all, Pascua is of strategic importance as well as being a sheep station."

That made Frank feel better.

Obregon then left Flight Operations to prepare for the captains of the two Chilean warships who were to come ashore later, as required by naval protocol. Things were quiet with no C-5s on the island and only one C-130 standing by for contingencies. Early on, Matt had decided to keep one Herk on Pascua at all times just to provide a quick airlift to Santiago if necessary. The C-5 explosion had made him very leery; he had been a green MAC pilot during the days of the pullout from Vietnam, and he knew that even military transport pilots could become involved in combat operations.

"Couldn't get Ingram MAC10s for you," Matt reported quietly to Frank. "But we've got a bunch of M16 rifles and enough ammunition to supply an army."

"Where'd you put them?" Frank asked.

Hubbard jerked his thumb over his shoulder. "Back there behind the crates some of our gear came in. I brought them in during a very busy time, and none of the Chileans noticed. And they'll never look over there."

"Bet they're all packed in cosmoline," Hap remarked. "I've never seen the government ship anything that wasn't sealed so tight or greased so thoroughly it couldn't survive thirty years under fifty feet of water in the Houston ship channel."

"Nope. These babies are ready to use. Got 'em on consignment from the Air Police armory at Andrews. The major in charge owed me a few favors," Hubbard explained.

"Pascua Tower, Redeemer Zero-One-Three, Ostra intersection, landing Mataveri," barked the loudspeaker.

"Redeemer Zero-One-Three, Pascua Tower. Pascua weather clear, visibility thirty kilometers, temperature two-seven Celsius, wind one-two-zero at five, altimeter one-zero-zero-four, using Runway One-Zero. Cleared visual approach Runway One-Zero. Report the aerodrome in sight."

"Redeemer Zero-One-Three."

Matt remained silent for a moment, then picked up a clipboard from the table and looked at the sheaves of paper on it. He looked back up at the now-silent loudspeaker. "I didn't think we had any airlift planes scheduled before NASA Nine-Oh-Five. Frank, did you schedule anything this morning?"

"No, and I don't think Lew did either."

Hap shook his head. "I didn't schedule an airlift plane this morning."

Matt picked up another clipboard and ran his finger down a list of assigned aircraft calls. "I don't think we've got a Redeemer Zero-One-Three assigned. Nobody wants that call. There's no Redeemer Zero-One-Three, and nothing scheduled before NASA Nine-Oh-Five!"

Jumping out of his chair, Matt began tearing the tops off crates stacked over in the corner. He pulled out an M16 rifle and tossed it at Frank. "Cram your pockets full of ammo clips from that box on the left, Frank. Then go find Obregon. Hap, grab this M16 and get up to Ororito City; alert the people there and have them shag-ass down here to pick up rifles. I'll alert my Air Force boys and Red Richardson." He checked the action on an M16 and slipped a clip of ammunition into the receiver. "The Palestinians tried to sneak one in like this at Aswan once. We'll handle this one the same way." He picked up a mike and snapped, "Tower, this is Operations. When Redeemer Zero-One-Three lands, direct them to taxi to parking on the south ramp." He put down the mike and added, "We'll be ready for them there."

Frank commandeered one of the Air Force pickup trucks parked outside and careened down the narrow dirt road toward Hangaroa and the military governor's quarters. All the while, he was thinking, *Where's Joyce? My God, I've got to find her so she doesn't get caught in this!*

He found Obregon just leaving his quarters. "Ernesto, red alert! We've got an unknown aircraft trying to sneak in with a nonexistent call sign."

Obregon didn't hesitate a moment. "Come with me," he snapped, and dashed back into his quarters. Frank followed, and Obregon led him to a part of the casern Frank hadn't visited before. The small room was equipped with quite modern and very sophisticated radio equipment.

"I didn't know you had this stuff, Ernesto," Frank said, noting that it was very new, single-sideband U.S. Navy gear from which nobody had even bothered to remove the markings or serial numbers.

Obregon didn't waste any time as he turned things on. He remarked, "Frank, I'm certain you haven't told me everything you and your people brought to Pascua either— for example, that M16 rifle you're carrying. I'm not ill-equipped or unable to defend the island. And there are marine detachments aboard both the *O'Higgins* and the *Serrano*. What arrangements have been made at Mataveri?"

"Hubbard's having the aircraft directed to the south-ramp area."

"Good—if the plane chooses to follow the instructions of the tower. Do we have enough time for Richardson to block off the entrances to the north ramp with construction equipment?"

"Should have. There's at least twenty minutes before that plane lands—depending on what it is."

Obregon shook his head. "But not enough time to get a marine unit ashore. I'll report to our ships and have my garrison up there right away. Find Richardson and have him block those ramp entrances where the *Atlantis* is parked. I'll get there shortly."

But Frank didn't go directly back to Mataveri. He went instead to the Hotel Hangaroa, but Joyce wasn't there. On his way back to Mataveri, he asked himself, What am I doing, chasing all over this island, trying to find a woman I shouldn't be involved with in the first place? Ellie, forgive me!

Joyce and Richardson were in the satellite ground station. Red was talking to Houston when Frank burst in. "Did either of you get the word?" he asked immediately.

Red looked up. "No, what's going on? I'm talking to Joe Marvin."

"Give me the mike, Red. I'll fill everybody in." Richardson moved to one side, and Frank sat down at the console. "Joe, we got trouble. I think we can handle it, but pass the word to Washington." He gave a quick rundown of the situation, then said, "We're ready for them, but we've got to get the hell out of this ground station. I'll talk to you when it's over." He put down the mike without waiting for a reply, then turned to Joyce and Red. "Get over to the Operations shack and pick up a rifle. You said you could shoot, and you may have to. Red, do you have time to move equipment to block the entrances to the north ramp?"

"I'll try," Richardson snapped, and moved.

Frank looked at Joyce. "I was afraid you wouldn't get the word and would stumble into this mess. Grab an M16, find Jackie, and get back to the hotel. Shoot if you have to."

"Where are you going to be?"

"At the *Atlantis*. She's probably the target if this is indeed a raid."

"It probably is," Joyce observed. "And you're going to need all the firepower you can get because you're on the defensive and don't know how many are coming in. This could be only the first planeload, Frank."

"I told you to get a rifle and go back to the hotel," Frank reminded her.

"And I'm telling you it's my job to get the *Atlantis* off Pascua, too. So I'll be over there with the rest of you, and don't try to pull rank on me—you aren't in charge here, Frank. There's no rule that says a diplomat can't shoot. In fact, it's about time we diplomats had the chance to shoot back rather than just cower in a corner. *Vamos!* Just don't stand there, Frank! That plane's getting closer every second, and we haven't got time to argue!"

There was hardly time to get everyone in position. Frank found Lew and Jackie sitting in the shade under the *Atlantis*. He and Joyce thrust M16s at them. "We were worried about terrorists? Well, they may be on their way. There's an unidentified plane coming in."

Jackie and Lew looked at each other, then both loaded clips into their rifles.

"Never thought I'd have to defend an Orbiter in a good old shootout," Lew remarked.

"There isn't much cover out here," Frank pointed out. "We'll have to see where they land and where they commence their attack. If we have to, we'll take cover around the trucks and the Manitowock crane. If they start throwing explosives or shooting rockets, get under a truck. Here come some of Ernesto's boys."

"Think a bullet can penetrate the side of the cargo bay, Frank?"

"I don't know, Hap. The ceramic HRSI and LRSI might stop some, but I'd guess seven-millimeter stuff would go right through the FRSI coatings."

"I hope nothing hits that Landsat. That's a real expensive and delicate piece of gear."

"I hope nothing hits *you*. You're more expensive and delicate," Frank pointed out. "And don't hand me anything about having been produced by relatively unskilled labor, either. Okay, here it comes!"

There was no mistaking the fat hull and the big high wing with two radial piston engines. It was an old World War II PBY-5 Catalina amphibious flying boat with no visible markings on it. Hundreds of them were still flying in various backwaters of the world, especially in South America, where they could land on rivers and lakes, or even on unprepared fields.

"Can't be many aboard," Frank said. "Maybe thirty people at most. We'll have them outnumbered and outgunned—and they don't know we know they're coming."

"Maybe they've taken that into account," Lew observed.

Obregon's voice boomed out over a loudspeaker near the tower, first in Spanish, then in English. "Everyone, take cover and hold your fire. Let them take the first action. We have them outnumbered. I repeat: take cover and hold your fire."

"That's going to be hard to do," Lew noted, "if and when they start shooting."

"Damn, Red didn't get his equipment in place in time!" Frank swore.

The Catalina was flying light. She had obviously burned off a lot of fuel. She was down, and stopped on the first 500 feet of Runway One-Zero.

"Redeemer Zero-One-Three," boomed the loudspeaker on the tower, "turn right—repeat, turn right—at the intersection and park on the south ramp."

The pilot of the PBY ignored the order. He turned left onto the north ramp, where the *Atlantis* was parked.

"Redeemer Zero-One-Three, this is the military governor of Isla de Pascua," the tower loudspeaker barked again as Obregon tried to make contact with the PBY by radio. "Stop there! Stop your engines. You are under the guns of the naval garrison of Isla de Pascua. Stop your engines and disembark with your hands in the air."

The PBY engines coughed and the propellers came to a halt. The plane sat not more than 200 yards from the *Atlantis*, pointed directly at the Orbiter.

Somebody opened fire with an assault rifle from the front turret of the old patrol boat.

Frank had heard that sound before. It was a Kalashnikov AK47 assault rifle, made by the millions by the Soviet Union and the Warsaw Pact countries, copied in China, and encountered all over the world in the hands of revolutionaries, guerrillas, and terrorists.

The burst hit the *Atlantis* over Frank's head. Chips of high-temperature ceramic tile spalled off the *Atlantis* where she had been hit. Frank and Lew opened fire from behind the two-and-a-half-ton trucks between the PBY and the *Atlantis*, aiming toward that front turret. It had been a long time since Frank had used an M16; his burst wasn't on target. Neither was Lew's.

Hatches on the aft hull of the PBY popped open, and there came the thud of mortar fire. The PBY rocked backward on her main wheels with the recoil.

"Under the trucks! Take cover! Mortars!" Frank yelled, diving for the safety of the truck and pulling Joyce down with him. He wasn't worried about getting hit until the terrorists secured the range; the recoil of the mortars rocking the PBY wouldn't help them attain accuracy quickly.

Then came the sound of two M16s firing in bursts from above. Frank squirmed around to see Jackie and Hap in the open hatch of the *Atlantis*, returning the fire from the PBY.

"How'd they get up there?" Frank growled. "The fools! They're prime targets in that hatch!" He knew why they were there. That Landsat was Hap's baby, and he was protecting it. As for Jackie, the *Atlantis* was something to be defended with her life, if necessary. Neither of them had been under fire before. Neither knew that the place to defend the *Atlantis* best was on the ground.

Two mortar shells landed on the ramp, well beyond the *Atlantis*. From the explosion, Frank knew they were up against light sixty-millimeter M2 mortars, again a type that was made in the Communist-bloc countries and supplied to guerrillas and revolutionary forces worldwide.

Someone inside the PBY lobbed four smoke grenades onto the ramp around the plane. Through the thick, enveloping smoke, Frank and Joyce watched as hatches flew open and two dozen armed men poured forth, screaming and yelling at the top of their lungs. It was difficult to see them through the smoke, but they were all wearing ragtag, unmarked, dark green fatigue uniforms with soft hats. They charged toward the *Atlantis*.

There was no need for Obregon to give the order to open fire. A hail of bullets from the Chilean SIG510 automatic rifles and M2 carbines ripped into the smoke, into the PBY, and into the horde of charging men, some of whom dropped to the ramp to provide covering fire for others running full tilt toward the *Atlantis*. Four more mortar rounds were fired from the PBY's aft blisters. All were overranged.

Frank's M16, on full-auto, bucked against his shoulder as he ripped off a clip toward the rushing men. Reloading, he saw Joyce run off semiauto bursts, carefully picking her targets.

One terrorist almost made it to the truck under which Frank and Joyce were firing. Frank shot his legs off.

Somebody hit the wing tanks of the PBY, and the avgas remaining went off in the billowing ball of orange flame.

The terrorists obviously had not expected or fully planned that their arrival would be greeted by the defensive force that was present. Either the terrorists were counting totally on the element of surprise, or the operation had been poorly planned, Frank decided.

Within a minute, it was all over. The 200 yards of ramp between the wrecked PBY and the *Atlantis* were covered with bodies, some of them writhing, some lying still. Five others had jumped from the burning PBY, but the Chilean naval garrison had cut them down almost before they hit the ramp.

Frank turned to Joyce. "You okay?"

"Yes. Scared, but all right."

"Welcome to the club," Frank told her. "I never joined NASA to do this."

"Did you kill anyone?"

"Yeah, that guy right in front of us. You?"

"I don't know. I don't think so."

"You don't need to know. Come on, let's get out of here. There's Ernesto and Doc Esteban. There may be some wounded. Maybe we can get them to tell us where they came from and who backed this little fracas."

The two of them crawled backward and emerged from under the truck. Obregon was walking around the ramp, looking over the dead and dying terrorists. Part of his garrison was with him, watchful lest some wounded terrorist attempted to shoot.

The military governor stood over one moaning man, looked at him, and muttered, "*Mi sentido me pesa, Luis.*" He pulled his Colt .45 from its holster and shot the wounded man in the head.

"My God, Ernesto must have known him!" Joyce breathed, turning her head away from the sight.

Dr. Esteban saw this and strode up to Obregon, arguing loudly in Spanish.

"He's telling Obregon that it's not right to shoot wounded men," Joyce translated quickly for Frank.

"And it's not right to blow up airplanes with people in them," Obregon said levelly in English. He pointed his Colt .45 automatic pistol and deliberately shot Dr. Esteban through the chest.

CHAPTER FIFTEEN

Before Frank and Joyce could react, Hap called out behind them from the open hatch of the *Atlantis*, "Frank, give me a hand here. Jackie's been hit!"

"Oh, my God," Frank groaned, "and Ernesto just shot the only doctor on the island."

It was Lew who reacted, dropping his rifle and sprinting back to where Jackie's nonregulation rope ladder swung from the open hatch. He clambered up and disappeared.

The welfare of his ship and crew came before anything else in Frank's mind, Obregon and Esteban notwithstanding. He turned and followed Lew.

The black and white tiled sides of the *Atlantis* had taken a few hits from the AK47 assault rifles. The impact had shattered some tiles, cracked others, and penetrated more of them than Frank cared to see. It would take some work to put the *Atlantis* back into shape for orbital flight again.

Jackie Hart lay unconscious on the floor of the mid-deck. She had been hit on the left side of the lower abdomen.

Hap and Lew both stood over her. "The slug went clean through her," Hap remarked. "I don't know if we can stop the bleeding or not."

"Dammit, Frank, get *some* kind of help for her," Lew growled. "We can't lose her. I can't lose her. Get some medical help here quick!"

Frank had never seen his copilot so emotional before. He had sensed there was something between Lew and Jackie, but neither had confided in him. Now Frank knew exactly what had been going on. He scrambled back down the rope ladder to the ramp and walked purposefully over to where Obregon was still examining dead and dying terrorists, pistol in hand.

"Ernesto," Frank said, "Jackie's been hit. She's bleeding to death up in the *Atlantis*. And you've just shot the only doctor on the island. So help me God, if Jackie dies, you're going to have to answer to *me* for it! Where can we get medical help for her now?"

Obregon snapped his head around to look at Frank. "Jackie? Hit?"

"That's what I said, Ernesto. And why did you shoot the island's only doctor in cold blood here?"

"Because he was responsible for the C-5 destruction, for the death of my admiral and Colonel Ríos, and, indirectly, for all these dead and dying men," Obregon explained, his tone suddenly sad. "Don't ask me how I know, but I did what had to be done. Esteban was the only person who boarded *every* airplane that landed here in order to conduct a public health inspection. I know that he could and did place a bomb aboard the C-5 Galaxy."

"What makes you so sure of that?" Frank asked.

"Because I know Dr. Victor Esteban was an agent of the Soviet KGB." He looked up at a sudden, new sound, and Frank followed his gaze.

A Bell 206 helicopter with a Chilean insignia and *CA-02 O'Higgins, Armada de Chile* on its sides was settling to the ramp. The door slid open, and men wearing white arm-bands with red crosses and carrying equipment poured out onto the Mataveri ramp.

Obregon holstered his pistol and put his hand on Frank's shoulder. "Don't worry, my friend. We'll have Jackie Hart in the sick bay aboard the *O'Higgins* in less than ten minutes. After all, Chile's not as backward and primitive as some of your media people think."

The Chilean naval paramedics went to work quickly once Obregon gave them instructions. Two members of the Pascua garrison had sustained wounds, but Jackie was the worst casualty.

Obregon shook his head as they lowered Jackie, on a stretcher, from the *Atlantis* to the ramp. "How did she get hit?" he wondered half aloud.

Frank sighed. "She's a seasoned fighter, but not with a gun. She was up there fighting for what she hoped would be hers someday."

As she was being taken across the ramp to the chopper, Jackie regained consciousness enough to recognize Lew alongside her. "You okay, Lew?" she asked him clearly.

"I'm okay, Jackie. And you'll be okay, too. I'm going with you to make sure."

"I knew you would, honey. I knew you would all along." She grasped his hand and held it in a surprisingly strong grip.

"She'll make it," Lew remarked to Frank as they passed him.

"Sure she'll make it, Lew. She's tough." Frank would have a lot to say about Jackie Hart to that clown, Duke Kellogg, when they got back to Houston. One whole hell of a lot, as a matter of fact.

A new sound intruded upon them: a Boeing 747 with red, white, and blue stripes along its sides and *NASA 905* on its rudder touched down on the runway next to the ramp, the sixteen tires of its main landing gear leaving a cloud of white smoke as they screeched on the asphalt, and its four fanjet engines roaring into the thrust reversers.

Jackie heard the sounds. A smile spread across her face as she was put aboard the Chilean helicopter, Lew at her side.

Red appeared, looked distastefully at the wrecked PBY-5

on the ramp, and handed his M16 to Frank. "Well, now that the fireworks are over and Nine-Oh-Five's here, I can get on with my job. And I guess you'll want me to get this wreck off the ramp, too, won't you?"

"Leave it where it is," Obregon told him. "I've got to go through it and see if there're any papers or other documents aboard that'll confirm what I know about it and where it came from."

"Where *did* it come from, Ernesto?" Frank asked.

"A place called Lake Rogagua, but the Bolivian government didn't know about it. It refueled at sea off Punta Coles, Peru, last night from a submarine that flew no colors but came from another Santiago a long way around Cape Horn. Richardson, I don't know if I'll find anything, but I've got to look. I'll let you know when to move it. Shouldn't be more than twenty-four hours."

"Okay, Governor, I'll work around you somehow," Red told him. "I don't like this game of international intrigue you people play. It almost caused me to get my ass shot off. When are you going to quit playing around with it and get to work on some serious problems? You know, maybe I ought to get involved myself. Maybe I could help spank some of those big playful boys with their guns and ships and planes and thermonuclear devices. Maybe I could. Maybe I will." He walked off.

"I hope he does," Obregon remarked, looking at the retreating back of the NASA mission manager. "There're plenty of people like Red Richardson who love to work with the problems of things. We could use more who like to work with the really big problems of people."

"Ernesto, I think you're something more than just the military governor of Pascua. You seem to know a lot about things that you shouldn't know anything about at all," Frank observed. "I think we need to go somewhere and have a little private talk, my friend."

Obregon shook his head. "And I don't think so at all, Frank. Your job is command pilot of the *Atlantis*, and your responsibility is to get it back to the United States. My job is to protect it and all of you while you're here. How I do my job is, frankly, my concern. But I'll tell you this much: I didn't expect this to come when it did, or I'd have been better prepared. As it was, they rushed me. Otherwise, Jackie would never have been hurt. So I must apologize for not doing my job very well in that respect. But the Armada de Chile will take care of her. And she'll be transferred to the *Kitty Hawk* when Task Force Sixty-Nine arrives tomorrow—escorting the two Soviet vessels, by the way."

"How'd you know? Did Joyce tell you about Task Force Sixty-Nine?"

Captain Ernesto Obregon chuckled. "Colonel King," he said, with deliberate emphasis on Frank's military title, "all military and naval organizations must have some sort of intelligence operation in order to function. Correct? The world today would be a much different place if, say, Admiral Kimmel had received that warning telegram before the attack on Pearl Harbor—or if Admiral Nagumo had known there was no air defense left on Oahu after his second wave had completed its attack."

"Nice try, Ernesto, but you didn't answer my question."

"Let's just say that the intelligence activities of the Armada de Chile are certainly not unsophisticated. And we have some help. We appreciate the fact that the United States is willing to send naval elements to assist us, but we will protect ourselves and our guests—Joyce, Frank, Hap, shall we go have some lunch?"

"Hold it, Governor." Casey had walked up, followed by a contingent of reporters and TV cameramen. "The media people have asked me to get you all together now that the shooting's over."

Some of the journalists were flushed, while others were still getting their color back. Some of them had been scared. For the real pros, this was the chance of a lifetime, an opportunity to get that Pulitzer-winning coverage. But not all were that good, not all were used to witnessing raw violence, and they didn't look well.

As a matter of fact, Frank thought, Casey didn't look too good himself.

Obregon glanced at Frank, then at Hap, then at Joyce. It was Joyce who replied, "Why not? These people have to do their jobs, too."

"Did you get good coverage, Casey?" Frank asked.

"Great stuff. Listen, the way the crew stood up there and defended the *Atlantis* was heroic. Some of the media gang now figure if a Space Shuttle Orbiter is so important that somebody'd try to blow it up, there must be something more to it than most people in the States think. We've got a bunch of real enthusiastic converts now. This whole Pascua affair has helped NASA immensely."

"A lot of it's been due to the way you've handled the reporters, Casey," Joyce told him.

"Maybe. I've just tried to keep them happy, that's all. So let's get this show on the road. Can we hold the get-together right out here where it happened?"

"Uh, let's move off a bit so that all these bodies on the ramp don't show," Herb Haynes remarked. "Sure, it was exciting, but let's not be macabre about reporting it."

"Why not?" It was Marty Soloman again. "A little blood and gore goes over great. TV audiences love it. Just look at the series with the top Nielsen ratings."

"And it makes some of us sick to our stomachs, Marty Baby." Surprisingly, this came from Alice Arnold. "Go shoot all the gore you want, Marty. You're right, Herb, let's move over a little bit, even though I don't file a video report."

"Speaking of sick, are you all right, Casey?" Herb asked.

"Me? Sure. Little indigestion. Gas pain up high here. Doctor once said something about a hiatus hernia, whatever that is. I get symptoms every once in a while." Casey thumped his chest with his fist. "Okay, Governor, how about you along with Frank and Joyce? Where's Professor Pérez?"

"I ordered him to remain in my quarters at the casern. No sense risking Chile's top astronautics expert," Obregon explained.

"Okay, troops, I'll arrange for you to meet with Pérez later," Casey told his media following. "Go ahead, gang, it's all yours."

Somehow, Frank managed to get through yet another press conference without blowing his cool.

The rest of the day wasn't any better, although it helped to get away from Mataveri and the reminders of what had taken place there. The captains of the *O'Higgins* and the *Serrano* came ashore by helicopter later in the afternoon, and Frank found himself accepting an invitation to dine aboard the *O'Higgins* that evening with Joyce, Hap, and Obregon.

"I'd like to apologize, gentlemen, but we didn't come to Pascua dressed for formal occasions. I trust that our flight coveralls will be acceptable," Frank said. The captain of the *O'Higgins* acquiesced because he had never entertained astronauts or a diplomatic representative of the United States aboard his ship. They were flown to the heavy cruiser in the Bell helicopter, and they saw Lew shortly after being piped aboard.

"She's still in surgery," Lew told them.

Frank didn't say anything.

"She's going to make it, isn't she?" Joyce asked.

"She'd better. I told her so," Lew remarked in a quiet voice, quite unlike him, "because I suddenly found out that I care very much whether she makes it or not. I never felt that way about any woman before. Do you know what I mean?"

"Yeah, I know what you mean, Lew," Frank acknowledged, suddenly aware of a very real problem in his own life.

"Can you stick around until she comes out of surgery?" Lew pleaded. "Jackie wants Joyce as her maid of honor, and I'd like to have you and Hap share the honor of best man. The captain of the *O'Higgins* said he's got the authority to perform the ceremony, but we want Father Francisco to do it, if he'll officiate over a non-Catholic wedding. If not, I'll ask Obregon."

Later that evening, after a very fine meal with the three captains of the Armada de Chile, they went back down to the sick bay. Jackie had made it. Lew had worried, but Frank never had any doubts.

It was a very simple ceremony, and Father Francisco did fly out to the *O'Higgins* to officiate.

Frank felt better the next morning. But the usual "how-goes-it" breakfast found the conversation centered around the actual job of recovering the *Atlantis*, a task that now involved several days of careful preparations prior to lifting the Orbiter into the air and towing NASA 905 under it. Red wasn't taking chances. "I'll check everything twice, and then do it again," he promised. "I've come this far, and damned if I want to drop the *Atlantis* now."

They were on the ramp at Mataveri, checking the strongback attachments, the stiffleg-derrick lines, the Manitowock crane, the tag-line masts, and the attachment points, when the big show took place.

Frank happened to be on the wing of the *Atlantis* and looked out to sea. Five ships were on the northwest horizon. "I believe the call is 'Sail ho!' But I don't think it's applicable in this case," he yelled down to Red. "Two groups . . . a carrier, a cruiser, and a frigate, and two other ships I don't recognize to the west of them."

"Pascua Tower, Soviet Navy One, flight of four, ten kilometers northwest. Request permission for low pass." There was a slight Slavic accent to the radio call broadcast by the loudspeaker on the Mataveri tower, but Frank thought the Soviet pilot had been trained very well in aviation English.

"Soviet Navy One, Pascua Tower. Low pass approved."

"Ah, Pascua Tower," came another voice with a slow Tennessee drawl that couldn't be mistaken for anything but an American fighter pilot's, "United States Navy Hawk Alpha, flight of eleven, following Soviet Navy One. Request permission to follow their low pass—*and we're right on your tail, Ivan, all the way!*"

"Hey, somebody get Casey on the ball!" Frank yelled. "Get the media out for this. It's got to be good with those Navy jocks tailing the Russkies!"

Casey was on the ball. Some of the cameramen missed the show because they weren't set up, although Casey had told them the Soviet and American naval vessels would be arriving at Pascua today.

In less than two minutes, the ground at Mataveri shook as a flight of four Yak-36 Forger STOL Soviet naval fighters barreled down the Mataveri airstrip not more than fifty feet off the runway. At the north end, the vertical takeoff fighters suddenly seemed to change course and go straight up as their pilots shifted the thrust vectors of the swiveling jet nozzles.

But right behind them were three F-14 Tomcats in the "missing man" formation: the slot position in the formation was vacant in honor of Colonel Amaldo Carlos Ríos of the Fuerzas Aéreas de Chile and the ten Americans of the U.S. Air Force who had lost their lives in the C-5.

Frank, who had joined Casey and the reporters to help provide background, hardly had time to explain the significance of this display before the second flight of Navy planes roared over, four F-18 Hornets that pulled up at the north end of the runway and climbed vertically right past the Soviet formation. The third and last flight of four, AV-8B SkyHarriers, thundered over Mataveri, then came to a dead standstill in the air, maintaining formation at 100 feet, their swiveling jet nozzles pointed down. The VTOL attack planes transitioned to forward flight again and climbed up to join the rest of the Navy formation flying alongside the Soviet Yak-36 Forgers.

"Pretty show," Frank remarked to the TV crews taping the peaceful aerial confrontation. He hoped it would remain peaceful, because the *Atlantis* was certainly a sitting duck, to say nothing of NASA 905. "This is probably the first time Soviet and American naval aircraft have been over the same island at the same time. It's interesting the Soviets are keeping a respectful distance. They're obviously doing their best to avoid any maneuvers to provide a comparison of performance between their Yak-36s and the planes from the *Kitty Hawk*."

"Why do you suppose the Soviet ships came all the way to Easter Island?" Herb Haynes asked.

Frank shrugged, not really wanting to tell what he thought might be the truth. Joyce had probably been right in her assessment. "Maybe they just wanted to get a good, close look at the *Atlantis*," he replied.

He noticed that Casey had suddenly sat down on the ramp. "Casey, you all right?"

"Yeah, I think so. Haven't gotten much sleep lately. Lot going on. Stomach's acting up again. Lots of gas pains." The NASA Public Affairs man, upon whose shoulders had rested so much of the world's view of the recovery of the *Atlantis* and the activities that surrounded it, looked very pale. He put his hand over his chest. "Hell of a gas pain—way up high this time . . . And my arms feel tingly."

Frank and Hap were at his side immediately. "Casey, lie down flat on your back. Lie down!" Hap snapped at him. "Those probably aren't gas pains. You may be having a heart attack."

"Somebody bring me a blanket," Frank called to no one in particular. "Red, there's one in the *Atlantis* if you can't scratch one up in a hurry. And get it in a hurry, please."

Casey's heart stopped.

Hap began cardiopulmonary resuscitation immediately. "Anybody else know how to do CPR to spell me?" he called out. Alice Arnold did.

Frank did the best thing he could do for Casey right then. He ran to the tower, climbed the stairs two at a time, and burst in on the Chilean tower operator. Almost completely out of breath, he said, "Call those American planes. Get in touch with the *Kitty Hawk* right now. We've got a man dying on the ramp!"

The young ensign froze, then handed the mike to Frank.

Ten minutes later, a Navy Sea Hawk chopper from the *Kitty Hawk* set down on the ramp with a paramedic team. They got Casey to the *Kitty Hawk* alive, but they had to defibrillate him twice en route. Hap went with him, spelling Alice Arnold and the Navy paramedics at CPR.

When the current emergency was over and the skies over Rapa Nui were empty again, Frank stood on the ramp at Mataveri and looked up at the *Atlantis*. "Are you worth it? Are you really worth it?" he asked the Space Shuttle.

It's always been worth it, something told him in the back of his mind. Did anybody ever tell you that a frontier never claimed any lives? Did anybody ever tell you that being a pioneer means discovering new and more horrible ways to die? You want to sail a new ocean? How can you if you won't risk losing sight of the shore?

"Red, I'm taking the rest of the day off. Just don't drop the *Atlantis*, okay?"

"I won't drop her. Where you going, Frank? Don't tell me this operation's got to you, too."

"You're damned right it has. I'm going for a walk. If I'm not back for dinner, come looking for me with a bottle of vodka. No, make that Scotch, and we'll both get smashed. I've got to think."

Rapa Nui isn't very large—only eleven miles long and fifteen miles wide at its greatest extent. It would be hard to get lost on it. But Frank didn't wander. Something drew him back to those seven huge stone statues, the *moai* on their pedestal facing the western sea, where five ships lay at anchor offshore.

As he approached, he noticed a small figure sitting impassively at the base of the *moai*. His first impulse was to turn and walk eastward to avoid the person. But he saw it was Juan Hey, who looked up and caught sight of him, then, without gesturing, turned to look back at the sea again.

Frank didn't know what made him sit down beside Juan Hey and look quietly at the ocean below them, the seven stoic shapes gazing out in the same direction.

It was Frank who finally spoke. "You come here often, Juan?"

"Yes, Miti King."

"Why do you keep calling me 'Miti'? Is it a Pascuan title?"

"It is the Pascuan way of saying 'señor,' Miti King."

"Why do you come here? Is there something special about this place?"

"Yes. No. Perhaps. Those of us who are left were never told. But it must have been a magic place to my ancestors because it still is. Why do I come? To watch the sea and the sky. To learn from them. To learn from the grasses. To learn from the stones. To learn from the *moai* and the gods."

"If the *moai* are responsible for the part of the world they face, are these seven responsible for those ships out there and the people on them?"

Juan Hey nodded. A long moment passed before he replied, "Jackie Hart and Casey Laskewitz will be all right, Miti King. These *moai* will watch and guard them. And your people have great *mana*. Jackie and Casey both have great *akuaku* with much *mana*."

"I wish I understood exactly what you're saying."

"You do. You are really a very great and powerful *ariki*. You may even be Makemake, except Father Francisco says it can't be true."

"Juan, I don't know your language. I don't know if you're calling me a saint or a sinner," Frank admitted.

"I do not understand your great ship *Atlantis*, and you do not understand that you are *ariki* with powerful *mana*."

Juan Hey remained silent again for a long minute, then continued. "*Mana* is great power and great magic, and an *ariki* like yourself is a person with very high position and *mana*."

"One man's *mana* is another man's technology," Frank muttered.

"But, Miti King, *mana* is more than your guns and weapons. True *mana* is the magic used by an *ariki* for the good of the people. And you have great *mana*."

Frank understood now. "Juan, *mana* isn't good or bad; it's the way *mana* is used that counts."

"That is what I said."

"Hmmmm. Yes, you did. My mistake. And we've made many mistakes here with our *mana*. It may not be true *mana* the way you just defined it."

"But it really is *mana*. Do you know what your *mana* has already done for us on Pascua?"

"Created problems for you."

Juan Hey shook his head. "Rapa Nui has seen many people come. Some took Pascuans as slaves. Some imprisoned and killed us here. And some brought us great *mana*, which we've remembered and cherished. But the world is changing, Miti King, because we have been brought only great *mana* since the days of my grandfather. The Chileans brought the beginning of the end of isolation for this island that was once at the center of the world. Now you have brought us even more *mana*, and we are again truly at the center of the world."

Frank was having trouble following the strange reasoning patterns of this man from an ancient culture. "Tell me what you think I've brought you, Juan."

The little Pascuan chanted a song:

> "*O Hotu Matu'a i-unga-mai-ai*
> *Ia Hau Maka, i toona tuura*
> *Ka-kimi te maara mo te ariki*
> *Mo te ariki, mo toma.*"

"What are you singing about?" Frank asked.

"A very old legend that is your story, Miti King," Juan Hey told him. "I cannot translate it exactly, but it means, 'The god Hotu Matu'a sent here/His servant Hau Maka/

To search for a landing place/For the king to land. And you did, Miti King. Not you alone, but also those who came after you once you discovered Rapa Nui as your landing place. You brought the people who brought more *mana*. Red Richardson has brought us the satellite ground station and television receivers. Now the rest of the world comes to us and we see it. *Mana*."

"I didn't know he'd done that," Frank said.

"You have been busy with other things. Now, for the first time, Pascuans are no longer isolated. And Casey Laskewitz has brought people who have made Rapa Nui again *te Pito o te Henua*."

"Juan, I'm afraid the things we brought you that you think are great *mana* right now may destroy what you have here," Frank remarked. "We didn't intend to change your home."

"What else is there but change? Rapa Nui changes every day. It may not look as if it changes, but it does. It has always changed with new people and new *mana*. We are not afraid of change on Rapa Nui, Miti King."

He rose to his feet. "Change is part of *mana*, just as change is part of each day. Even the sunset changes and is different. Thank you for your *mana* and for those who brought more of it after you, Miti King. All change does not destroy, and this change will not destroy us. We are stronger than that. One must be strong to live at the center of the world.

"I must return to the hotel. *Ia orana korua!*" And he was gone, leaving Frank to try to puzzle out exactly what he had heard. He didn't think he was at the center of the world but somehow at the cusp between two worlds.

Well, the Pascuans would have to handle things the best they could. If Juan Hey was right, they would make it. They would grow. They would survive. They would perhaps even prosper now that they were no longer isolated. How much longer could the military governor of Isla de Pascua impose the restrictions required by the old regulations? Not very long, once the Pascuans discovered what the rest of the world was like.

He shook his head. "But the price . . . the price . . ."

"What price?"

He looked up as a shadow fell over him.

"How'd you find me here, Joyce?" Frank asked.

"What makes you think I was looking for you?" she replied, sitting down beside him, asking as she did so, "May I?"

"You already have."

"Rhetorical, polite social question," she pointed out, "since I already knew the answer."

"I wish I knew some answers."

"First things first. You were saying something about price. Care to elaborate?"

"Maybe. Maybe talking about it will help me get it straight in my mind. I was thinking aloud about the price of change—in human effort, in human lives."

"TANSTAAFL," Joyce said.

"There Ain't No Such Thing As A Free Lunch. So?"

"So it applies to change, too. Trouble with you fighter pilots, you're so interested in where you're going that you never bother to watch your tail. You don't think about where you've been or what got you where you are." She tucked her skirt under her and smoothed it across her knees. "Whoever said change was free? Or even cheap? Change any system, and it costs you something. Change? That's energy flow, Frank. And without energy flow, without entropy, there's nothing. And nothing in the future, either. No change, no world, no universe. And it costs in terms of human effort and human lives—or even universal life force, if you want me to go mystical on you."

"You're mystical enough as it is," he told her. "Let's get off this approach before we dive into our belly buttons contemplating Nirvana."

"Yes, it would be easier if we could remain children all our lives, wouldn't it?"

"Huh? Joyce, let me tell you something: If I had to go through childhood again, I wouldn't. Being a kid was the toughest time of my life. I was a second-class citizen being told I might be able to do it myself—fly, make love, whatever—when I grew up. Well, I grew up."

"And it was so nice when you did, and everything settled down and stabilized on an even keel without any worries or problems, right?"

"Uh . . . no. Dammit, it's been interesting only when things were changing."

She smiled at him. "Okay, Frank, I'll stop now. I've managed to lead you down the garden path and around the complete circle. At least I've gotten you to admit to yourself that you've changed, and that maybe I've been part of that change."

"But what am I going to do about Ellie now?"

"You've got lots of love you haven't even used yet. Go back and love her, Frank. I think you'll find you love her even more now."

Frank was taken totally aback. "You mean you're turning me loose, just like that?" He snapped his fingers. "Wham, bam, thank you, man?"

"Oh, no, Frank! I never had any claim on you. Never! I loved you, I love you now, I'll love you again, and I'll love you for a long time. But I don't own you or any part of you. I only cherish you. Can you understand?"

Frank looked out at the sea, confused. "I'm not sure. Joyce, it's like growing up all over again."

She reached over and gently caressed his cheek. "Hello, Frank. Welcome to the world."

A long time later, he looked at the *moai* again and spoke to them, "You're gods and supposed to look out on that part of the world for which you're responsible, huh? But you're not responsible for us any longer. Some of us can make better *mana* magic now. We'll get along without you. We'll eventually give people a world in better shape than it was given to us. In the meantime, we'll take what we've learned is good . . . and we'll take it to the stars . . . but we won't forget our childhood."

CODA

"NASA Nine-Zero-Five, Pascua Tower. You're cleared for takeoff, left turn out. *Adiós, amigos. Buena suerte y volved otra vez.*"

The Mataveri runway stretched almost two miles in

front of the windshield of NASA 905. "*Gracias, señor. Adiós!*" Hank Hoffman put away the checklist and nodded at his copilot, Jake Stanley, then turned to where Frank was sitting in the observer's jump seat behind him. "Ready?"

"I was sweating less when I landed the *Atlantis* here than I am now," Frank admitted. "*Vamos.*"

"Okay, let's see if the world's largest biplane flies again. Takeoff power!"

The runway began to move.

"Ah, Houston, brake release. Nine-Oh-Five's rolling," Hank reported via the S-band satellite link.

"Nine-Oh-Five, Houston. Roger," came Joe Marvin's quiet reply.

Frank found himself back in a world of instant communications again. He was separated from Rapa Nui now, and the island seemed an unreal place that was merely a scene in the windshield of the 747 with the *Atlantis* on its back.

"Rotation," Jake Stanley called.

The nose came up, and the runway and Rapa Nui vanished from sight as sky took its place.

The *Atlantis* was airborne again.

To Joyce, Red, and Ernesto Obregon, watching from the ramp, it was an incredibly beautiful sight.

"Incredible that anything that big can fly," Obregon remarked.

"Beautiful," Joyce said. "Just beautiful."

"Yeah," Red added. "We got her off—two days ahead of schedule."

As the complex of landing-gear struts and wheels retracted into the belly of NASA 905, she was joined by four F-14 Tomcats from the *Kitty Hawk*, still on station with the *Cochrane*. The Navy was taking no chances, although the Soviet ships had left days before on the remainder of what one Soviet captain called a "world-circling good-will tour."

Matt Hubbard stepped out of Flight Operations. "Ready to go, Joyce? Wheels-up in fifteen minutes. We're following Nine-Oh-Five into Santiago."

Joyce turned to Red Richardson. "When will you be leaving, Red?"

"Couple more days. Stiffleg's down and stowed in your C-5. I'll get the trucks and the Manitowock crane out in another C-5 later today. Then I've got to spend a few days cleaning up," Red told her. "Governor, you're sure you want us to leave the ramps intact? We'll plow them up as we agreed, if you want."

"Leave them, Red. We may need them if a Shuttle ever has to land here again."

"Yeah, next time we'll know what to do because it'll be in the procedures manual." Red had a moment of hesitation. He took Joyce's hand, started to raise it to his lips as he had seen Obregon do, had second thoughts, paused while he debated whether to kiss her good-bye, and finally compromised by holding her hand in both of his. "Joyce, thanks. I couldn't have done it without you. You . . . you're one hell of a woman. Come see me if you ever get to Houston."

"Come see me when you get to Washington," Joyce said.

He held her hand a moment longer, then walked off across the ramp.

She looked at Ernesto Obregon and told him in Spanish, "Don't say good-bye, Ernesto. I'll see you again in Washington or New York. You will not be on Isla de Pascua forever. You're a very good man, and Chile needs you elsewhere."

"Perhaps," he replied. "Who can tell?" He took her hand and started to raise it to his lips.

She stopped him and added quietly, "I *know* you will, Ernesto. Shall I give your best wishes to the people in Langley, Virginia?"

"You knew?"

"Not at first, but you gave yourself away to me when you shot Dr. Esteban. I knew there was a CIA contact on Pascua; I just didn't know who."

"That's why you probably will not see me in Washington or New York, Joyce. The KGB must also know about me by now. They'd use it against me in Washington."

"Don't try to anticipate those things, Ernesto," she urged him, still speaking in Spanish. "You must also consider the possibility that it might work *for* you, because they'd hesitate about applying pressure, knowing who and what was standing behind you."

"Joyce, coming?" Matt Hubbard called from the door of the C-5 on the ramp.

"I'll take good care of Professor Pérez also, because I know he's one of our special friends, too," she told the governor, still in Spanish. "I'm sorry that Ríos was not."

Obregon nodded and replied in his native tongue, "Ironic, isn't it, that Esteban destroyed one of his own by accident?"

"Are you certain it was by accident, Ernesto? Or that Professor Pérez was the original target? Or that the KGB wouldn't sacrifice one of its agents for bigger game?"

The military governor nodded. "They had been known to do that. Such are the ways of the world. Joyce, I'm disturbed to see you leave Pascua and return to that dangerous world. Please take good care of yourself. You are a special person."

Joyce took her hand out of Obregon's. In a most un-Latin farewell, she threw her arms around him and kissed him. "*Adiós, Ernesto. Me gusta a Usted muchísimo. Vaya con Dios!*"

She turned and ran toward the plane so that he couldn't see the tears in her eyes.

Captain Ernesto Obregon watched her go. *How fortunate are the Americans to have a woman with such capacity for compassionate love of all!*

In Houston, there was a quiet celebration in Mission Control. It wasn't the exuberant boisterousness of a lunar landing, but a quiet round of congratulations, mostly to Joe Marvin, while Duke Kellogg sat quietly by, wondering why it was Joe who was the center of respect.

Duke knew he had tried to follow the book and keep these people pointed in the right direction. Sure, there had been the unanticipated times when Marvin wouldn't follow procedures and threw the book away. Duke had spoken to Joe about that, and they had had a little confrontation in Mission Control. But, by and large, Duke was pleased with himself and what he considered to be his people. He was still confused about what had happened to Jackie Hart and why Lew Clay insisted on coming back with her aboard the *Kitty Hawk*. And why Hap Hazard wanted to ride back to Houston with Frank in NASA 905. He would call

Frank into his office in a day or so and get the full story—
or so he thought.

Alfred M. Dewey also watched the takeoff on the little
TV set he had brought to his office. He put off the urge to
telephone the Chilean chargé d'affaires. Later, perhaps.
Joyce Fisher would be back in a few days, and he would
give her the continuing job of working with the Chileans.
Maybe he could even get her a boost in grade, if not a step
increase. He would have to put in the request for Nash
Sullivan's replacement. Dewey had known from the start
that State wasn't the place for that young man; he had
been too eager and far too familiar with current technology
for State. Nice that Sullivan had been asked to join the
staff of the UN Committee for the Peaceful Use of Outer
Space; he would do well, and they needed him there.

At 400 Maryland Avenue S.W., Roger Service stepped
behind the podium in the sixth-floor conference auditorium. "Ladies and gentlemen," he announced pontifically
to members of the media, "the *Atlantis* is on its way
home, as you saw in the TV transmission via satellite from
Easter Island. We expect the *Atlantis* to be operational
thirty days after NASA technicians have carefully inspected her and replaced the damaged tiles.

"As for the crew of the *Atlantis*, the Administrator is
pleased to announce that the President will award the Presidential Medal of Freedom, the nation's highest civilian
award, to each for meritorious contribution to the national
interest of the United States in saving the *Atlantis*, which is
one-fourth of our nation's manned space capability."

Casey Laskewitz didn't hear the takeoff of NASA 905
from Mataveri, nor did he know of the press conference in
Washington. He lay in an intensive care unit in the sick
bay of the *Kitty Hawk*, alive, barely conscious under heavy
sedation, and wired to a bank of instruments that were saving his life—instruments that had come from the space
program he so dearly loved and that had almost cost him
his life.

Nor was the takeoff of NASA 905 audible to Jackie
Hart and Lew Clay in the trauma unit of the *Kitty Hawk*'s
sick bay. In any event, the two of them had other things
on their minds, mostly each other. They didn't know that the
carrier was making more than thirty knots toward San

Diego; they only knew that each had found something neither of them had ever had before in their lives.

NASA 905 continued her climb in a left turn that brought Rapa Nui into Frank King's view.

Frank looked closely at Rapa Nui as it swept astern.

He knew he would never see it that way again. The hurricane of change would now pass over it.

Rapa Nui dropped from sight behind the 747, and he turned to the business of being flight observer, relief pilot, and the commander of the *Atlantis*, responsible for getting her home again.

It was time to go. He had never wanted to return to Seabrook so badly before. He had to get there as quickly as possible. His life and the world would never be the same again because they had grown immensely on the Island at the Center of the World.

Hap Hazard entered the flight deck through the aft bulkhead door, closed it, and leaned against it. "She's riding fine, Frank," he reported.

"How are you holding up, Hap?"

"Okay. Uh, Frank, I—uh—kind of got a new perspective on a lot of things in the last few weeks."

"Welcome to the world, Hap."

"I did. Really. Maybe Landsat-XIII's more important right now than that space station I've been all hot about—and madder than hell that nobody takes it seriously, even with the Shuttle lift capability. How's a lunar base going to help the Pascuans? On the other hand, the Landsat may do them some good."

"Hap, old buddy, I've got news for you. *Both* things can't help but do some good for the Pascuans and everybody else. This is a big, complex system we're in, and it's impossible to figure out how something's going to affect something else. Whoever thought that the *Atlantis* would affect the world's most remote island the way it did? Don't try to figure out the future in detail, Hap. The world's changing. Even Pascua's changing. We can't stop it. I'm not sure we'd want to. We can't freeze the world in the condition it's in now, not when people kill each other even on Rapa Nui."

"Amen, brother. Frank, I've never figured out that terrorist raid. Why'd they do it? Why'd they want to destroy the *Atlantis*? Why'd they pull a suicide raid with no way to get off the island if the Catalina was damaged?" Hap sounded perplexed because the lack of apparent rationale behind the raid had bothered him.

"Are you sure it was a suicide raid, Hap?"

"What do you mean?"

"They pulled it off the morning the Soviet ships were originally supposed to arrive—if it hadn't been for that typhoon. There were inflatable rafts in the PBY, Hap. Maybe they'd planned to be picked up by the *Kharkov* or the *Sverdlov*."

"And they got caught by the Law of Comrade Murphy," Hap added. "But I still can't figure out *why* somebody would want to destroy the *Atlantis*."

"I'm not sure I want to take the time to try to figure that out, Hap. If the world's changing, I've got to work like hell to make it change the way I think might make it a little better instead of making it worse. The way people have been running it can't possibly work in the long run. I like to think we're growing beyond that."

Hap looked at the command pilot of the *Atlantis* for a moment. "You're right. Things have changed. You've changed. Never heard you talk like that before. It's been a rough time for all of us."

"Hap, growing's always rough." Frank stretched, the tension of weeks now beginning to drain away. "Hey, any place below to grab some sack time? It's six hours to Santiago, and we don't meet the KC-10 tanker for about two hours."

"Frank, have you ever tried to sleep on a fuel bladder?"

"You mean NASA can't even keep the john working on this airplane?" Frank asked, then paused a beat. "Sorry. I thought you said something else."

"Come to think of it, they're something like a firm water bed at that. Could be worse on a long flight. And Pascua's a long way from everything."

"Don't be so sure, Hap. Everything important just might have been right there at the center of the world—at least for a few short weeks."

ABOUT THE AUTHOR

Better known under his real name, G. Harry Stine, Lee Correy is a rocket pioneer, a futurist, an expert in space industrialization and high-technology marketing, and the author of or contributor to more than twenty books on science and technology. He uses his pen name "Lee Correy" for fiction to separate it from his nonfiction.

He has been the director of an industrial research laboratory and the marketing manager for a small industrial company. He is an instrument-rated private pilot with over a thousand hours, owns his own Cherokee (N95439), and is an aerospace historian and a consultant to the National Air and Space Museum.

He lives in Phoenix, Arizona, with his wife, a cat with twenty-four toes, and three golden retrievers.